BRAND
Brand, Max,
Silver trail :
33277003106577

SILVER TRAIL

SILVER TRAIL

A WESTERN STORY

MAX BRAND®

FIVE STAR

A part of Gale, Cengage Learning

GALE
CENGAGE Learning™

Detroit • New York • San Francisco • New Haven, Conn • Waterville, Maine • London

GALE
CENGAGE Learning

Copyright © 2009 by Golden West Literary Agency.

The name Max Brand® is a registered trademark with the United States Patent and Trademark Office and cannot be used for any purpose without express written permission.

The Acknowledgments on page 265 constitute an extension of the copyright page.

Five Star Publishing, a part of Gale, Cengage Learning.

Set in 11 pt. Plantin.

Printed on permanent paper.

LIBRARY OF CONGRESS CATALOGING-IN-PUBLICATION DATA

Brand, Max, 1892–1944.
   Silver trail: a western story / by Max Brand. — 1st ed.
    p. cm.
   "A Five Star Western."
   ISBN-13: 978-1-59414-740-1 (alk. paper)
   ISBN-10: 1-59414-740-X (alk. paper)
   I. Title.
PS3511.A87S47 2009
813'.52—dc22
                              2008049391

First Edition. First Printing: March 2009.

Published in 2009 in conjunction with Golden West Literary Agency.

SILVER TRAIL

CHAPTER ONE

At timberline, John Signal paused. Before him, the pass narrowed to a gorge, dark and silent as a throat of iron; behind him, the slope dipped and folded like a sea heaped up by some prodigious wind until it descended to the green of the valley, far off, and quiet as standing water. By shading his eyes and peering, he could discern that glimmer of green clearly in spite of the blue mist of distance, and clear as a streak of quicksilver he made out the face of the river. Where the bright mark divided, there was the village that had been home to him. He never would see it again!

At that thought, John Signal made his face as stern and as hard as the black cliffs before him; young Westerners refuse to melt with emotion, and Signal was only twenty-two. But he wondered, now, why he never before had appreciated the beauty of the white streets of the town, smoking with dust at every touch of the wind, or the narrow gardens on either side, and into his memory all the houses looked like the faces of dear friends, and all the hours of his life seemed to cling about those buildings, like plants rooted in rich mold. Suppose he went back to face them, rode to the sheriff's office, and gave himself up?

He turned his horse about with a sudden twitch of the reins, but, in so doing, he noticed how much thinner the gelding was across the shoulders, how much sharper the ridge of the neck. All the sleekness of the pasture fat had evaporated in the labor of lifting his rider from that far-off gleam of water to this upland. Should all that labor be wasted? Besides, if he returned, his friends would look at one another and smile, and say that John Signal's nerve had failed in the great pinch. They would point out that it often happened before, and that the hero of the schoolyard and the vacant lot and the bunkhouse grew soft of heart when real danger came.

Thinking of the town itself, John Signal was about to rush back in surrender. Thinking of the people in it, he became grimly resolute and turned the gelding back toward the throat of the pass.

He was on the verge of timberline, which ran along the deeply incised profile of the mountains like a water mark—a stain left, as it were, by the lower atmosphere with its fogs and vapors and climbing mists. He, like some amphibious creature, for the first time was lifting his head and shoulders from the deep and breathing the pure air of the upper region. This thought pleased John Signal, and he turned and returned it in his mind, like a toy. Sometimes a metaphor is like a pack, bending the back, sometimes it is like a sword in the hand. The boy, much heartened, looked about him.

The outermost line of the trees, in their unending battle against mountain wind and mountain cold, was flung forward, groveling to the ground, clinging desperately; limber pine, and alpine fir, the quaking aspen, black birch, and arctic willow still marched against the height and lived on where they had fallen. The air was as calm as the waters of a standing pool, but the trees seemed to be still fighting against the wind that had dwarfed, and broken, and distorted them, and yet it could not drive them back.

It seemed to John Signal that he could understand this battle in another way. Where the forest could climb, man could climb, also, and the laws of man, and all beneath this water mark upon the mountains was the dominion of sheriff and judge—but now his horse was carrying him out of the lower region to a place above the law. He looked up to the dark portals of the pass as if to a gate on which he expected to read some inscription. Once inside the rocky throat, darkness fell over him.

The echoes raised by the shod hoofs of his horse came faintly, hollowly upon his ear, floating upon air so thin that it hardly would bear up the sound, and the snorting and breathing of the gelding was like the puffing of another animal, pursuing him at a distance. John Signal felt as though he had ridden into a dream, and he was more than ever startled when he came to the end of the narrow pass and saw before him the treeless gardens of the upper mountains.

He could see, now, that, although he had gone over one ridge of the world, he was not yet at the summit, but in a sort of half land, between the bottom and the top. To his left he looked up the face of a thousand-foot cliff, and at the top saw a mountain sheep—very like a tuft of cloud lodged on the rough edge of the rock—and beyond that lofty mass there were other peaks, but all before him and to the right was a comparatively level plateau without a tree, without a bush, but so thickly stippled by ten million flowers that it appeared not painted, but streaked with bits of tinted atmosphere. And for the first time, having passed the dark gate to this land above the law, John Signal understood that it was not only cold and mighty, but also that it possessed a radiant and a lonely beauty of its own.

The winter was not ended here, and never would be, even in August heats; all the northern slopes were agleam with ice or dazzling white with snow, but the flowers that covered the upland meadows—spring beauties, the daisy, the forget-me-not, purple asters, the goldenrod, and many more—advanced to the edge of the icy slopes. Yes, they even blossomed on the backs of the boulders, and through the very ice itself the avalanche lily pushed up to the sun, drilling its way by miracle to the air and to the light.

He rode on past a whole slope of paintbrushes, white-pointed by wild buckwheat, and now he observed that these gardens had their own peculiar music, as well. Here rose a cloud of buzzing sounds and drifted down the wind—bees, filling the air with a sound of sleep, and yonder a flock of ptarmigans, startled from a feast on the buds of arctic willows, rose on noisy wings, whirled in a circle, flashed in the sun, and settled again to their banquet. Butterflies, too, were everywhere adrift, like unbalanced leaves, trying to settle to the ground and rarely succeeding, and then only to be tossed up again to waver in the air.

This was all a very pretty scene, but the boy was hungry, and three or four hundred pounds of mutton was looking blandly down upon him from the heights. He uncased the rifle that he carried in a long holster beneath his right knee, the muzzle down. His hands were a little cold—this was not an atmosphere or a light in which he had been accustomed to shooting—but he told himself grimly that he must not waste ammunition. Suppose yonder puff of white wool upon the rock lip were a man with a rifle leveled in return? At this, with narrowed eye like a fighting man, he jumped the butt of his rifle into the hollow of his shoulder and fired. The sheep stood unmoved, but he lowered the gun without a second shot. One bullet a day would have to keep him in meat; otherwise, he simply would starve himself by way of punishment.

Providence, one might have said, had heard this resolution as it was registered in the heart of Signal, and now it tipped the mountain sheep from the ledge. It went down a four-hundred-foot slide, cannoned out into empty air, and fell with a *crunch* not fifty yards away. Signal went to it curiously, rather than with an outburst of savage appetite. He turned the heavy body. He had aimed at the right shoulder, a little back, and in that spot, exactly, he found the bullet wound.

When he saw this, he looked up and stared at the dark mouth of the pass through which he had come, and he smiled in content, and in something more than content. Then he set about butchering the sheep with care, for if he could preserve this meat in part by jerking it, he would not have to go hungry for weeks—it was a three-hundred-and-fifty-pound ram.

For fuel he had to go back through the pass and use his short-hafted axe on the tough, timberline trees, and, returning with a load of this firewood, he set about his cookery. Even then he dared not unsaddle his horse, and many a glance he cast at the shadowy mouth of the pass, for if they were following close upon his heels, they would have to come at him through this doorway. No matter how many, he was grimly confident that he could close that door and bolt it with bullets from the rifle.

By noon he began his cookery; he did not finish it until evening, which came on early and cold when the sun got behind the western heights and all the valley was flooded with chill shadow. It had not been a very neat job. His fingers were scorched, and half of the meat was rather burned than cooked, besides a great deal of it would have to be seasoned yet more with heat before he could hope to preserve it. However, he felt that a day or two of the fierce white sun of these uplands would finish the cure, and so he rolled up the rest of his supply in the big sheepskin and prepared to find a shelter for the night.

He was drawing up the cinches of his saddle when a shadow of danger crossed his mind, and, whirling about, he saw a horse-man coming toward him, not from the mouth of the pass, but in the opposite direction. Even at that distance, he could see that it was a big man, on a big horse, and through the shadows he made out a horizontal gleam balanced across the pommel of the saddle—a mountaineer with a rifle in readiness, then.

John made no secret of his own precaution, but threw his

gun across the hollow of his left arm and placed a finger on the trigger. Then he watched the other come up as a look-out watched the approach of a strange ship at sea—a ship at sea in the days of pirates and the buccaneers.

Looming first as a tall, imposing form, the stranger now appeared at close range rather a gaunt figure, his face overshadowed with a beard of many days' growth, and his clothes loose and ragged to a surprising degree. With a keen eye he looked upon John Signal, a keen and sunken eye, and then made a little gesture of greeting, half a wave of the hand, half a military salute.

Signal merely nodded, and kept the gun in readiness. "You raised quite a smoke, young feller," said the man of the mountain. "I see that you got a bighorn. Your first?"

And his lips twitched a little in a very faint smile beneath his beard. Signal suddenly felt very keenly his youth and his inexperience. He freshened his grip upon the rifle, as the thing that made him equal to any man. And then his sense of good manners returned to him.

"If you're hungry," he said, "get down and eat."

CHAPTER TWO

The unshaven mountaineer did not hesitate. "I could use a bit of mutton," he said, and swung his leg over the cantle of his saddle. He moved slowly, very like a man who is numbed by cold, and then sat down, cross-legged, on a stone beside the cooked meat that was pointed out by Signal.

"It's coming on cold, ain't it?" asked the stranger.

"It's pretty cold," admitted Signal, and kicked together the last embers of the fire, so that a blaze jumped up. And, doing this, he kept his face constantly, watchfully, toward the stranger. He had laid aside his rifle, but he had a Colt loose in the holster at his right thigh, and his right hand was never far from the projecting handle.

He felt that he had some reason for this caution. There was something wolfish about the manner of the stranger in eating—something wolfish also in his way of turning his eye upon Signal. Part by part, the boy felt himself surveyed—his boots, even his revolver—the rifle he had put aside, the heavy belt of ammunition that loosely sagged about his hips.

With amazing speed, the mountaineer had devoured a quantity of the mutton. Now he leaned back against the rock. "Got the makings?" he inquired.

With his left hand, Signal extracted brown papers and tobacco from his pocket and passed them over, watching critically while the other made his smoke with fumbling fingers, lighted it, and drew in great drafts, so deep that very little of the smoke appeared again when he blew it forth.

"You hunt, maybe?" asked Signal, allowing his curiosity the satisfaction of a single question.

"I hunt now and then," said the other. He nodded after he had answered; his eyes had grown strangely sleepy, and a vague smile appeared beneath his beard. Then he jerked up his head, suddenly awake.

"You don't pack a knife, I see."

"I have a knife here."

"That'd never pass for a knife . . . not if you have to live up here for a spell. Look at this one. It's the best German steel." He displayed it accordingly—a hunting knife with a long and a heavy blade. "I'm a little short," he said. "I'm a little short of bullets. I'd trade that for a handful out of your belt, youngster."

"It's worth a good deal more," answered Signal.

"I know it is. But I can't expect to make a good trade at this end of the world. You throw in as many bullets as you want."

"And where shall I get more up here?" asked Signal.

"Why, you'll have enough to see yourself through, I suppose. You're not going to camp up here forever, young feller?"

"No. But ammunition may be worth more than gold," said Signal.

"Why, then," replied the other, "I've got another knife. I can get along without this one. Suppose we say only half a dozen cartridges?"

"And I take the knife?"

"I've got another as good," explained the stranger. "A few cartridges would be saving me from a long trip."

And he looked with such earnestness at young Signal that the latter hesitated and, for a fraction of an instant, turned his eyes upward in thought. Charity is highly commendable. He could live very well without another knife, but this ragged man of the mountains seemed desperately cornered. So thinking, with the scales turning to the side of kindness, John Signal saw a floating bird high above him, and knew the flight of a golden eagle—drifting across the range, perhaps, to drop on some prey in the richer lowlands.

Then his glance flickered down, and he was in time to observe the last of a lightning movement that brought a Colt from somewhere about the person of the stranger and leveled it at the head of his host. There was hardly more chance to outspeed that gesture than there would have been, say, to beat the flick of a cat's paw when it has started toward the mouse. And young John Signal was too bewildered even to attempt resistance.

"I tried to treat you white," said the other, "but you wouldn't have that. Now you're gonna get trouble instead. I'll take that whole gun belt, kid. Just unbuckle that belt and let her drop, will you? Bein' special careful about what your fingers do at the time of unbuckling?"

Totally outraged, the boy exclaimed: "You've been fed when you were starving, stranger! Is this your comeback to me?"

"Son," said the other, pushing himself up to his feet with the same clumsy movement that Signal had noticed when he dismounted, "I'll tell you how it is. There's some that's able to do the way they're done by . . . and there's some that ain't got a chance unless they do a mite more."

He rendered justice to his own wit with a broad, slow grin, and this was the thing that unbalanced the scales for Signal. If he had been one of those cautious and thoughtful beings to whom probabilities mattered in a pinch, he never would have done the thing that, in the first place, drove him away from his home—but now he was in loftier regions—above the law. And he felt a pain in his temples, which was the beating of his blood there. Then he went for his Colt.

He was well covered at the instant. There was no chance that he would escape being shot through and through. But he merely gambled savagely against fate that the bullet would not strike him in a fatal spot, or would, at least, leave him enough life to enable him to send home his own shot. So he twisted himself sidewise as he snatched out the revolver.

And the gun of the stranger remained silent! Instead of firing, he raised his own weapon like a club and lurched in at the boy. Far better for him if he had run at an upreared grizzly—a young grizzly, say, unhampered by fat, unwieldy bulk, sickness, or wounds.

The gun of Signal was ready for work while still the stranger was plunging in and a rash or careless workman would certainly have pulled the trigger, but Signal was one of those rare creatures who can drop an old thought and find a new one in the course of a single second, or a split part thereof. So he noted that the game of bullets had been thrown aside and another sport put in its place.

It was not for nothing that he had grown up in the streets of a town where the tough jaws of hard-fisted young Mexicans had to be cracked, and where the boys from the range came in for a fight or a frolic like troops of young lions. In that town he had been the acknowledged master. If there was a hard look about his stern young features, it was because, perhaps, they had been beaten to that texture by the knuckles of his peers in many a grand battle.

So he abandoned the thought of using his trigger finger, and instead he shot a well-timed uppercut just under the chin of his guest. It lifted the hat from the head of this stranger and tossed all his long, unkempt hair upward as though in a puff of wind; it stopped his rush; it caused the revolver to drop from his nerveless hand; it made him waver in a balance from toe to heel. Then his knees buckled and he sank slowly down.

Signal picked up the fallen revolver and stepped back, with both hands armed, but the instant his left hand took the burden of the other's gun, he knew what had happened. The Colt was totally empty. It had been merest bluff that had caused the bearded fellow to draw the revolver!

Half stunned, as yet, the stranger supported himself upon one hand and knee while his eyes slowly cleared. He shook his head like a dog trying to get the water out of its pelt, then he staggered to his feet again.

"What's wrong with you?" asked Signal sharply.

"Kid," said the other, facing the pair of guns undauntedly, "I tried a crooked move on you, and you called me. Well, you hold the cards. I never had a play in the game, anyway. My gun was as empty as the belly of a starved wolf."

"You hadn't a shot left. I could tell that by the heft of your Colt. But what's paralyzed you? I never saw a man go down so dead from such a tap."

"Tap?" The other grinned with surprising good nature. "You may call it that . . . it felt like the tap of a sledge-hammer to me. But I haven't had a mouthful of chuck for five days, son. That's what softened my joints, if that's what you mean."

Instantly Signal believed. It explained the slowness of the other's movements—except that lightning flash when the gun had been drawn. It explained the wolfing of the mutton, and the sunken eyes, and the gauntness of the form that made the coat fit so loosely.

"I'm sorry," he said. "If you'd come cleaner, this wouldn't have happened. Are you feeling better now?"

"My jaw'll be loose on its hinges for a couple of weeks," replied the other, still with perfect good nature, "otherwise I'll soon be all right."

"Will you tell me why you had to starve?"

"I'm up here waiting for pals," said the stranger.

Signal stared. "Up to starving time?" he asked, astonished.

"My pals would never go back on me," replied the other.

"They may be slow in coming, but they're sure to arrive."

"Then why not live on horse for a while?" asked Signal.

The other turned and regarded his horse. It was a tall, clean-limbed bay, sleek and trim from living in the mountain pastures. "That horse and me," he said, "have played tag with trouble together too often for me to tap on the head because of hunger. I've sure envied him that there talent for living on grass the last week. But outside of that I've never given him a hard thought. Live on Shanks, there? It'd be like cannibalism, partner!"

Signal hesitated no longer. From his cartridge belt he took out a dozen cartridges—more precious than gold, perhaps, they might prove to him. And he presented them together with the empty gun to the other.

"For the price of the knife?" asked the stranger eagerly.

"For the sake of your horse"—John Signal smiled—"and for your sake, too, partner."

CHAPTER THREE

Friendship is not sold by the yard; neither is it traded for merchandise; but it is rather like gold, and sometimes the hardest rocks give the richest strike. These two who had stood on the verge of a life-and-death battle now looked upon each other with kindly eyes. Unhesitantly Signal turned his back upon the stranger and finished the cinching of his horse, conscious that his back was guarded from danger by more than leveled guns.

And he said, as he turned: "You'd better help yourself to some more of that meat, old man. You may need it before you get in your next shot."

"Where are you bound?" asked the other with curiosity.

"Yonder," said Signal.

"Over the range?"

"Most likely."

"To Monument, I suppose?"

"Monument? What's that?"

"You ain't heard of that?"

"You mean the mining town? The silver mines?"

"What else?"

"I've heard of that. Whereabouts does it lie?"

At this the stranger stared at him in some wonder. "You beat me," he said. "As sure as my name is Henry. . . ." He paused, cutting himself very short, and went on: "You don't know Monument?" It was as if he had said: *You don't know the sun?*

"I don't know the place. I've never been there."

"You're from the hind side of the range, are you?"

"Yes, from over there."

"You don't have to cover up with me," said the other, smiling most disarmingly again. "You're on the run, kid, I suppose. Well, that's your business. I'm on the run, too. This is to say, more or less. I've had to hop a dozen times in my life. I still hop now and then. If you want to tell me who you are . . . it goes. If you don't, I shut up. But my name is Henry Colter."

There was enough force in that name to make Signal, who had just buckled the last cinch, wheel about, his shoulders flattened against the ribs of his horse. "You're Colter!" he exclaimed.

"That's me."

"Well, I'm hanged!"

"To think you had me down, eh?" The other grinned. "I suppose it does seem a little funny, but, as you've seen for yourself, I'm not as hard as they've made me out all these years."

His words came dimly to the ears of John Signal, who was seeing many strange images that rushed up into his mind. There was a picture of a big, rugged fellow, riding a mustang through the street of the town, burdened with revolvers and a long rifle. That was Dan Garrison, bound outward, men said, to ride until he found death or the life of Henry Colter. Dan Garrison never had come again. He had found the end of his trail, and Colter's superior gun had won. And there was Ned Levis, famous for his dapperness and his savage fighting, who had been brought down the Bender Creek to the town, five long years before, and had lain for three days in bed before he died more of exhaustion from the loss of blood than because of the terrible wounds that the bullets of his conqueror had driven through his body. Henry Colter was that conqueror.

Those were two overt pictures, so to speak. But there was much else, such as the wild tales of robbery and murder that, from time to time, drifted upon the tongues of men, not quite enough substantiated to appear in the public press, which rather referred to Colter as "celebrated" than "notorious". He was one of those men really wanted for a hundred crimes, but not yet outlawed because he had not actually been tried and found guilty of any important action. For he had lived not on the hind side of the range, but on the western front of it, where the law had not yet established itself. He had kept ahead of the sheriff, so to speak. And, though all the world knew that he was a criminal, there was probably not a warrant in existence for his arrest.

So famous was this Henry Colter that young Signal looked upon him agape.

"Oh," he said, "but I've heard a lot and a lot about you, Colter."

"Have you?" said the other, not unpleased. "And pretty near all bad, I take it?"

"They say that you shoot straight . . . and you're square with your pals," said the boy, who had much to learn of diplomacy in this strangely tangled world of ours. However, he was talking with one who was quite indifferent to most criticism.

"If they say that, they say enough," said Colter. "I don't ask for any more. I shoot straight, and I stand for my pals . . . all them that stand for me. Now, kid, where d'you aim to ride that hoss tonight . . . or are you still mistrustful of me?"

The boy hesitated a little, not only because of what he would have to say if he answered at all, but because there was a weight upon his heart when he even thought of the thing that had sent him from Bender City to the highlands. He sighed, and instantly the words came.

"They want me for murder at my home town. That's my story. My name is John Signal."

The other nodded. "I knew it was a killing," he said, unshocked.

"Will you tell me how you happened to guess that?" asked Signal anxiously.

"You haven't got the story branded on your forehead." The other smiled. "That needn't bother you, if that's what you mean. But folks have to have a reason for coming up to this section of the world. And after I saw the way you tickled that revolver and danced it out under my nose, why, I didn't have to ask any more questions. It was guns that made you leave your home town . . . and you'd shoot too straight not to kill your man."

This simple analysis left Signal a little bewildered.

The other went on genially: "They ran you out, then?"

"I didn't stay to be run out," he said. "I knew that they'd be after me."

"Self-defense, son," said the experienced Colter. "That's the gag to use on them . . . so long as the shooting is done from in front."

The boy shrugged his shoulders. "It was done from in front. But it was the son of the judge who dropped." He exploded angrily: "Damn him! He'd been trading on his father's name all his life. He tried to walk on me."

The other grinned broadly. "And you couldn't reach him with your fists?"

"It was poker," said John Signal. "He began to talk and tap the table with his Colt. A man can't stand for that."

"He had his gun out?"

"He did."

"Did other people see it?"

"Two sneaking cronies of young Bill Hampton."

"They'd testify against you?"

"Of course they would. They're both employed by the judge. I didn't have a chance."

Colter held his peace for a serious instant. Then: "What do you aim at?" he asked.

"A new start in life," said the boy gloomily. "That's the only thing that I can do."

"And why not a start in Monument?"

"I've got to avoid towns . . . and the law."

Colter laughed. "You think that they'll pepper the whole countryside with men looking for you, and a thousand-dollar reward. They won't. On the hind side of the mountains the law's a growed-up man. But over yonder it goes on bare feet and ain't as big as a baby. In Monument there ain't any law to speak of. Not for a man that wears two guns and can use 'em. Monument, my boy. That's the home that's waiting for you."

"What would I do?" sighed Signal. "I'm not a miner."

Colter laughed again. "Who goes to a mining town to mine? Only the suckers . . . and five or six lucky ones. The rest go there to get their honey without working."

"I don't know what you mean by that."

"You know me, kid."

"Yes."

"What sort of work do I do?" Then, as the boy was silent, he went on: "Your best plan is as plain as the nose on your face. The thing for you to do is to stay here with me until my chums come along. Then throw in with me. That's the absolute ticket! Why, kid, I'll roll you in money." He explained during the pause that followed: "That sounds a lot . . . from a starved man that didn't have even a bullet for his guns, eh? But wait and see. Today or tomorrow, the boys I'm waiting for, will be up here. We head straight down for Monument. I'll show you who's king there, old-timer."

Signal shook himself like a man rousing from a profound sleep. He said rapidly: "That's a kind offer. I take it that way. But the fact is that I want to go straight. You see how it is . . .

I'm willing to work. I don't mind work. I've worked before."

The other chuckled, unabashed. "Is that it?" he said. "Well, they all start like that, and feeling that way. The books say that the crooks have got to go down. Sure, because the books only know about the ones that have been caught. Well, I'm forty, and never saw the inside of a jail. You try working. But on Saturday night you come around and talk to me!"

CHAPTER FOUR

Like a hot toddy, the sense of his own virtue warmed the heart of John Signal through three bleak, beautiful days among the highlands during which he shuddered at night beneath his blankets in the cold, and during the day drove gradually across the range. He came, on the third afternoon, to a lofty platform, held up as upon stilts, and stopped to view the lower regions around him. And he saw almost as far as the human eye can reach, for the mountain air was pure and still—distance made objects dwindle in size but hardly obscured their features, except to the south where a reddish haze, like smoke, continually poured upward from the earth to the upper air. That was the desert, as he knew, over whose face the wind is never still, picking up the sands and sifting them eternally through the sieve of the air.

Out of that desert mist, while he watched, he saw a streak of black moving, making a pencil line that broadened and evaporated toward the rear as it ran straight on in front toward a range of hills—ran very slowly, but never stopped. He marveled only for a moment, but then he knew it was a train heading north. The patience of the mountains was upon Signal, and he watched, amused, while the pencil stroke ran on to the foot of the hills where a gap opened among them. There it stopped at a number of houses, clustered close.

Where was the railroad pointed? Not surely at this insignificant village that, nevertheless, seemed to be the terminal of the

25

line. But beyond the broad heaps of the hills there was a small valley with a curving gleam of water down its center, and, where the river flowed from the western hills, a town appeared, stretched out along the river's edge. Still farther west, the hills ran against the knees of great mountains that suddenly stood up against the sky, one of them loftier than all the rest, with sides more rigidly straight and a great white hat upon its head. By many a description he knew that mountain. It was Monument, and, therefore, the town beside the river had likewise the same name. That was Monument, to which Colter had commended him.

He frowned at the thought. In making that recommendation, Colter had clearly pointed out that there was little likelihood of proper work being found in the town, except for a gunfighter, or a hanger-on.

But the rigid sense of his own virtue that had supported the boy so stoutly during these past days now faltered a little. What, otherwise, was he to do? Ride on into the unknown and, at last, find obscure work on a ranch, riding herd? All the miseries of that labor came up in his mind—the blinding hot August days, the winter blizzards, the weaklings of March that had to be tailed up endlessly, the continual labor, the dirt, the ignorant companions, the poor food.

And suddenly the boy put his conscience asleep by saying to himself that he would venture down to the lowlands and find Monument, and then—see what might happen to him. Not that he deliberately chose a lawless life, but having once ridden to the highlands above the law, it seemed a dreary descent to go back to the common ways of common men.

So he rode down for Monument.

It was no easy ride. That which his eye had seen, striking straight across the valley as a bird might fly, was in reality many a long mile away. He was down to the level, however, in the dusk of the day, and there he camped; in the gray morning he rode on up the valley, keeping close to the bank of the river when he had reached that water. It flowed with a hurrying murmur and he smiled a little as he watched it, wondering how much he could have learned from that continual whispering.

The valley narrowed to a pass between two hills, the river cutting a gorge, and following a trail over the first hill, he came to the top and had his first near view of Monument laid out like a little map at his feet.

He was amazed by it. For the stories he had heard of mining camps usually figured forth scanty shacks of thin wood, collected largely from packing cases, and patched with canvas—jumbles of dug-outs, lean-tos, dog tents thrown confusedly together. But Monument was different. There appeared before the startled eye of the boy a city of broad streets, and structures up to three stories, built of adobe, frame, or brick. Even while he watched, he saw a long procession of wagons loaded with lumber come trundling down the main street on the right bank of the river, drawn by great teams of mules. At the chuckholes the teams paused, shocked to an instant's halt, and then lurched ahead again, all hitting their collars with one rhythm, while the loud voices of the drivers and the crackling of the big wheels came up to John Signal clearly and yet at such a distance that he was reminded of the music of the bees and the whirring wings of birds in the tableland of the mountains through which he had just passed.

It was no straggling frontier town, but seemed built for permanence and pleasure as well as utility. Each bank of the river had been made into a park, the tall trees that originally stood there in imposing files, having been miraculously preserved from the hungry axes of the miners. And Signal at last shook his head in doubt, for it seemed impossible that such a place should be free from the influence of the law.

He jogged his gelding down the slope, still scanning the town and the country all about it. It was a mining town set in the heart of a cow country. All the hills, at a little distance, were freckled with livestock, and, as he came down again toward the river, he saw a pair of cowpunchers bringing in a hundred beeves toward the town—for the butchers, no doubt. And even those scores of fat steers would not last long among the thronging crowds of the city of Monument.

When he joined the trail, he fell in with the rearward cowpuncher and helped him round into the crowd a runaway steer.

"Are you an old hand here at Monument?" asked Signal.

"I'm about as old as any," said the cowpuncher, who was a man of thirty-five. "I've worked cows around these parts for eleven year."

"And worked silver, too, I suppose?"

"I never took nothing out of the ground," answered the other. "What I say is . . . if you want to stay above ground, you better work there. Them that take the cash out of the rocks, give their bones in exchange before very long. That's a bang-up hoss you got there."

"He's not bad," admitted the boy, pleased.

"A cuttin' hoss, I'd say, by the way he pointed that hunk of beef back into the herd."

It was an ugly roan that Signal bestrode, with jutting hip bones and a ewe neck and a great Roman nose and ears that perpetually sagged back. "It's a cutting hoss, too," said Signal.

"Looks a pile more like a camel than it does like a hoss," went on the cowpuncher, "but by the looks of its legs, I could tell. Give a hoss a middle piece and four real legs, and he's worth something."

"He stands over some ground," pointed out the boy, well pleased by this appreciation of a favorite.

"And you gotta use plenty of canvas to make cinches for him."

"He can last," agreed Signal. "He can run all day. Can't you, Grundy?"

Grundy tossed his head and snorted, and flicked his ears back and forth, annoyed.

"He's got the temper of an old woman," commented Signal. "He'd as soon eat you as a bale of hay. His idea of a good game is to get a man down and walk up and down his frame. But he's all horse, and he has a head on his shoulders. That's what counts, I suppose."

"Of course it is," agreed the other. "I wouldn't mind owning a horse like that myself. He's got a turn of speed, I'd hope?"

"Yep. He'd surprise you."

"What kind of a price would you put on him?"

"More than you'd want to pay, partner," said the boy amicably. "He's worth more to me in my line of work than he would be to you in yours."

"Is that so? And what might your line of work be?"

Signal hesitated. What, after all, was his line of work? To keep his hide and head intact, first and foremost, and for that purpose, of course, the horse was invaluable to him. "I'm drifting on a long march," he said in indirect answer. "I'm piling off on a mighty long march, and of course I wouldn't be selling the best thing I got before I start."

"Are you gonna make a richer strike than Monument?" asked the cowpuncher with a grin. And he looked Signal up and down with a flick of his eyes that might have meant nothing, and might have meant a great deal.

The second cowpuncher came up.

"Here's a kid," said the first one, "who's about to make a long march. A mighty long march. I dunno that he knows where."

The heart of Signal began to beat fast and his color altered a little, for he saw that they were beginning to suspect something about him.

The second cowpuncher laughed. "Maybe it ain't what's before but what's behind that makes him ride," was the latter's comment.

Signal reined up his horse. "What are you fellows driving at?" he asked in resentment.

They made no answer, but worked slowly on after the herd, talking to one another, and not to him.

He looked after them in some dismay, and, making a grim resolution that he would never again allow himself to be tricked into conversation about his own goals and destinies, he cantered up the road again, passed the herd without giving the drovers a glance, and rode on toward the town.

And in a few moments he was within the verge of the city of Monument, and the sounds of the place gathered about him like the ripple of water about the ears of a swimmer. So, determined to keep rigidly upon his guard, and to set a special watch over his tongue, he moved on, glancing to the left and right, and feeling extraordinarily like an escaped prisoner, returning to his jail.

Who would attempt to lock the door upon him?

CHAPTER FIVE

He found the streets of Monument broad and fairly clean, though deeply rutted by the wheels of the great wagons that constantly were jolting and jarring through them, in all weathers of the year. The plan of the town was pleasant enough—the upper stories of the buildings projecting out well above the lower, and being supported on strong pillars of adobe or brick or wood that rose from the outer edge of the sidewalks. In the shade of the arcades thus made, the citizens of Monument walked to and fro, sometimes almost lost in the shadow, but at the street corners emerging suddenly into the brightness of the sunlight, and the boy was amazed by such types of clothes and people as he never had seen. Looking down from the height of his saddle, he stared at the headgear in particular and observed derbies, high silk hats most absurdly out of place, common felts of gray and brown, and the sloppy, wide-brimmed, black felt so common all through the West, turning green with age and much sunshine; there were caps, and the peaked straw hats of Mexicans, and the flatter straw hats of others; there were sun helmets, and there were the towering, massive sombreros, sometimes flecked with metal work of varying kinds.

He had many glimpses of the faces that flowed along, making those hats bob up and down, and he saw peons, and high-class Mexicans, and half-breeds and full-blooded Indians from both the north and the south of the Río Grande—and he saw Negroes, and all the shades up to the octoroon whose blood

31

was betrayed only by the smoke in the whites of his eyes, and perhaps by a certain frightened look—and for the rest, there were all the nationalities of white men, and all the grades, and all the classes, from the laborer to the affected gentility of the professional gambler, from the dour-faced gunman to the youngster from England, in riding boots and breeches, unconcerned by the glances of amusement cast after him.

John Signal was so amazed and delighted by this stream of life that he felt that he could have gazed at it during the rest of his days. But here he came to a great sign: *Jenkins's Employment Agency.*

And suddenly he remembered that he had to work in order to live. He had exactly $8 in his pocket, and he already gathered that $8 would not lead him far in such a community as this. He halted the roan horse with a sigh and tethered it at the hitching rack, where already there were half a dozen other horses tied.

Then, resigning himself to the lot of man, he passed into the employment agency. It was a small room, and there was not a soul in it, except a single fat fellow with one arm, who leaned at the center table upon his single hand and seemed to sleep. Young Signal touched his shoulder and was rewarded by a grunt, a start, a whirl of the little man, and a big Colt jabbed into his stomach.

But the other instantly realized that he had made a mistake, and he backed away, grinning shamefacedly. "I was havin' a dream," he said.

"I'm sorry I woke you up," said Signal, good-natured. "You almost put me to sleep for good and all."

"Not me! Not me!" said the other. "But what d'you want with me, son?"

His hand gestured toward his bosom, and the big Colt disappeared.

"I want to talk to the employment agent."

"That's me."

"Are you Jenkins?"

"Thank goodness I ain't. The crook beat me out of my money. All I got is his business. And you see how thick that is."

"Are there a lot of other agencies in the town?"

"There ain't another one."

It was again an occasion for the boy to gape in bewilderment. "How can you keep everybody in jobs?" he asked.

"How can't I? Who wants to work in Monument? Do you?" He looked in open wonder at the boy.

"I do."

"What can you handle? A drill and a singlejack? Know how to break ground long? There's a place for practiced hands at that, but they collect more blisters than dollars, and bust their backs besides."

"I can ride a little and use a rope."

"Are you handy with a rope?"

"I can daub it on a cow now and then."

"You'll find plenty of bulls in this here town, but not so many cows." The fat man chuckled. "But now and then I get a call for a 'puncher on one of the places near here. Shall I write you down?"

"Yes . . . no," hesitated Signal. He had not yet decided upon a name that he could assume. "John is my name," he said.

"John what?" asked the fat man, leaning over a large book that he had opened.

"John what? John nothing."

"You only got one name?"

"That's all."

"There's a million Johns," protested the owner of the business. "Why, if you want something short and snappy, don't you call yourself Red-Eye or Whiskey John, or something like that. People could remember you then."

It appeared to the boy that he had made a ridiculous mistake. He should, of course, have thought of something else to go with his own real name. But all that could pop into his mind at the moment was Jones or Smith, and it seemed to him that the combination would smack too much of an obvious alias.

"Red-Eye John, alias Whiskey John, I like the name of that, old son," went on the employment agent.

There was a rushing of hoofs, a confused bawling, as a herd of cattle poured down the street, casting up clouds of dust that boiled against the door of the agency and sifted in through the screen.

"I can do without the alias," said Signal shortly.

"Hold on!" cried the fat man. "I gotta name for you. I gotta beaut. And it stands by itself. There ain't any other like it. John Alias! How's that?" He rejoiced in the name with loud laughter, smiting his paunch with his open hand until it resounded.

"It's all right," answered Signal, casting his dignity aside, and chuckling in turn. "Call me John Alias, if you want to."

"Alias what?" roared the agent. "They'll always say that. It'll start conversation. You'll never have a dull time . . . not around this part of the world." He laughed again, and there was something other than good nature blended with his mirth, which the boy could hear in the laughter but could not exactly analyze. "John Alias," said the employment agent, "wants a job punching cows. Got his own hoss?"

"Yes."

"A good one? That counts."

"A cutting horse."

"Got a cutting hoss, too. That'll land you a job inside of a week. So long, John Alias." And, still laughing, he followed Signal to the door.

Inside of a week! And how to lodge and board on $8 for a week? That was the problem.

John leaned against a pillar outside the agency and rolled a cigarette, frowning in thought, but, as he lighted the smoke, he noticed with amazement that the roan horse was gone. He looked wildly about him, certain that he must have mistaken the hitching rack, but, stare as he would, he could not spot Grundy. This, indeed, was the rack. He could not be mistaken. Yonder was the mustang that had neighbored Grundy on the right, with a tuft of dirty white forelock thrusting out under the brow band.

He turned to a pair of idlers standing nearby. One was a short, broad man, the other tall, pale, handsome, dressed in a frock coat and a high hat.

"I had a roan horse here!" exclaimed the boy. "Did you see anyone take him . . . by mistake?"

They looked at him with curious intentness. Then they looked at one another.

"Have you any friends here in Monument?" asked the broad fellow.

"No. No one. I've just ridden into town."

"It's a bad town to ride into," said the tall man, and turned deliberately away.

The blood of John Signal was just a little slower to take fire than a train of oil and powder commingled; he wondered if this attitude on the part of the stranger was not enough to justify him in taking offense, and, as he paused, he noticed a Negro in a leather apron, sitting cross-legged at the entrance to a small shop with a sign—*First-Class Boot Repairing*—above the door. In the eye of the Negro, who was looking straight at him, there was a certain message, although the man looked down again in haste.

So John stepped to the door of the shop.

" 'Morning, Uncle George."

" 'Mawnin', son, 'mawnin'," replied the man, and his broad

35

grin was lined with shining white.

"I had a roan horse hitched out here. Did you see anybody take it?"

"There's two kinds of takin', son. There's takin', and there's stealin'."

"I have no friends here. Nobody was authorized to take that roan."

"That remembers me of a story about a kid from Denver that rode in last week. Sullivan was borrowin' his hoss and gettin' into the saddle when the kid runs out of a saloon.

" 'Git off that hoss,' says he, 'you thief.'

"Sullivan shot him through the head. 'Borrowin' ain't robbery,' says Sullivan, and the sheriff seemed to agree."

CHAPTER SIX

If this story made it clear that accusations of theft were dangerous to scatter abroad in Monument, it did not help the boy to find the person of the robber, if robber he were and not "borrower".

"You leave me in the dark," John commented, therefore.

"They's a good many mighty smaht men in this heah town," said the shoemaker, "who doan think nothin' of losin' a hoss. Hosses is cheap heah, son."

"Not horses like my Grundy."

"A good one, was he?"

"The best I ever sat on, and we have good horses in the part of the country that I come from."

"What part is that, son?"

"Yonder," said the boy hastily, and waved in a gesture that embraced half the points on the horizon.

"Come to think," said the other, "you gonna find a lot of neighbors right heah in Monument. Mos' of the gemmen has come from jes' that place." And he laughed, strange, throaty, high-pitched laughter.

"He had a lump of a head and a ewe neck and plenty of hip bones," went on Signal, "but he was all horse, and a yard wide, at that."

"It would've took a hossman to tell his points, Ah'm thinkin'."

"Just that, it would," agreed John heartily.

"Well," said the Negro slowly, "Sim Langley has the name of

37

being a judge of hossflesh."

"Who's Sim Langley? Is that the man who took him? Where shall I find him?" demanded the boy in haste.

"Langley? Ah dunno nothin' about him," said the other, and bent over his work with a scowl.

Plainly he had already said more than he wished, and would not add a word to his statement. Therefore, Signal waited no longer. He went slowly down the street. To his left was a gun shop, and into this he stepped.

A very lean little man, with a rat-like face, furnished with a long nose, met him in the middle of the floor. "What'll you have?"

"I'm looking for a man by name of Sim Langley," said John Signal. "Can you . . . ?"

"D'you think that I got him in here?" snapped the other. "Have I got him in one of those bins, maybe? Do I keep him here and feed him lead and gunpowder, maybe?"

Signal retreated a step before the condensed fury of the other. He began to feel that the people of Monument were one half mad and the other half purely insulting. The long, striking muscles along his arm twitched and hardened. But then he controlled himself.

"People may get guns in your place, but they don't get manners," he said.

"And what might you mean by that?" asked the little man. The ferret-like fury seized upon him again. Actually his hand jerked back to his hip, and he glared with red-stained eyes at the youngster.

It would have frightened most men. Size makes no difference in a gunfight, except that a smaller man is apt to have quicker nerves and a bigger target. But John Signal had the temper of a bull terrier, which leaves the stranger unregarded until the stranger picks up a rock.

Now the boy said with simplicity and directness: "You poison little rat!" And he waited for that speech to take effect. For an instant he felt that the convulsed face of the gun salesman would twist itself to bits with rage, but then the beady eyes grew dimmer. They wavered to the side. And with that, Signal turned upon his heel and left the place.

He accosted the first man who passed, a free-swinging cowpuncher by the look of him, with his sombrero pushed back from a round, red, moist, cheerful face.

"Stranger, can you tell me if you know a man named Sim Langley?"

The other halted, suddenly serious. "Who don't?" he asked. And he passed straight on.

Signal leaned a hand against the nearest pillar and gritted his teeth. He was fast losing his temper completely, and he felt that the next rebuff would bring a gun jumping out of his holster to start talking the only language that this mad town, apparently, could understand. But still he fought hard and controlled himself.

He sauntered on down the street, his face a little pinched and white with the relics of his passion, and so he came to a door beside which, inscribed on a brass plate, were the words: *Sheriff's Office.* And beneath: *First floor up.*

Signal went one floor up and turned to the left down a narrow hallway, the floor giving in noisy squeaks beneath his feet. He reached a door, the upper half of which was of frosted glass, with black letters painted upon it. The letters read: *Sheriff Peter Ogden. Walk in.*

Signal walked in. He saw a dingy room, a roll-top desk in one corner, a round table in the center, and at the table a shirt-sleeved party playing poker. The chips were stacked in small piles. Evidently it was only a friendly game.

Five men sat at that table. Five cigars tilted as the men turned their heads toward the stranger.

A narrow counter enclosed the door, as though to keep the press of business from overflowing into the room itself. Upon that counter the boy leaned his left hand. Already he had been in the town long enough to realize the necessity of keeping the right hand free and ready.

"I want to see Sheriff Peter Ogden."

A large and rosy man removed his cigar. "You're seeing him, my boy."

"Then I want to talk to you about a stolen horse."

"A stolen horse?"

"That's it."

The sheriff rose with a sigh and approached the counter. "I'll take down the particulars," he said. "First time that a stolen horse is picked up, I'll let you know."

This touch of irony brought the teeth of young John Signal together with a *click*. But the sheriff did not appear to notice. He had taken out a sheet of paper.

"Kind of horse?"

"Roan gelding."

"That the only description?"

"Roman-nosed. Fifteen three. Ewe-necked. Prominent hip bones. Good legs. Keeps his ears back."

"That's a lot to write," said the sheriff, "about a ewe-necked horse." But, looking up, he encountered a blaze of dangerous light in the eyes of the boy. At that he pushed the paper to one side. "How long you been in Monument?"

"About two hours."

"*A-h-h-h,*" murmured the sheriff. Then he added: "Where'd you leave this horse?"

"At a rack outside the employment agency."

"You're looking for work?"

"I am."

The sheriff tapped upon the counter with his soft, fat fingers. "What sort of work?"

"Horses and cows. That's my line."

"You can ride?"

"Yes."

"Pretty well?"

"I'm not a bronc' peeler. But I can ride 'em."

"You come out of the agency and your horse is gone?"

"Yes. He's gone."

"Anybody standing around?"

"Yes."

"What did they say?"

"That I ought to keep my horse in my pocket when I came in to Monument."

Again the teeth of the boy *clicked*, and the sheriff banished his smile.

"I'll tell you what," he said, "there are about twenty horses a week stolen in one way or another around Monument."

The retort of Signal was hardly courteous. "Are you the sheriff?" he asked.

The latter tipped up his head, and, so doing, he showed a bull neck with lines of great power beneath its fat. A cold light appeared in his eyes. "I'm the sheriff," he said. "What about it?"

"Twenty stolen horses a week are what about it," said John Signal. There was a little stir at the table. He paid no heed, but his bright, angry eyes glared at the fat man. The latter's mouth twitched.

"You're young," he said. "You have no line on the thief?"

"A man said it might be Sim Langley. Who's he?"

The sheriff started erect. "You don't know that?" he asked.

"I don't know that. Why should I?"

"Young fellow," said the sheriff, "take the chip off your

shoulder, or are you here to try to make a reputation out of me?"

"I want nothing out of you or the rest of Monument," said the boy, "except my horse back and a job if I can get it."

"Who told you about Langley taking the roan?"

"A man who doesn't want his name used."

"Do you want me to arrest Langley without anything on which to make out a warrant?"

"I want my horse."

"My boy," said the sheriff, "it's not hard to find Langley. If he's got your horse, take it back. And when you bring it in . . . I'll give you a job . . . as deputy sheriff . . . at a hundred and fifty a month!"

CHAPTER SEVEN

This remark of the sheriff was not made to the boy alone. Rather, it was delivered to the entire room, for he turned halfway from the counter in order to let all hear what he had to say. From the four who lolled in their chairs at the table came appreciative laughter; they had been enjoying this scene with the dull eyes of content, putting by their impatience for the game in the superior pleasure of listening to the follies and the conceits of a very young man. It was not difficult to hear everything that young Signal said. He spoke crisply, biting off his words, like a man who controlled his passion better than his voice.

But now that the sheriff had delivered this rather amused ultimatum, Signal brought all attention back to himself by tapping upon the counter with the stiffened fingers of his left hand. "Suppose I take you up on that proposition, Sheriff? Suppose I just take you up on that?"

The sheriff looked back at him, round-eyed, and the youngster discerned, in the corners of the eyes, a faint stain of yellow, caused, perhaps, by too much smoking of cigars, or, on the other hand, by a dash of Mexican blood. Who could tell in this border land? At any rate, those eyes now blinked at the boy in amazement; there was chiefly astonishment and a sort of persistent disbelief in that expression, but also there was a goodly measure of amusement. Yonder at the table, however, the four smiles had settled down a good deal. A big, handsome man got up and came to the counter. The very fact that the sheriff played cards with such a fellow as this raised Signal's respect for the former.

"My boy," said this newcomer, "what's your name?"

"John Alias," said Signal defiantly.

"Alias what?"

"Alias nothing."

"John . . . alias Nothing," murmured the new speaker. "Why, we've got a firecracker in town again, Sheriff!"

"It ain't the first," said the sheriff rather wearily. "You go an' explode yourself under the nose of Sim Langley, will you?" he added to John. "And bring back your horse that you lost."

"Will you tell me the way to his place?"

"He has all sorts of places," said the sheriff.

"He's spending a good deal of time on the Esmeralda," replied his tall companion.

"Is he going that way to perdition?" commented the sheriff. "Well, if you want to find him, young fellow, go straight across the first bridge over the river and head straight on. You can't get off the main road. Two or three miles out, you'll come to a ranch house, Mexican style, spread out long and low, white-washed adobe with a lot of vine climbing all over it. That's maybe the place around which you might find Sim Langley."

John Signal stepped to the door.

"Hey, Alias!"

Signal turned.

"The kid answers to the name, all right," said the sheriff's companion. "Alias, d'you know the sort of game you're apt to get from Langley?"

"Guns?"

"And shotguns. Good bye and good luck!"

He waved his hand with a graceful gesture, and John Signal went down to the street.

He got to the first bridge across the river as the leaders of a fourteen-mule team began to clamber up the arch of the farther side, and he stood aside to watch them tugging all in rhythm, while the muleskinner, with his long whip, strode beside them, cursing magnificently. The wheels of the two wagons that trailed behind this laboring team ground and rumbled on the upgrade. Then as the crest of the bridge was mounted, they began to gain impetus. The wheelers were forced to hasten, then to trot. The yell of the driver forced the pointers to take up the swifter pace, then the swing, then the leaders themselves were jogging while the wagons rolled with thunder down to the level road, struck a bump with a crash, rocked perilously from side to side, and then settled again to a monotonous progress up the street.

This small affair held Signal enchanted, for he was an imaginative youngster, and he thought he saw in this tiny interlude something that cast a light upon the whole course of human affairs. That is to say: all deeds have an upgrade that takes labor, and when the crest of the labor is reached, then caution and skill are needed to keep from going too far. Yes, at the very shore of success, we often find the bumps that wreck us.

And he turned out the road that led away from the town of Monument to the southern hills with a feeling that perhaps his task would be exactly the same. Sim Langley was a gunfighter, it appeared, a thoroughly dangerous man, and yet a brisk, determined approach could do wonders with the most danger-ous of fighters.

He had fully three miles, then, of dusty road to cover, before he had sight of the ranch house. It made a pretty picture, set well back from the road, with an avenue of poplars pointing toward it. In fact, the white walls showed very little, and even the red roof was nearly lost under the shade of the trees and the host of green climbing things that swarmed across it. Behind it were the barns, and the corrals, and, circling a little around the house, he approached the latter.

He did not have far to look. The ugly head of Grundy was thrust over the fence toward him, and at the sight of his master the roan whinnied softly in recognition.

Signal went into the barn, and the first thing he saw was a pair of Mexicans, working on the braiding of rawhide whips—and the second thing he saw was a rack of guns to the side—and the third thing he saw was his own saddle, hanging from a convenient peg.

He did not hesitate, but, nodding to the pair, he went to the saddle and picked it off its peg. With the saddle comfortably propped against his left hip, he stepped to the gun rack, and he knew his own Winchester in a flash. He drew it forth.

He had come back to the door of the barn before one of the Mexicans said in a broken English: "Chief you send here?"

John replied in perfectly good Spanish: "Langley has a little job on his hands."

The other stepped back at once, and Signal went on with a faint smile. For it was perfectly true that he expected Langley would soon have a job on his hands, though not exactly of the sort that the pair of Mexicans might suspect.

Inside the corral there was no difficulty in catching the roan. Grundy came gladly to the bridle and even abandoned his usual complaining grunting and swelling of the stomach when the cinches were tightened on him. And so, with the rifle in the long holster and the saddle in place, young John Signal passed out through the corral gate with the feeling that a cheap triumph was in his hands and that the crest of the bridge already had been passed. Then, as he turned from shoving home the bolt of the gate, he saw one of the Mexicans hurrying toward him from the house, and beside him was that same tall, lean, hard-faced fellow who he had met earlier in that day, bringing in the five-score beeves to the market.

John remembered instantly the rush of cattle and the bellowing down the street when he had been inside the employment agency. He remembered also how highly he had commended his roan to the same cowpuncher during the course of their conversation. That made the links of understanding complete.

Over his bended left arm the cowpuncher supported a rifle; young Signal went straight toward him.

Then, as though changing his mind—or his tactics—the other passed the Winchester to the Mexican at his side and advanced with empty hands. But it could be noticed that he wore two Colts, each slung low down on his leg so that the handles were most convenient to the touch. Signal understood perfectly. His own gun was carried in exactly the same position.

"Hello, young feller," said the other. "You've got a quick eye for a trail, I see."

"I'm glad you see that," said Signal.

"But about that horse," went on the cowpuncher, halting at a significant ten paces, while Signal stopped the horse. "I've gotta say that you can't get away with it."

"Can't I?"

"How do I know that you own it?" went on the cowpuncher brazenly.

"How do I know that you own the guns you wear?" countered Signal.

"Kid," said the other, "that don't need any proving. If you want it proved, lemme ask you, do you know my name?"

"It's Langley, I suppose."

"You know my name. D'you know me?" He asked this with a great deal of satisfaction.

"I don't know you," answered Signal. "But I gather that you're what's called a bad *hombre*."

"Do you?" asked Langley. "Now, lemme say this. Gents have seen me ride this hoss in here . . . what would they think if they

47

saw you ride that hoss out . . . and me not raise a voice?"

"I don't give a hang what other people would think," declared Signal.

"I'll tell you what I'll do. I'll pay you a fair price for that hoss and that outfit. Not that I care about the outfit . . . or very much about the hoss. But folks have seen me take it, and it's gotta be mine."

Signal took note that the Mexican was drifting to the side, rifle at the ready. And he, in turn, slipped around the head of Grundy, putting the horse between him and danger. He still could confront Langley.

"Langley," he said, "you never had a better chance for fighting than this. Are you going to take it?"

"Why, you young fool!" cried Langley in the tone of one bewildered.

There was a little trick that Signal had learned on his father's ranch from an old half-breed. It was to mount a horse's side and cling like an Indian, with nothing showing in the saddle. His right arm remained free to manage a revolver under the neck of the horse if need be. So, having delivered his challenge fairly and getting no immediate response, Signal leaped at the side of Grundy, who lurched instantly into a run.

Langley leaped backward to avoid being trodden underfoot, and, springing back, most unluckily, his right spur caught in a tiny hummock, and he landed flat on his back with enough force to jar most of the wind out of his body. Signal, seeing that, turned the head of Grundy a little, and, as he did so, a rifle *clanged* and a bullet *hissed* past.

Under the neck of Grundy he saw the Mexican upon one knee, the rifle drawn level and steady for another shot, and Signal fired without taking aim. He saw a spurt of dust spring up just in the rifleman's face; that weapon exploded wildly in the air, and the Mexican leaped up and bolted, yelling, for the barn.

And, in five more seconds, young John Signal found himself galloping into the avenue of poplars, tearing up the sod of the garden on the way. He heard a muffled, faint cry, and on his left he shot past a very pretty girl with a pale face and dark, fine eyes regarding him intently.

That was the Esmeralda, perhaps, of whom the sheriff and his companion had spoken, and, even while he galloped, Signal wondered why it should be that those who chose to call upon Esmeralda were said to have chosen a particular way to perdition. For so it had been inferred in the sheriff's office.

However, there was no need for further speculation. The next moment he was *clattering* down the highroad, and now Monument held out its arms to him again.

CHAPTER EIGHT

To his mind, there was no better way of expressing the difference between his first entrance and this one, for when he first rode into the place, he had been surrounded by sneers and short answers, but now he knew beforehand that all this was altered.

He had proof positive as he *clattered* across the bridge, for as he reached the arch of it, he passed a small boy who cried out to a companion: "Look! He's got it again!"

Their voices followed in Signal's ear as he rode on.

"He must've bought it back!"

"Bought nothin'. Would Langley sell?"

After this, Signal reduced the pace of his horse to a jog trot, because he was anxious to hear any further comments that might be made.

The town of Monument was large enough to have two newspapers, which lavishly abused one another, but the papers were not needed to spread about the local news, it appeared. They could comment, but they could hardly spread any tales. Before Signal had ridden three blocks, he was aware that the entire city knew about the stealing of his horse. Men and women stopped short upon the street and stared at the roan, and at him. And when he came back to the sheriff's office and dismounted to tether his horse at the rack, a little crowd gathered—but across the street, as though they did not wish to come closer for fear of committing themselves.

Now, stepping onto the sidewalk, John felt reasonably sure that the roan would not be stolen again. He could tell that, as it were, by the signs of the times, and those signs he read in the little murmur that ran before him and behind. Upon the sidewalk he passed the same tall, pale man in the frock coat who had treated him with such rudeness before. He now gave Signal a cheerful smile and a nod that said, as clearly as though words had been used: *Well done!*

Signal went up the stairs to the sheriff's office and walked in upon a moment so tense that no head turned toward him. He waited. He could afford to wait.

And so he saw the sheriff's big friend rake in the stakes with a smile, and then, turning, exclaim: "By the long arm of Aaron! The kid is back already."

The sheriff turned with a grin. "You lost your way, kid, I suppose?"

Said Signal: "I've come to be sworn in as deputy sheriff."

He had been turning over that sentence in his mind on the way back to town, and the spectacular quality in it pleased him enormously. As for the sheriff, he seemed thoroughly staggered. He got up from his chair and came to the counter with a frown.

"You went out there and found your horse at the Pineta house?"

"I don't know the name of the house."

"Langley wasn't there, then. But what about the greasers?"

"Langley was there. There were only a couple of greasers."

"Langley was there? But you slipped the horse away without anybody seeing? That's smart work, my boy!"

"They saw, well enough, but Langley tripped and fell down at just the right time for me. There wasn't much shooting . . . I don't think anyone was hurt."

"Langley was there . . . and the greasers . . . and still you got that horse away!" The sheriff summed up in a puzzled voice, as one to whom a conundrum had been proposed, a conundrum incapable of solution. Then he said quietly: "My boy, if you're what you seem to be, you're what I want as a deputy. I don't know exactly what happened at the Pineta place. But if you've brought back your horse, that's enough for me. We'll swear you in right now, if you want. And you can take down two weeks' advance pay, if that will please you!"

In five minutes, Monument received a new deputy sheriff, named John Alias.

"You stick by that name?"

"It's as good as another."

"As good as any other to start trouble, but that's your business. What do you know about Monument?"

"Nothing."

"You have to know everything. You know the Eagans and the rest of 'em?"

"I never heard of any Eagans of Monument. I've only heard of a Fitzgerald Eagan."

The sheriff turned to his companions. "The kid has heard a lot," he said. "He's heard of Fitzgerald Eagan."

And a white-whiskered, elderly fellow remarked: "He must've been plumb diving into the old books of lore, I'd say. He's been hunting the newspapers pretty close, if he's heard of Fitz."

By which Signal was wise enough to understand that he had mentioned one who, for one cause or another, was a great celebrity.

"You boys clear out," said the sheriff. "I've gotta talk to this lad. Run along. We gotta be alone in here."

"Teach him how to shoot and how to pray," said he of the white whiskers. "I got an idea that he'll need to do both before he's many days older."

They trooped away. Signal sat down at the center table in a shaft of sunshine; the sheriff sat down in the shadow, out of which the fume of his cigar ascended and made a strange, blue-brown writing, like the scrawl of a child, across the pathway of the sun.

"Now, John Alias, we'll talk shop."

"I suppose we'd better."

"You've lodged yourself here," said the sheriff, "in a house where trouble is served up boiled for breakfast, and fried for lunch, and hashed for supper. You know that?"

"I guessed that," observed the boy. "Nobody glad-handed me when I came in."

"You didn't look worth a tumble, or you'd have had plenty of lying, sneaking crooks around, trying to pick your pockets or to lead you into one of the gambling houses . . . or to dope you in a saloon and roll you afterward. You understand what sort of a place Monument is now?"

"I begin to read a few of the headlines. I don't know the whole article as yet."

"You won't, either, my boy. Not for years. Not even then. I've been here for three years, studying everything like a book, and still I don't know much. Hardly anything at all as a matter of fact. Do you follow that?"

"Yes, of course."

"Where were you raised? Back East?"

"No. Just on the other side of the mountains." He hesitated to say this much, but, after all, "the other side of the mountains" included a large sweep of country.

The sheriff, noting this hesitation, smiled in turn. He grew more amiable with every moment. "You didn't come here for fun, my boy," he suggested.

Signal shrugged his shoulders.

"Don't talk, then," said the sheriff. "Don't say a word, if it hangs on your tongue a little. What people were before they came to Monument hardly matters at all. It's what they turn out to be here that bothers me. I've seen the hardest-boiled crooks in the world tame down and turn white inside of two days in Monument. And I've seen the straightest lads that ever left good homes come out here to have a little fun and to take a whack at silver . . . and they've gone bad quicker than meat in hot weather. So I say that you never can tell. Only, I want you to open up your ears and listen to one piece of advice from me."

"I'm listening," said the youth.

"You've been raised to shoot and ride. I can see that. Ride straight and shoot straight. There's nothing better than that. But remember this. If you never crossed those mountains before, this is your first trip to the West. This is your first trip to Montana days, to California in 'Forty-Nine, to fury and fire. They've got the railroad and the telegraph spilled all over the country, now. They've got newspapers in Monument, and they've got a dog-gone' opera house, and everything else that a man would like to see. But I'll tell you, under that flossy front, this Monument city is as wild as ever any camp in California or Montana . . . it's as crazy and as hot as Abilene or Dodge City ever was in their palmiest days . . . which ain't so long ago at that. Discard all your first ideas, while I take you by the hand and lead you up to meet Miss Monument."

Chapter Nine

This peroration of the sheriff having been finished, he rose from the table and sauntered to the door. There, standing to one side, he jerked the door suddenly open, and into the room stumbled a startled, blinking youngster.

"Hey!" he said. "What's the idea?" He rallied himself as the sheriff looked down sternly upon him, and in silence. "Mister Ogden, I come up here to tell you that I've been rolled in Mortimer's saloon. They fixed me up and trimmed me proper, and. . . ."

"What's your name?"

"Hovey."

"Hovey, what did they roll you for?"

"My whole wad! Two hundred and twenty-five dollars."

"Who rolled you?"

"I dunno. I was a little woozy with booze yesterday and I. . . ."

"I'll keep you in mind. If anybody comes around here with two hundred and twenty-five dollars that needs an owner, I'll take it for granted that it belongs to you. So long, Hovey."

Mr. Hovey slunk silently from the room.

And the sheriff, turning the key in the lock, came slowly back to the table and sat down. He had his back to the wall, and his face toward the door. "I never know when that glass will be smashed through and the nose of a rifle poked in at me," he declared. "They'll get me someday, of course. You saw how that young cur was spying on me?"

"Why didn't you collar him?" asked the boy hotly. "Why didn't you collar him and find out what he meant by trying to eavesdrop?"

"What good would it do?" answered the sheriff wearily. "I know who sent him, I think."

"Who, then?"

"Fitz Eagan, probably. No, Fitz is above that sort of thing. But some of the other Eagans are not. One of them sent him."

"And what was he to learn?"

"What I said to you, of course. Do you suppose that every man and woman and child in Monument doesn't know at this instant that there's a new deputy come here to file his claim on a grave?"

The youngster pricked his ears at this cheerful speech.

"You have to know the truth," said the sheriff. "I've had three deputies inside of the past year. They've all been hard-fighting, straight-shooting men. They've all gone down. They've all been salted away. You'd better know that before you go any further."

"I've sworn myself in," said the boy bitterly.

"I'll swear you out again, my lad. Don't let that stand in your way. Don't let any false pride stop you."

"Four other men heard you swear me in," protested Signal gloomily. "I didn't know that Monument was as poison as all this . . . but now that I'm in the job, I'll stay with it."

The sheriff puffed his cigar for a moment of silence. "You saw how I had to turn that kid away?" he said. "Rough, wasn't it?"

"Not if he was a spy."

"How can I tell that?"

"Sneaking at your door!"

"He might be an honest fellow who came up here, and I simply happened to jerk the door open under his nose. The chances are in any other town that would be the right explanation of him. But here in Monument it's a great deal different."

Signal nodded.

"The law says that every man is innocent and must be so treated and so regarded until it's proved that he's guilty. That's what the law says, and I try to obey and respect the law. But in Monument you have to look at things from another viewpoint. Every man in Monument is guilty, or else he wouldn't be here . . . and in any sort of trouble."

"That explains," murmured the boy.

"Explains what?"

"The way people treated me when I asked questions on the street when I first rode in."

"Ask nothing! That's the first rule in Monument. Everybody knows what you're after. If they want to tell you what they know, they will. If they don't want to tell you, they won't."

Signal nodded.

"Now, then," said the sheriff, "you've been introduced a little to Monument ways. I'll give you the map of the land as it lies today, seven years since Billy Shane found his mine and called it Monument."

"Because it was on a ledge where an Indian monument had been piled up?"

"You know that much? Well, Billy Shane's strike started loose into the world a lot of money, and a lot of trouble. This is the way things are lined up here . . . Monument is marshaled on two sides. I'm the weight that tries to keep things balanced in the center of the scales. On one side there's the Bones and their crew. You've heard of the Bones?"

"Never."

"You *have* had a mountain range between you and Monument, son. Old Bone has a long white beard. It's fifteen inches long. He's killed a man for every inch of it, they say. And he has a pair of sons who are growing up to follow in papa's footsteps . . . Jud and Billy. Jud is a bully, and sometimes a coward. Other times, he's a fighting fiend. And that's one thing to learn. The man you can bluff with a wooden gun one day will charge a Gatling and its whole crew the next. Usually whiskey makes the difference. These fellows are generally drunk and foolish . . . or weak with getting over the liquor . . . they're normal in the times between sprees. You never know how you'll catch them. Some men fight sober. Most men fight drunk. You have to know your man. Then there's Charley Bone. He's dead game by nature. He laughs when he fights. A wicked sort of a scrapper that makes, as you may be able to guess for yourself.

"Along with the Bone tribe, we count in Doc Mentor and Joe Klaus, who most people call Santa Claus. They're a pair of crooks who have done everything from stage robbery to Mexican raiding. They're great pals of the Bone family. But the biggest card that the Bone outfit has in its pack is Colter, of course. You've heard of Henry Colter, at least?"

Young Signal said not a word, but his eyes grew a little brighter, and he nodded.

"Colter is a great man in this part of the world. He can snap his fingers and call twenty hard-riding, straight-shooting fellows to follow him. Some of them are worthy of hanging. Others are young fools who simply like adventure. They're apt to be the most dangerous of all. Others are honest men who follow Colter because he has the whip hand over them. But what makes Colter feared and worth fearing is that he has the ability to win the confidence of the men behind him. They'll steal or kill exactly as he bids them. In short, Colter is the Napoléon of this town of Monument."

"A fellow like that," said the boy, "is surely an outlaw. How can he live in Monument?"

"I'd need five regiments of United States regulars," said the sheriff, "to arrest every recognized outlaw in this town. We run on different rules. We arrest the men who commit crimes in Monument, if we can find them. As for what happens outside, we have to blink our eyes at it.

"Now I want to tell you the other side of the story. There's the Eagan faction. Fitzgerald Eagan is a famous man. He tamed down Dodge City when it was boiling hot. He's the town marshal in Monument at this minute. And he wants my job as sheriff." He paused to allow this information to sink in. Then he went on: "Behind Fitz Eagan is Major Paul Harkness. He's a consumptive gambler and all-around crook. There's only one good spot in his whole rotten heart, and that's his love for Fitz Eagan. Those fellows have saved each other a dozen times. Behind Harkness and Fitz are the four other Eagan boys. They are Dick, and Jimmy, and Harry, and Oliver, who's the oldest of the four. Every one of the Eagan tribe has accounted for at least two men during the course of his life. The Eagans, led by Fitzgerald Eagan, hate the Bone tribe. The Bone tribe hates the Eagans."

"It seems to me," suggested Signal, "that the Eagans are the better crew. But why shouldn't the whole crowd of both sides be run out of town?"

"I couldn't do it," answered the sheriff. "Neither could you. Neither could any man. There's hardly a man in Monument who isn't lined up on one side or the other. Take your friend Sim Langley, for instance. He's a devoted Bone advocate, and one of the most dangerous. That will probably throw you on the other side."

"I'll be on no side at all," said the boy fiercely. "I'll be on the side of law, against everyone."

"In that case, you won't live two days."

Signal was silent, breathing heavily, and all the fight in him mounted to his head and made his face a burning red. Yet there was no answer that he could make to the sheriff. Plainly he could not fight every gunman in Monument single-handed.

"On one side or the other," said the sheriff, "you will certainly find yourself. Pick your party as you please. For my part, I'm inclined toward the Bone party, and most people know it."

At this strange statement, Signal fairly gasped.

"You think the Eagans are a cleaner lot," said the sheriff. "And in many ways they are. But one can't tell. Men say that Fitz Eagan is responsible for most of the stage robberies around here, that Dick Eagan is the expert yegg who has been cracking safes. And we know that the whole tribe are killers. In the meantime, through the Bone-Colter faction I'm able to lay my hands on the new crooks who drift into the town. Everybody has to take a party, here. So do the papers. The *Ledger* writes always for the Eagan party. The *Recall* works for the Bone group. And there you are! Walk out and take the air, young man, and try to pick your side of the fence."

CHAPTER TEN

So John Signal went out into the air to pick a side. He had no more idea of how to go about it than an eagle would have a thought about the best way to dig a mine. Of one thing, however, he was perfectly sure, and that was that the roan horse would be waiting for him at the hitching rack. And there, in fact, he found him. Sim Langley had not rushed into town to take vengeance.

But, no, he was wrong.

A hand touched him on the shoulder. A voice whispered in his ear: "Sim Langley is in Mortimer's saloon, swearin' that he's gonna shoot the eyes right out of your head."

Signal half turned and saw a man with a lean, yellow, weak face, now drawn with fear and yet ecstatic at the thought of the mischief that was in the air.

"Where is Mortimer's saloon?" asked Signal. "I'll go there and talk to my friend Langley. I've been wanting to see him, in fact."

"You'll . . . go . . . there!" ejaculated the news-bearer. And he turned and dipped into the crowd, doubtless intent on carrying back this fine tiding to the saloon.

A little group of people had collected to overhear as many of these words as possible. Not that they actually halted, but they slowed their steps, so that they would be longer in passing, and thus there was formed a small swirl of humanity, and all the eyes flashed cornerwise glances at the youngster.

John Signal is our hero. We frankly avow it. In many ways, such a man is a less desirable citizen than a royal Bengal tiger—such a man is like a roaring fire in a forest. Sooner or later, the wind is apt to blow that fire into the great trees, and then will follow a conflagration that will waste millions in dollars, and the work of ages in noble beauty. But still John Signal is our hero in spite of his faults, or perhaps to a certain extent on account of them. Too many of us are little, twinkling points of half-discernible light—only now and again one finds a beacon.

But it is with shame that it must be admitted that Signal was pleased by this attention from all around him. It pleased him so much that he stiffened his back and looked straight before him, trying to appear unconscious of all the questioning, half-admiring and half-frightened glances. The hard faces of fighting men, as they passed, gazed at him with the same expression as the mildest boys. Definitely he had stepped upon the stage of Monument and was somewhere near the center of public attention.

And John Signal was only twenty-two.

"If you go to Mortimer's saloon, you're a fool," said a quiet voice.

The tall, thin, consumptive form of Major Paul Harkness stood before him. Upon the lips of the sick man there was usually a slight sneer. He wore it now, as he stood before Signal.

"What's wrong with Mortimer's saloon?" asked Signal, very surprised and depressed.

"You want to go there and break into a couple of columns of print by killing Langley."

"I haven't said that."

"You don't have to say it. Why else would you be going there?"

That silenced the boy.

"Mortimer's place is the hang-out for Langley and all the rest of the crooked tribe of Bone," declared the major. And, saying this, he turned his head a little, and raised his voice, so that the words could be heard plainly through all the slowly drifting mass of bystanders.

"I said I'd go there. I have to keep my promise," said Signal.

"Go and be hanged to you!" said Harkness contemptuously. "At least, I don't have to buy your coffin."

He regarded Signal from head to foot with the coldest pale-gray eyes that ever fell upon a human countenance, and the boy was chilled to his marrow. Then Harkness turned away and moved through the crowd, turning neither to the right nor to the left, but, although he was heading through the thickest mob of the lingerers, yet in some manner a way was opened before him, deftly and mysteriously. He walked on with slow dignity, and presently disappeared.

And the boy, rousing as from a dream, asked of a bystander: "Do you know the way to Mortimer's saloon?"

"Mortimer's saloon?" asked the other, startled. "Of course! Right down that next street, about three blocks, I suppose."

And John Signal went out to his horse and mounted, while he heard a secret little murmur behind him:

"He's going to go. He's going down to find Langley. In Mortimer's saloon."

He heard those whispers and knew, now, that nothing could prevent him from going down there, and, therefore, that nothing could possibly keep him from dying in Mortimer's saloon. For it never occurred to him to doubt the truth of what the cold-faced major had said. The very essence of deadly truth was breathed forth by that chilly presence.

So, hating the foolish pride that drove him on, John Signal untethered the roan and swung into the saddle. He hardly had dropped into it when the roan gave him something else to think about.

There had been a day when that roan was considered a most

promising young outlaw, with a broken fibula, a cracked collar bone, and half a dozen cracked ribs to his credit. At the cost of a dozen hard tumbles, and with infinite patience, Signal had been able to master that vicious spirit, but it left Grundy with a brain packed full of subtle invention, and with a lasting contempt for all mankind tucked somewhere in a corner of his spirit.

All those subtle inventions, all that hearty contempt, now suddenly exploded. Grundy lurched into the air as though a gigantic springboard had been released beneath him. He came down in true sun-fishing style upon stiffened forelegs, and thereby snapped the startled and unprepared John Signal half out of his saddle.

This flourish thoroughly awakened him, but he had no good chance to get back into the saddle. The yell of delight from the onlookers stabbed into his ears. He told himself with grim humor that it hardly mattered whether Grundy killed him here in the open street, or the Bone murderers disposed of him in Mortimer's saloon. And then he strove to wriggle back into the saddle.

Grundy, however, was not waiting for developments. He bucked for two blocks as fast as another horse could have run, and then he began to spin like a top flung from a boy's hand. Presently the feet of the rider were disentangled. His body began to stream out to the side. And then a convulsive pitch settled the business.

The world, comprised of blue sky, a shining white cloud, a hitching rack, fronts of houses, faces of humans, and the reckless, fighting head of Grundy—all this world was shuffled before the eyes and in the brain of young John Signal like a pack of cards.

He struck the ground heavily—heavily enough to have broken his back, had not the blow been glancing, so that he was merely rolled over and over at tremendous speed, beating up the dust into a great cloud about him.

He lay still, then, his wits spinning, and heard the *boom* of a revolver, and dust spat against his face. He rose swaying, upon one arm, and promptly his hat rose from his head, jerked off by a second bullet, and sailed some feet distant.

He managed to bring out his revolver, but he dared not shoot into that spinning sea of faces, although he marked the would-be assassin with perfect clarity. It was a man whose face was puckered upon one side with a great red scar, a never-to-be-forgotten vision of perfect ugliness.

Then a tall fellow, a mighty man, stepped from the crowd to the gunman and struck up his Colt, so that the third bullet whistled harmlessly high above the head of Signal. A brief scuffle—and then the scar-faced warrior had disappeared, and the deliverer was alone.

And then a crowd washed out into the street and surrounded Signal. He got to his feet, pushing away the hands that offered to assist him, and went with a weaving course and a staggering gait.

Grundy, snorting with excitement, actually pranced to the master he had just discarded, and, while the onlookers shouted with delight, allowed Signal to take the dangling reins and support some of his weight on them. So they came up together to the big fellow who had routed the killer.

"I don't know you, stranger," said Signal.

"You don't?" The big man smiled.

"By Jiminy, he don't know even Fitz Eagan," said the whisper of the crowd.

"I'm Fitzgerald Eagan. I seen this rat of a Doc Mentor about to clean you. That's all. I don't like to see a good man go with a crooked shuffle of the cards."

"I want to shake your hand," said the boy. He found the

hand of Fitzgerald Eagan and gripped it hard, and as he did so, as by magic, his brain cleared from the hard fall he had received, and his eyes saw before him the most real picture of manhood that ever he had encountered, that ever he had dreamed. Fitz Eagan was not a giant, but it was easy to see that he possessed a giant's strength, and he had the lordly manner of one who is master of himself and of all his passions. A perfect sword in the hand of a perfect swordsman—so appeared Fitz Eagan to the astonished and delighted eyes of young John Signal.

Ordinarily he was not a particularly demonstrative boy, but now, unsettled by his fall, filled with bursting gratitude for what this stranger had done for him, he broke out with an enthusiastic cry: "Are you Fitz Eagan? By heaven, you are a man!"

The crowd laughed joyously, sympathetically.

"*Aw,* he's a man, all right!"

"This is where Eagan picks up a right good man with guns!"

But Fitzgerald Eagan himself smiled on Signal, and nodded his acknowledgments, not in the least upset or crimsoned by this flattery.

"What happened to your hoss?" he asked, and approached the roan.

CHAPTER ELEVEN

"He used to be a bad actor," said the boy. "He's got a brain filled with all sorts of tricks. He was just trotting out a few of them today."

"Does he trot 'em out every day?"

"No. Not for months, in fact."

"Been working him hard?"

"Most of the time, he's loafed around. Lately he's been worked down a little. You can see for yourself."

He was rather surprised by these questions, but it did not occur to him to doubt the wisdom of anything that this lordly man might say. He took note that the other was admiring the legs of Grundy.

"He stands pretty well," said Fitzgerald Eagan.

"He'd never fall down under you," declared the boy with warmth.

"But what made him bust loose? What's happened to him? A hoss don't go mad in two minutes after being straight for months." He felt under the blanket. Grundy snorted and winced—and then Eagan drew forth a great bur, deeply stained with red. His face was dark as he handed it to Signal. "That's your first token from the Bone tribe," he said. "The murderers! They fix your horse. Then they put gunmen along the street to get you when you're helpless. They're organizers, are the Bones. Organizers of murders, the yaller, yappin' coyotes!"

He, delivering these words with a separate dignity of

emphasis, impressed John Signal that the Bone family and all their adherents were the lowest of the low.

"You were going to the Mortimer saloon?" asked Eagan.

"Yes."

"Of course, they heard that. They decided that it would be better to get you in the open air. It would have made a bit too much talk, if they'd murdered you within doors. But let me tell you something, John Alias. . . ."

Very strange that name sounded upon the lips of Fitzgerald Eagan; from that moment, as though he had received a title from a king, John Signal felt that his new name was real, and that a new personality, almost, went with its bestowal.

"You're not going to the Mortimer saloon. You're coming along with me."

"You know a lot more about this town than I do," consented Signal gladly.

Someone among the ever-present bystanders was chuckling. "He knows a lot more about it than anybody. Whoever wanted information would have to ask the opinion of Fitz about this here town, I'm thinking."

But Signal went off down the street, walking at the side of Fitz Eagan, and leading Grundy. He went proudly. He did not have to be told that he was at the side of the lion of Monument. Something the sheriff had told him; something he had gathered from the awe and the admiration of the crowd—but a thousand times more than this he had seen and felt for himself.

They twisted out of the business section down some side alleys and came to a house that fronted on the river. It was a pleasant little cottage, drenched with vines. A shower of honeysuckle poured its spray of white blossoms above the porch, and the bees were laboring patiently among the blossoms. Upon the front steps a cat slept, curled into a pool of black. And before the door, there was a mat into which letters had been woven that read: *Welcome.*

Suddenly it seemed impossible that this little house could be no more than seven years old. It had about it the atmosphere that usually comes only from generations of habitation, and young Signal wondered at the house no less than he had wondered at the master of the place.

He was invited to take a chair on the porch. Fitz Eagan sat in another beside him and the cat leaped into his lap, and then stretched out along his thigh. They lighted two of Fitz Eagan's cigars, and smoked in silence.

Signal fell into greater and greater suspense. He felt that a revelation was about to be made to him.

Then Eagan said: "Honeysuckle is fast growing, ain't it? Look how it's been working there, and putting on a head."

Signal nodded. He was keeping himself well in hand. He did not want to say anything boyish and enthusiastic. He wanted to be a grave and serious man, and so accepted by this hero.

"It was a naked little shack when we got it," said the other. "But some things do pretty well in Monument. Some things will put down root and blossom a lot, like this here honeysuckle. Some men are that way, too. They flourish a lot in Monument. But others just dry up quick. A baby could take them and pull them up by the roots."

Still John Signal was silent.

"Of course," went on Eagan, "it depends mostly on the sort of soil that you plant a bush in . . . or a man. You can see that. You can't make oak trees grow in the desert, and cactus doesn't do well in heavy rains."

Gradually Signal was beginning to see some point in this conversation, but he did not commit himself.

"I've seen," continued Eagan, "a good deal of Monument. I've been here for six years, about. That's about six generations. I mean to say, the way that I live. Other men have come here, and six years to them mean no more . . . well, not a pile more'n six years, plain and simple. But other folks get speeded up. They live fast. I've growed pretty old in Monument."

He turned his head toward the boy, and the black cat turned its head, also, and looked at John Signal with yellow, glowing eyes. Yellow were the eyes of Fitzgerald Eagan, also—or hazel, flecked thickly with yellow spots. Those eyes never could be dull, but at the least effort of the will, they began to glow and gleam. Very hard eyes to face, Signal thought them.

"And," continued the big man, "I've seen a good many of the boys come into this town and dry up fast. I've seen big fellers with plenty of life in 'em dried up and blown away inside of a few days. You never can tell. Sometimes iron cracks at the first whack of the hammer, and sometimes it's the hundredth blow that breaks it, and sometimes all the hammering of a long life ain't going to more'n temper that metal and make it closer and closer to steel, and tougher, and more true. Men are like that. Like iron, all kinds.

"Here's young John Alias," went on the speaker. "Alias what? John Alias . . . alias a clean kid, a straight liver, a straight-shooter, that rides straight up, and that wants a straight chance. Is that right?"

"I don't know," said the boy. "I don't suppose that I know very much about myself. But I'll tell you that I've. . . ."

The other raised a hasty hand. "I don't want to know about your past," he said. "I don't want to know a word about it. The minute that a man comes over those mountains and drops down below timberline again, he's walked out of one section of his life, and he's walked into another one. One part of him is dead, and the new part is all that Monument cares about. And I'm part of Monument." Having said this, he paused again thoughtfully. He looked back at the river, and the cat looked back, also, and, unsheathing her claws—ten narrow sickles of silver brightness—she buried them in the cloth that covered the leg of her master.

"You've taken on with the sheriff?" said Eagan.

"I'm a deputy now."

The other nodded.

"You're a deputy sheriff. That usually means a pretty short life. You've heard that."

"I've heard that."

"But you think that you can beat the game?"

"I don't know," said Signal. "Look here, Eagan . . . I don't think that I'm better than anybody else. But I think that I gotta have a chance to work at something. I want action. I want heaps of action. I'm tired of sitting still. I've sat still almost all of my life."

"I understand." The older man nodded. "You're how old?"

"I'm twenty-two."

"I'm twenty-eight myself."

Signal could have gasped; he controlled himself with an effort. The stern, lined face of the other had seemed to him at least ten years older than the age he mentioned. And then he understood in a flash; the extra ten years—the extra hundred years, perhaps—all had been crowded into the life of this man of twenty-eight. He looked as if he had conquered worlds, or, at least, as though he had beheld the contest for them.

"There are two sides in Monument."

"I know that."

"Well, then, I've brought you here to ask you what soil you'd grow best in. Bone or Eagan?" Then he explained: "Don't think that I put this question to every man who comes to Monument. I wouldn't look at most of them, and there are four hangers-on of the Bone tribe to one who stands by me and my friends. Very well. I don't want the thugs and the cheap gunmen. I want the real article. You're the real article, John Alias. I've brought you here to tell you that I'd mighty well like to have you with us."

This speech sent the blood in a crimson surge into the face of the boy. "That's the greatest compliment that I ever had . . . I'll never have a finer!" he exclaimed.

"Well, then? It's settled?"

"You were talking about soils and . . . bushes, a while ago."

"Yes, I was."

"I've done one bad thing," said Signal. "I never want to do another. I want to go straight. I want to be a good man."

The black cat turned its yellow eyes upon him, but Fitzgerald Eagan continued to look out toward the river. He did not smile at this simple confession from his companion, but a slight frown gathered on his brow.

"If I side with you . . . what about it? Would I have to do any crooked work? Would I even have to know about any crooked work?"

Fitz Eagan began to hum softly to himself. And, still looking out upon the river, he nodded slowly in his thought.

"Yes," said he at last, "you would."

CHAPTER TWELVE

It had been far from the mind of the boy that his question would receive any answer of this nature. He had been on the verge of softening the query, explaining it, so that it should not appear in the light of an insult. Now, the moisture sprang out on his forehead. He tried to find words; there were no words to find. Miserably he sat and suffered.

Then the other turned a calm face toward him. "It troubles you a little, John," he commented. "Well, of course. It would have troubled me even as little as two or three years ago. But you see I'm iron now."

He smiled at John Signal, and the boy said in a shaken voice: "It's a blow to me. But no matter what . . . what you. . . ."

"No matter what dirt I've dipped my hands into? Well?"

"Dirt? I don't mean that! You've done . . . I don't know what. Whatever you please. I know that it's never been really low. I want to say that I liked you the first time ever I laid my eyes on you. I'll like you to the finish. I only want to say that."

"Why, that's fine an' liberal," said Fitz Eagan. "Thank you a lot, John. But I could laugh when I think of the fine, large hopes that I had when I invited you here." And laugh he did cheerfully, his bass voice booming into the quiet air beside the river. The cat shuddered, and the hair along its back bristled.

"No, I didn't think that it would turn out like this. . . . Hello! What's that?"

Far off, wind-borne, uncertain, they heard the high-pitched

voices of men yelling in angry dispute. Those voices were cut short by the sudden chatter of revolvers. This ended, and then, wonderfully near it seemed, came a cry of mortal agony.

Every nerve in the body of John Signal leaped. He turned pale. But the big man beside him said: "Monument is going to have a man for breakfast, as usual."

"Great Scott!" cried the boy. "Is it as bad as that? Is there a murder here every day?"

"A murder every day? More than that! More than that! It used to be a great deal worse. Three times as bad before our fat sheriff got the job. He cut things down. Only the privileged classes can murder today." And Eagan laughed again. "There'll be even fewer, when you get on the job, John Alias."

"It makes me a little dizzy . . . and sick," admitted the boy frankly. "Of course it does. Sometimes even I. . . ." He stopped, frowning. And then the boy asked: "Is the sheriff a . . . a right sort of a man, Mister Eagan?"

"I'd rather that you call me Fitz," said the big fellow.

"Thank you."

"The sheriff? He's an enemy of mine," preluded Eagan.

"Then forget that I asked that question, of course."

"No, I can do him justice, I think. The sheriff is a fellow that likes to hold down a high job. That likes to hold down a dangerous job. He likes to have guns and men wearing guns around him. But . . . he ain't a real fighting man, John." He shook his head decisively. "That's why I don't like him. I like to see real gamblers play cards. I like to see bull terriers at work, if it's a scrap between dogs. But the sheriff ain't that kind. He likes his job, and he tries to work it by politics, pretty largely." He laughed again. "What'll his paper have to say when it speaks about you? You that have become deputy sheriff by taking back your horse from Langley . . . because Langley's a Bone man, and therefore he's behind the sheriff."

"If the sheriff is straight," asked the boy, "why should he deal with people like the Bone tribe?"

"Can he work with nothing? He has to have tools. He would have worked with me, when he first came in. He offered to, but I didn't like his style. And there you are. He did the next best thing and threw in with the Bone outfit. I don't hate the sheriff, mind you. Only I'm not a pal of his. But we both work, off and on, at the same job of cleaning up Monument."

Young Signal threw up his hands. "I don't understand!" he exclaimed. "It beats me!"

"That I should make an income out of crookedness and still try to clean up Monument?"

"Yes. Exactly that."

"Mind you, Alias, you're the first man I've made a confession to. Other people suspect. Nobody knows."

"It's dead and buried with me. It's as if I hadn't heard a word," Signal assured him.

"Of course I trust you perfectly," answered Fitz Eagan. "I had to tell you the straight of things before I got you in with me. But let me tell you what both the sheriff and I are trying to do. We're trying to keep the straight men from trouble. Colter and the Bone outfit who make their money mostly out of Mexican raids . . . they hardly matter. And as for the gunfights, mostly they take place between crooks, and either way the fights turn out, the law is the gainer, and Monument that much better off. But when I first came here, there were a lot of sneaking murderers and bullies who would stick up people at night and blow their brains out if they didn't like the sum of coin that they got out of the other fellow's wallet. Well, we changed all that. We've strung 'em up thick."

He stood up. The black cat scrambled up his coat and stood on his wide shoulder.

"It'll do you good to spend much more time with me," said

Egan. "You'd better get back into town. The Bone outfit will be wanting to make a proposal to you."

Signal rose and held out his hand.

"You'll find me a friend to the finish," he declared.

And the quiet answer was: "Don't make promises. Get the taste of Monument under your tongue before you order up a full meal of friends and enemies."

Signal went back to his horse and mounted. The sun was sloping westward, the full brilliance of it striking against his eyes. And it seemed to him that he had passed through an equal confusion of mental light, in his talk with Fitz Eagan. He never in his life had met a man he was more drawn toward. And for the frank confession he had heard, he admired the big man all the more. And yet it had established a gulf between them. What was the illegal work of which Fitz Eagan was guilty? To what did it lead? Was it the robbing of trains? The smashing of vaults in well-guarded banks? Something on that scale was all that he could conceive of as worthy of the attention of such a man as Fitz Eagan. And again he shook his head in wonder. To him, a deputy sheriff, that confession had been made.

The road wound down by the river, following a gentle incline until it was only a few feet above the level of the water, and at this point a brilliant figure rode out from the trees and fell in beside him. He was dressed like the beau ideal of the Mexican dandy, in a short and closely fitted jacket blazing with metal lace, with a decorated sombrero, and huge silver conchos down the outer seams of his trousers. He bestrode a beautiful black horse that *jingled* with twenty little silver bells, attached to the saddle and the bridle, and tied to the woven mane.

"You're John Alias?" he said cheerfully.

"Yes."

"Alias, I see that you didn't take on with Fitz Egan?"

Signal narrowed his eyes. "What makes you think that?"

The other said with astonishing openness: "I was watching you through a glass. The way you shook hands was no 'see you later and we'll arrange things' farewell. You said good bye in earnest. Respect on both sides. Everybody happy. Good friends forever. But not partners."

He laughed in appreciation of his own cleverness, and even Signal could not help smiling at the accuracy with which these deductions had been drawn. "Well?" he asked shortly.

"My name is Charley Bone. You've heard of me?"

"I've heard of your family," said Signal most decidedly.

"And you haven't heard anything very sweet, eh? As a matter of fact," went on Charley Bone, "when we thought that you were going to make trouble, we would just as soon have put you out of the way."

"You fellows arranged to have me dropped, then? You had the bur stuck under the blanket of my horse?"

"I don't know a thing about that," said Charley Bone. "But now that you've had a chance to talk things over with big Fitz Eagan . . . grand man, isn't he? . . . and since you haven't come to terms with him, we want you on our side."

Signal merely stared.

"You don't understand what it would mean to you. A hundred hands and a hundred guns ready to work for you any minute. Nothing demanded from you except to be kind to your friends who are kind to you. That's all! Everyone buries the hatchet. You see what it would mean? Besides, we'd show you all the ropes immediately, and there's nothing more worth knowing while you're holding your present job."

Signal cut short this glibness. "I don't want to insult you," he said, "but I think that the Bone party stole my horse, and I think, since that, they've tried to murder me. I want nothing to do with your tribe."

"That's short. That's sweet. That's final," said Charley Bone.

"I'm glad it turned out this way. I have to do something to make a bigger and a better reputation."

"Here's a grand opportunity for you!" offered Signal fiercely.

"*Tut, tut.*" The other smiled. "Here on a lonely street? With no witnesses? I want a crowd, old fellow, when I'm to die or when I go out to kill the killer."

He waved his hand and rode straight back toward the trees that had been sheltering him.

CHAPTER THIRTEEN

A trained eye is an almost omniscient tool. And, walking to the office the next morning, John Signal read the papers as he went down the street. His eyes were continually lifting from the print—returning, fumbling at the place they had left off, and continuing for a flash, then taking another glance that printed upon his mind all that was near him, and all that was far.

In part he wanted to know what was in the papers, and in part he was practicing, for he knew that he walked in the midst of the most constant danger and he strove even to print upon his mind the faces that appeared behind windows, blurred and streaked by the uneven glass. The very footprints in the dust before him might have a vital meaning.

So, in the midst of this danger that strove to wear the face of an ordinary morning in an ordinary city, Signal, being what he was and very young, rejoiced in the city, in the danger, and in the stern work that lay before him. How much, he said to himself, the people of Monument would be amused when they learned that their new deputy sheriff was, in fact, a man with a death already credited to his gun. That would be the time for him to flee away to fresh pastures. So said the boy to his heart as he stepped into the business section of Monument.

He had a copy of the *Ledger* under his arm; he was reading the *Recall*. The account of the *Ledger* was friendly from the first line. That of the *Recall* was astonishingly hostile.

Said the *Ledger*:

UNEXPECTED BOOST FOR LAW AND ORDER

And as a subhead it declared:

Sheriff Ogden Gets the Right Man by Mistake

These pleasant sentiments the *Ledger* reporter expanded all down a column on the first page of the newspaper, so that young John Signal rivaled in the morning papers the tidings of a new and rich strike in the mining hills, and the suicide (?) of Monument's most influential banker.

Said the paper, in part:

> *He came, he saw, and he made himself wanted. He called himself "John Alias", with a straight face.*
>
> *On the other hand, notorious Sim Langley came, and saw, and mounted the roan horse of John Alias. The latter pursued. He took his horse back again, ran Langley, bellowing with fear, into the Pineta house, and scattered half a dozen of Mr. Langley's ruffian Mexicans. Mr. Alias, as he chooses to be called for the present, then rode back to town and called the sheriff's bluff.*
>
> *Ogden had sworn to give the young stranger a place as deputy sheriff—though at a beggarly small salary—in case he should bring in his horse from Langley. The sheriff thought it would be impossible. For him it would have been. But back came John Alias.*
>
> *The sheriff was sick at heart. The last thing he wanted in his office was an honest man. But he had to have this one. At times there is a grim look in the eye of young John Alias. The sheriff saw it yesterday, and was bluffed into keeping his word—an extraordinary state of affairs!*
>
> *Going to press at a late hour last night, we rejoice to know that our brave young deputy is still alive, and that the knives*

and the guns of the Bone faction have not yet reached his heart.
*Long life and happiness to you, John Alias, and may you
give us at last a taste of honesty in the execution of the law!*

So spoke the *Ledger*, and, although he was familiar with the
efforts of small-town journalism, and all its petty spites and
wrangles, still it appeared to Signal that this was carrying the
liberty of the press to a singularly advanced point. It could be
seen that the *Ledger*, supporting the Eagans, wished to be
friendly without complimenting the sheriff, and it had succeeded so well that Signal could be reasonably sure of finding
trouble not far before him.

But the *Recall* made the effort of the *Ledger* seem puny. It
roared and thundered for the opposing faction:

MYSTERY MAN GETS MYSTERIOUS JOB

In this manner it began.
Hastily it shielded the sheriff while preparing to attack his
new assistant:

*The heart of our sheriff is as big as a house. Yesterday it
moved him to take into his office a nameless wanderer who
chooses to call himself "John Alias".*

*Remember, Peter Ogden, that kindness is sometimes out of
place in the sheriff's office!*

*We want to know something about this stranger who is now
given power over life and limb in this fair city.*

Where does he come from?

What has he done before?

*What doctor operated on his name and removed the last part
of it?*

*We humbly propose these questions to Mr. John Alias. Not
that we expect a reply!*

The first thing the new deputy did was to fall into a brawl with our well-known fellow citizen, Simeon Langley. The excuse which John Alias trumped up was that Langley had stolen his horse!

At this, the Recall *is forced to smile.*

We interviewed Simeon Langley. Mr Langley was quiet and dignified. He merely said: "I have heard that the so-called John Alias has spread a scandal about me. All I have to say is that the next time I meet the low hound, I am going to run him out of town."

We compliment Sheriff Ogden on the excellent work he has done for Monument, but we are forced to say: Put your house in order, Peter Ogden! And remember the story about the man who brought the snake back to life!

It was very hard for the boy to realize that these words had been written about him. He had been raised with a great deal of reverence for the printed word. What happened in a newspaper had, to him, a peculiar dignity and truth, and he flushed and grew cold in turn as he read the tirade. This was his real introduction to the life of Monument.

He turned a corner and stepped aside to avoid a crisply pretty girl walking beside a middle-aged man of fine, soldierly bearing.

"That's the new ruffian who's been made deputy sheriff," he heard the man say.

And the face of the boy burned hotly. He was glad that few people were in the streets. Monument remained awake very late at night and was correspondingly tardy to begin the day. In the entire office building where the sheriff had his rooms, there was only a yawning janitor at work when John Signal arrived. But the yawn disappeared in a broad grin when Signal came in. With a pass key the sheriff's door was opened. Then, in the open doorway, the janitor lingered for a single instant.

"Keep 'em backing up!" he said, and suddenly closed the

door and was gone.

It heartened Signal enormously to have this kind word, but he settled down straightway at the roll-top desk. There was much to be learned, and, most valuable to him, there was a complete picture gallery of snapshots of all the most prominent men in Monument. In this gallery there were many gaps, several pages of the big book being empty because of death or removal, but enough remained to give him a busy morning, printing in his mind the features of all the Bone crew and their adherents, as far as he had heard their names, and all the Eagan tribe, much fewer in numbers.

The sheriff arrived a little before noon, bustling in with the morning papers under his arm and his usual fat black cigar in a corner of his mouth. He seemed highly pleased with the two reports. The abuse that the *Ledger* had heaped upon him did not move him at all.

"You have to keep your name before the people," he assured Signal. "Give them a chance to forget you, and you're dead in a day. Keep them stirred up. Keep fire under the pot. That's the way to get on in this little old world of ours. If I could get this much space, I'd hire a new John Alias every day."

He was much amused, also, by the manner in which the *Recall* had handled, or rather juggled, the case of Langley and the stolen horse.

"Sim isn't such a bad fellow," said the sheriff. "I've had him twice in my posse rounding up rustlers, and I never saw a man fight harder or ride better. By the way, Charley Bone tells me that you've refused to talk friendship with him, or to bury the hatchet. Is that right?"

"How could I?" asked Signal. "I'm not here to make trouble for anyone. But I'm not going to be gathered into either side of this affair. You've made me a deputy sheriff . . . well, I'm going to do my duty and stand for the law. That's all."

The sheriff listened with attention, and amusement. "You're going to clean up Monument?" he asked.

"I can't do that," admitted Signal. "But I can do the jobs that come my way. I can do them straight. That's all."

The sheriff answered obliquely: "You've only been here a day, and that's not a long time in any town. Have you learned those faces?"

"I've learned them. I mean, I've an idea of them, mostly. I've studied the Eagans and the Bones."

Here feet *clattered* noisily down the hallway, and the door to the office was flung open. The same meager fellow who had apparently been spying at the door the preceding day now appeared again, exclaiming: "They're bringing in a wounded man here, Sheriff!"

"What're they bringing him in here for?" asked the sheriff with irritation. "Ain't there a hospital in this town?"

"He wants right bad to see you. He's been shot up!"

"We're going to have a dying confession, I suppose," said the sheriff. "There's the weak point of all these crooks. They fade away and lose all their resolution when it comes to rubbing elbows with death. They have to talk. They have to talk."

Stumbling, burdened steps approached. Two men, carrying a third between them, squeezed through the doorway. He who they bore was a boy of no more than sixteen, his face streaked with crimson, crimson dripping from one leg, also.

"Lay me flat," he gasped in Spanish. "I must save my strength for the words I have to speak."

CHAPTER FOURTEEN

The indifference of the sheriff disappeared instantly. "It's young Pancho Pineta," he said. "You . . . Bill . . . run for Doc Hotchkiss, will you?"

"It's only a greaser, Pete," said Bill to the sheriff. "And he's leakin' his life away as fast as water through a sieve. What's the good of bothering the doc? He hates to get up before noon."

"The poor old doc is bucking faro lately," commented the second of the pair who had borne the wounded man into the office.

The sheriff, busily cutting away the clothes of the boy, merely shouted: "For heaven's sake, one of you two move, will you? Call Doc Hotchkiss and say that I want him on the run. Maybe we can stop this. . . ."

Young Pineta had fainted. He lay on the center table. From its edge, crimson dripped upon the floor.

But the sheriff, in the meantime, was working like a Trojan. "Only a greaser," he muttered. "Ain't a greaser a man, the same as you and me? Ain't he been born of a woman, and can't he die like a man? Look at this here kid. Drilled through and through. But he had the nerve to keep from laying down to die, the way that most white men would've done."

John Signal said not a word, for the sight of so much blood made his brain spin and he was in deadly fear lest he should faint. A fine article that would make for the *Recall*—the fainting of the new deputy sheriff at the mere sight of blood! He had to grit his teeth and hold himself hard, and a sort of a tune began to beat with his failing pulse through his mind, saying like a voice with words that he was too young for Monument—he was far too young for the horrors of this city.

They stripped the Mexican boy. Through the left shoulder and through the right thigh he had been cleanly shot. The sheriff worked those limbs anxiously and muttered that no bones had been broken. There was only the loss of blood to fear, and at this point the doctor arrived. He was very old, very withered, but straight as a string and with an eye as bright as the eye of a bird.

Iodine poured in the wounds brought a groan from the unconscious boy. Then bandages were swiftly applied, and the doctor leaned with a stethoscope over the heart of young Pineta.

"*Tush*," he said. "He'll live without any doubt at all. Men don't die out here from flesh wounds. They're like grizzlies. The heart and the brain, yes. But nothing else matters very much. Yesterday I cut out of the back of a man a bullet he'd been carrying about with him for five years. Good bye, Sheriff. I'm going back to sleep. Faro needs a fresh eye. Give this lad a shot of whiskey."

Whiskey, accordingly, was poured down the throat of Pancho Pineta, and it revived him almost at once. He asked to have his head supported; a rolled coat was placed beneath it. Then he rallied himself, his eyes still half closed.

The sheriff said gently: "You take your time, son. You're not going to die. You've got lots of time to say what's on your mind."

"Every moment they are riding farther away . . . every moment they are closer to safety," said young Pineta. He opened his eyes. "It was the San Real Cañon," he said.

"What broke loose there?" asked the sheriff. "I've been waiting for years for something to bust loose there."

"All the mules were coming up the San Real, well loaded. It was our greatest expedition, *señor.* We came well up into the cañon. It was time to think about the next camping ground and we hoped to be up to the plateau. We came to a place where the cañon grows very narrow, and it begins to twist like a snake."

"I know the spot as though I'd built it," said the sheriff.

"In this place the trail was very narrow, also. As narrow, *señor,* as the trail where you and your men surprised us two years ago." He chuckled a little as he said this, and the chuckling turned him suddenly black in the face. He choked, and it was only after a moment that his breathing became natural, as he lay back in a dead faint.

"This boy is walking a tightrope," said the sheriff. "He ain't got more'n a quarter of an inch of rope beneath him and he's walking over a whole dog-gone' gulf. He sure is a game little feller."

"Is he related to the Pinetas who are. . . . ?"

"Who live near town? Langley's friends? He's a cousin. He and his two brothers have been smuggling from Mexico, and back, for years. The older two are Manuelo and Gregorio. Tough nuts! But I cracked 'em all one day. I laid for 'em and scooped up eighteen thousand dollars' worth of stuff in cash and goods. I thought that that would've broke the boys, but inside of a year they were back at work again. Oh, a smart greaser is the smartest thing in the world."

The boy suddenly opened his eyes again. "Down the trail toward us came a tall man on a mule. He was a *gringo* . . . I beg your pardon, *señor.*"

"Go on, kid. You ain't stepping on my toes. Go right ahead and tell your yarn."

"He was very good-natured. He saw that the trail was narrow and that the sides of our mules bulged with the packs. He moved aside among the rocks and watched us go by. To every man he had something to say. Every word that he spoke was cheerful. We all laughed. We talked back to him and were glad to see him. We thought that perhaps he would follow onto our camp that night, and buy some of our goods."

"I understand," said the sheriff.

"I asked Gregorio if that was it, and if he knew the man. Gregorio, *señor*, was always a suspicious man. . . ."

"*Was?*" asked the sheriff.

"Alas, that is what I am about to explain. Gregorio said to me that he had seen that tall man somewhere, but he did not know where . . . and that he would not trust him. You know, *señor*, that Gregorio always had a very dark mind."

"He would not trust the *Americanos*. Well, I don't blame him. He's had enough rocky deals from them."

The boy smiled on the man of the law. "It is easy to speak to you, *Señor* the Sheriff," he said. "It is easy as to speak to my father."

And Signal, standing by, curious and watchful, could not help agreeing. He wondered, indeed, if he had not found the key to Ogden's character in the universal kindness that he appeared to feel for everyone. A kindness, therefore, that was a little too catholic, in that it embraced both sides, more or less, of every faction.

"My brother Gregorio," said the boy, "was so solemn that I told him it was no good to have doubt about everything, and that there were many good men in the world . . . and that this was one of them. At that, Gregorio only shook his head. 'For travelers and merchants,' he said, 'there is only one friend in the world, and that you should learn at once.'

" 'What friend is that?' I asked him.

" 'This one,' he said, and he touched on the band of his sombrero, in front, the golden image of Saint Christopher that he always wore there."

"I've seen it myself," said the sheriff. "Saint Christopher with a staff, carrying the Child on his shoulder."

"Yes," said the boy, "carrying our Lord upon his shoulder. He is in the middle of the stream. It is not big, but it is beautiful work, and all in gold. This my brother touched, telling me that Saint Christopher was our only friend, and then he commanded me to go back to the rear of the mule train and see that the stranger did no harm as the tail of the herd went by.

"Of course, I did as he told me to do. I came to the rear of the train, but I paid no attention to the stranger. Why should I? There were eleven of us, altogether. There was only one man. How could he dare to do any harm to us? I hardly looked at him after I had waved as the last mule passed him. I was looking across the valley at a rabbit running up among the rocks and wondering if I could take a shot at it. But my brother Gregorio never liked to have shots fired along the way. A silent road was the best road, he would always say, and the most pleasing to travelers under the care of Saint Christopher. Therefore, I did not touch my gun, and the next instant a revolver spoke behind us. I saw the man just ahead of me throw up his arms, and heard him cry out, and then he began to topple to the side, still with his arms thrown over his head, and still crying. It was as though he had frozen in that position, and died so.

"I looked about, snatching at a revolver, but I was only in time to receive this bullet wound through the shoulder, and the shock of the bullet tipped me out of the saddle to the ground. There I lay still. I was half stunned by striking my head against a rock, but still I could see what had happened. From among the rocks rose many men with masks upon their faces. They fired rapidly from repeating rifles, and everywhere my friends were falling. The man who had shot down us two at the rear of the procession now rode up and leaned from his horse above me and fired into my body."

"The cowardly skunk!" said the sheriff hotly.

"By grace, he only shot me through the thigh. I did not stir. It was as though he had passed fire through my leg, but I dared not stir. And he went on, shooting at others who had fallen. I heard them shouting. They were murdering every one of the wounded. When I saw that, I got to my feet. There were several pack mules between me and the murderers. They screened me so that I was able to get into the saddle. I rode into the rocks. I tied myself into the saddle. I made a great prayer to Saint Christopher that through me some sort of vengeance might come upon the murderers, and then I gave the horse the spur.

"I began to grow faint. After a time, I was riding between sleep and a dream. At last, daylight rolled back across my eyes once more, and I saw that my horse was cantering wearily into a city. I saw that it was Monument. I remembered then the great and good sheriff who keeps one law for Americans and Mexicans, both. See, *señor*, I am here. May Saint Christopher lead you to find the murderers."

CHAPTER FIFTEEN

They carried young Pineta to the hospital—there were half a dozen volunteers for that work of mercy—and he was taken off, raving violently, and shouting: "All is lost!"

Peter Ogden, in the meantime, was left behind with his deputy. The sheriff was in great trouble and confusion of mind, apparently. He said, with bitterness: "They drive me to the wall, John Alias. They drive me to the wall. Haven't I showed them that I'll put up with smaller things, but I won't stand for murder?"

And Signal could not help asking tersely: "Is it true that men are killed nearly every day in the streets of Monument?"

The sheriff turned a clouded eye upon him. "And why not?" he said. "Isn't it better that they *should* die every day . . . crooks killing crooks . . . poison fighting poison? But the honest men . . . and here are ten of 'em butchered, by heaven."

"How do you class smugglers?" asked Signal quietly. "Are they among the honest men?"

"You can't be too absolute," answered the sheriff, sighing. "Of course, they're doin' crooked work, but not so very crooked. I bust them up when I can, but I don't hunt 'em too hard. They bring in goods that we need. They take out goods that they need south across the border. What harm did these Pinetas do? By their way of thinking, it was as honest work as any man could want, with just enough danger splashed in to make it fun. And ten of 'em murdered. Ten!" He raised his fist above his head. "I'm going to smash somebody for this!" vowed Peter Ogden. "I'm gonna smash somebody!"

Then he turned to the boy. "Scatter down into the town. Keep your ears open. Find out what you can. Pick up some sort of a trail. Ride to San Real Cañon, if you have to. It's only five miles out. Look over the ground."

Nothing was more to the mind of young Signal. He took the roan horse and rode out to the place, quickly directed by the first passer-by.

He found it all that the wounded boy had claimed. A narrow trail, worn deeply into the rock, descended into the cañon, which wound back and forth uncertainly. It was a naked, sun-blasted place, with not a tree in sight, only shrubs that had taken a precarious fingerhold here and there among the boulders. And along the trail the dead lay. Ten men, as the boy had declared, all Mexicans, seven of them ragged peons, and two others—the brothers of Pancho, no doubt—dressed with more care. Every item of value had been stripped from them.

On the trail was also a dead mule, and four others lay in the hollow of the cañon, where they had fallen, toppling from the trail above. All was silent. And overhead the buzzards were circling in narrow loops, ready to settle to the feast.

But as for clues, they were hard to come at. There was a jumble of sign of men and horses. It was only by dint of careful trailing that he was able to find the place back among the big rocks where the horses of the killers had been held while the butchery went on.

Anger such as had possessed the sheriff now was rising in the young deputy as well. With all his heart he searched the sign that remained between the rocks for some token worthy of following, but there was nothing to be discovered, except, where the trail thinned out at the point where the victors had ridden off in single file, a small bit of iron—the calk and end of one side of a horseshoe. It was recently broken. There was no doubt of that. The crystallized metal shone, sparkling in the sun. So Signal sat down to think over the thing. It was a shoe for a right forehoof, snapped at this point by being planted with force on the face of a hard rock, and there was no doubt that very skillful trailing might enable him to run back this clue to some important source.

He could hear men coming down into the cañon, now, men sent out by the sheriff from Monument. The sheriff himself was among them, but the boy did not waste time talking with them. He hoped that this clue might lead him on to some deed of importance, that he might prove to Monument that he stood definitely upon the side of law and order, and so choke off such further articles upon him as the *Recall*, in its venom, might be apt to print.

For a quarter of a mile he had no difficulty at all. Again and again, where the animals stepped on impressionable ground, he discovered the incomplete mark of the broken horseshoe. And his heart was beginning to rise high when the sign showed where the whole procession entered a region of well-compacted gravel—hardly gravel, indeed, but rather a strewing of small rocks such as are rounded and milled by the action of running water. There he lost the trail utterly.

He rode in circles, beginning at the center, but although he found several of the trails again, issuing from the rocks, he could not find the sign of the broken shoe.

Might it not be, indeed, that the rider had dismounted here and pulled off the telltale shoe?

For two long hours he labored, and then, with deep disgust, he gave over his work and turned the roan back toward Monument. If that eagle-eyed man, his father, had been with him— ah, that might have meant a different result.

Back to Monument, then—hungry, hot, and tired. For it was

a blazing day, with no wind blowing across the hills. Where the big teams were hauling up and down the grade to Monument, the dust they raised mounted slowly straight up. Every wagon was lost in an unpleasant mist, with the leaders of the team walking continually out of it, powdered white. Monument itself glistened in the sun and the windows flashed blindingly where the rays struck them. And there appeared to the boy something so monotonous, so humdrum about this picture, that he felt despair of ever accomplishing any feat worth recording. Other men, keener and stronger than himself, filled that city. Men keen and strong enough to murder ten men, and wound another, and come off clean. And this within an hour's ride of the town!

A down-hearted man was John Signal as he entered the streets of the town, keeping to the shady side and using a bandanna to mop his streaming forehead.

As the horse went on, he was aware of other riders coming behind him. He turned a little and saw that one was Charley Bone, dressed as brilliantly as ever, snapping a quirt with his left hand and controlling his beautiful black horse by means of his knees alone. He seemed quite uninterested in Signal. For that matter, so did the man across the street from Charley Bone. He could recognize him well enough from the photographs that he had studied in the office of the sheriff earlier that morning. It was Doc Mentor, famous among the adherents of the Bone tribe for relentless ferocity, and the man who had shot at him the day before.

What kept the two riders in this fashion just behind the deputy sheriff?

Signal turned down a side street, and instantly there was a sharp whistle, twice repeated, behind him. He did not look back. He was tempted either to put the spurs to his horse, or else to back against the wall and draw his guns to settle the matter then and there. Instead, he took the more moderate course of bearing straight forward, not letting the roan hasten a step.

He was halfway down the block when he saw a rider jog on a piebald, ugly horse into the middle of the street at the next corner, where the anvil of a blacksmith was *clanging*. And this rider dismounted quickly, threw the reins of his horse, and stood at the head of the animal, resting on a rifle.

It could not be said that in this town such a maneuver was suspicious. The man might simply have dismounted to enjoy the shade here, while waiting the turn of his horse to be shod. But then again, it was very doubtful if he had not some connection with that sharp and repeated whistle that Signal had heard from the rear.

The deputy sheriff turned his head enough to glance back down the street again, and there behind him, still riding as far apart as the width of the street permitted them, he could see Charley Bone and Doc Mentor.

It was good tactics that separated them as much as the street allowed, of course. For in case the man they stalked should turn, he could not cover them both with one gesture. He would have to swing his gun in a wide arc, if he attacked one and then the other. Bitterly Signal wished, then, that he had mastered two-gun play. His father had spoken scornfully against it.

"Two guns are like two tongues. If you had 'em, what would you do with 'em? Speed is mostly bunk, too. Accuracy, my boy! Accuracy is the thing. Hit a dime at twenty yards . . . punch a button through the chest of a man at the same distance. That's what wins a fight!"

Signal was plainly cornered. No matter what explanation might be made of the man who stood in the shade of the tree at the next junction, it was very odd that he should need to sling his rifle across the crook of his left arm, which was exactly what he was doing now.

John Signal grew cold. If a fight started against two such men, so skillfully placed, he would have to go down, and he knew it. And now he saw to his right a narrow, open gate that led into the rear yard of the blacksmith's shop. He did not hesitate, but turned the roan straight into it. A convulsive shudder went coldly up his back as he approached the gate. From the tail of his eye he saw Charley Bone bringing his horse to a trot.

But no bullet was fired, and he rode safely through the entrance. Once inside, however, he well understood why he had been allowed freely to pass into this cover. For the yard behind the shop was entirely closed around with a smooth wall of wood, six feet high. The roan could jump, but he could not jump that. He might, of course, abandon the horse, and go on alone over the fence, but he felt that this would wreck his reputation as a fearless man in this city of men without fear.

So he dismounted and walked straight into the shop itself, leading the horse behind him.

CHAPTER SIXTEEN

It was by far the largest shop in Monument. Two thirds of the mule teams passed through the hands of the smiths here, who stripped off the tattered shoes and trimmed the hoofs and hammered and banged the new shoes into place. When Signal stepped inside, he was caught on a wave of crashing sound that never died. Shouting voices—for ordinary speech would never be heard—and the screeching of bellows, and the trampling and snorting of horses, and above all the ceaseless shower of blows that fell, with eight- or twelve-pound hammers, upon six echoing anvils.

In the bright sunshine of Monument, this shop was a sort of little Hebrides, perpetually dim with clouds of smoke that rose from the six forges as the flames bit through fresh feeds of coal. Blue-white, thick, and stifling, the mist curled outside the chimney hoods that vainly strove to draw up the smoke, and the great rafters above were seen by glimpses, clotted with soot. The great double doors at front and in the rear were always open, and through them wisps and puffs of smoke continually rolled, so that the only sunshine that entered was sifted through that veil. It left the interior a place of shadow in which men and horses were confused silhouettes and through which the red pulse of the fires gleamed wildly. This babel of voices and action and hopeless confusion made Signal feel as though there had just been an explosion—the smoke of it was aloft, the ruin of it was scattered upon the floor.

Along the walls appeared a tangled frieze of horses, ever shifting as they swung from side to side to avoid the blacksmiths, kicking, stamping, whinnying with terror. The smiths, hot iron shoes glowing upon their drill points, advanced upon their victims with one hand extended soothingly, and imprecations upon their lips, and in the center of the floor were impatient cowboys and teamsters waiting for the completion of their individual jobs, bribing, entreating, threatening to have the thing pushed through more briskly.

Signal, passing down the center of the shop without haste, glanced back, and he saw behind him the outlines of Charley Bone and of Mentor, with the gleam of their rifles still in their hands as they entered. They were following to the finish, whatever that finish might be. And, staring forward, he saw the third rifleman standing with gun ready at the other mouth of this inferno.

Panic jumped up in the throat of Signal. He set his teeth and quieted himself with an iron effort of the will. If the thing had to be fought out, what better time than now? He halted the roan, and put his shoulders against its ribs. Then he dropped a hand on his hip, conveniently near the handle of his weapon, and waited.

One would have thought that a blacksmith's shop would halt its business for the sake of looking on at a first-rate murder, but not this one. The hammers *clanged* and the voices roared as loudly as ever.

"Hey, you brindle-faced fool! Here's half a dollar, old-timer, if you'll . . . Jerry! Oh, Jerry! You said eleven. Look what time it is now! I told you calks! You poison bronc'! You jerry-built man-eater, stand still!"

Roaring nearby, or wildly shouted in the dim distance, so these voices rushed through the mind of Signal like the sound of the ocean among hollow rocks. He felt as one feels wakening from a delirium, or sinking into the fever again.

And still the three advanced straight toward him, and still he waited. He could see their guns more plainly now, and now he could make out their faces. He ought to begin. He made up his mind that he would take a snap shot at the single rifleman first of all. Then, pitching forward upon his face along the floor, he would open upon the other two—and heaven send him luck.

With danger walking so close upon Signal, finally some hint of what was coming dawned upon the other men who were grouped and clustered about him. For they gave suddenly back, with oaths and exclamations.

"What sort of a place is this for a fight?"

"Give 'em room!"

"They'll be some good hosses shot up before this is over!"

"It's the kid deputy! It's that John Alias, the fool!"

He heard such phrases as these, and they seemed to him detached sounds, without meaning—voices, let us say, out of the sea. For all that was in his brain, burning bright, was the advancing picture of those three warriors. Should he open fire now?

Someone had said, somewhere: "Don't fire till you see the whites of their eyes." He remembered that now. He would wait until they came as close as that. Then he would get one of them first. Of course, two bullets would plunge through and through his body, but, as he fell, he would be deliberate, certain—if there were any life in his body—and try to bring down all three before his death. That would be a fall worthwhile.

A greater space had opened now when from the side, straight toward him, walked another man. Four, then, to finish him off? He could have laughed. It was too perfect and too complete a trap, and with what ease they were prepared to swallow him.

Let him kill but one man before he fell.

Upon either side the three killers were terribly close, when the newcomer stepped up to Signal and turned toward the pair who advanced cautiously from the rear.

"Hello, boys," he said. "What you come for in here? Me?"

It was Colter!

But how different from the ragged, tattered, hunger-pinched man of the mountains. He was like a cavalier; he needed only plumes in his lofty sombrero. Even young Charley Bone was not more splendid. Yet, within this casing of glory, there was the same lean, hard, handsome face. He stood now with his feet spread a little apart, and his hands dropped upon either hip, which was girdled with the most brilliant of silken scarves. And, strapped to his hips, there were two guns, just under the tips of his fingers.

"Henry, what the deuce do you mean?" cried Charley Bone, angered at this unexpected interruption.

"I mean what I say. Have you come here for me?"

"It's the deputy. It's that damned new one. I'm gonna get him now!"

So said Bone, and Henry Colter nodded.

"All right, boys," he remarked. "You can have him any minute, when you're through with me. But not until I'm down . . . and I'll go down smoking, I warn you that!"

They had halted,

Signal, dizzy with relief, turned toward them. Their features contracted and worked with malice now. But the fellows had halted.

Suddenly Signal cried over his shoulder softly: "Colter, if you'll stand with me, let's clean them up! The sneaking murderers! They laid the trap for me. Three to one!"

"Come, come," said Colter. "These ain't bad boys at all. I know 'em all. They're all friends of mine, I tell you. Don't you go worrying and bothering about them. They're all right. Look here, I'll introduce you."

"Henry," said Mentor, seconding Charley Bone, "are you really going to gum up this here deal? We got him spread out for a wind-up."

Colter replied genially: "The man that takes a shot at John Alias is taking a shot at me. And the man that takes a shot at me is gonna live in an atmosphere that's blowin' lead for a considerable spell. Now, I tell you boys the straight of this, and I mean it. Step up here and shake hands with my friend, John Alias."

They had come to a pause. They formed a tight little circle of five, glowering at one another. In the distance, the spectators no longer crowded back against the horses along the walls, but moved nearer, to hear what they could, now that it appeared there would be no shooting.

"You all ought to know each other," said Henry Colter. "Here's Doc Mentor. You can tell him by the scar on his face. And here's Santa Claus. He's got a kind face, ain't he? All he needs is the whiskers. And of course you've met Charley Bone before. Shake hands, boys."

"If you're right with Henry," said Charley Bone, "you're right with me. If you're good enough for Colter, you're good enough for Charley Bone. And let's shake hands on it, John Alias."

"Good for you . . . ," began Colter.

But Signal struck the proffered hand away and stepped closer to the handsome face of Charley. In the smiling youth of Bone he felt now more danger than he ever had felt before in any man—unless it were Henry Colter himself, and great Fitz Eagan. But he welcomed that danger with a wholehearted hatred.

"I'd rather," said Signal, "shake with a sneak of a coyote just in from killing chickens. I'd rather shake hands with the fangs of a rattlesnake than touch you . . . except with my fist, Bone."

Charley Bone looked him up and down, contented, still smiling. "You take it hard," he commented.

"They would have murdered me," said Deputy Sheriff John Alias. "You hear me, Colter? They trailed me through the town. Three against one is their idea of a fair sporting chance and an even fight."

"The point is," said Colter soothingly, "that you ain't been touched. Don't you let your imagination start running away with you. These here boys, I'll swear, was only playing a little sort of a game of tag with you. They was trying out your nerve."

"Of course," agreed Santa Claus, smiling in turn. "And we found that the kid was made of the real stuff . . . he didn't run."

Said John Signal: "I've heard your say. I've seen all your lying faces. Mind you this . . . the next time that I see two of you together, I start shooting, and I shoot to kill. You, Bone, I've written down 'specially big and clear. And you, Mentor. This is the second time that you've tried to get me. And the third time, one or the other of us will have to leave town."

An angry answer came upon the lips of Mentor, but Henry Colter waved him away.

"Get off, the three of you," he said. "I'll handle this colt, if I can."

And the three drifted off in one ominous group.

CHAPTER SEVENTEEN

Now released from the presence of the would-be killers, it appeared to Signal that the rest of the crowd would soon flow back toward their old place in the center of the room, but there seemed to be no desire on the part of anyone to come too close to them.

Colter was saying quietly to his companion: "You've made a big mistake today, son. Those boys would have been your friends. They would have stuck to you through thick and thin."

"I don't want such friends for a gift," replied Signal. "Every one of the three is capable of mob murder. You saw them all come at me. Thank heaven I had you here, Colter. And that's one thing that I'll never forget. Mind you, I'm going to show you what I'll do to all of 'em, before the finish, and I'll try to show you that I never forget a friend, Colter. It was a fine thing to see you stand them off."

Signal was on fire with enthusiasm, but Colter said quietly: "I wasn't in the least danger. Those boys are all old friends of mine. And whatever I've done, it doesn't more than balance against what you did for me in the mountains. You took me in, kid, I tried to double-cross you, and then you gave me another chance. Any way you figure up this account, I'm still in debt."

Signal protested.

"You're in the sheriff game for what you can get out of it?" asked Colter suddenly. "Or are you in it for glory?"

The boy laughed lightly. So great a burden had been lifted

from him in the past few minutes that he could have laughed into the face of a dragon. "I'm here for the glory," he said.

"Well, then," said Colter, "I don't know how you and me are going to get along together."

"Because I work for the sheriff?"

"No. Ogden is a good friend of mine. I never bother Monument, and Monument never bothers me. There you are. How are you going to stand toward me?"

"I've taken an oath," answered the youngster. "Lord knows how close I'll come to living up to it."

"And friendship, John?"

"Aye, that's the other thing. But after what's happened between us, how could I ever want to lay a hand on you, Colter?"

Said Henry Colter gravely: "You know my line partly. I'm not a saint. I've raised a good deal of trouble. I expect to raise a good deal more. I won't ask you in to cut the melons with me because I see that you ain't that kind. But if it's agreeable to you, suppose we say friend, and shake permanent on that?"

"I never was gladder to do anything," replied the boy, and their hands closed strongly.

Colter nodded, highly pleased. "That's that," he said. "We'll have to solder that handshake with a drink . . . but first I want to see how that bone-headed blacksmith is gonna fit my hoss with shoes. Will you come over and take a look?"

Colter's mount was a splendid bay, wedged sideways against the wall, head thrown high and strained back, ears flattened, nostrils dilated with fear.

"*That's* a horse!" commented the boy with much enthusiasm.

"That's a horse," agreed the other. "I can't afford to ride cheap horseflesh. I have to cover too much ground. This brute is a little too nervous."

The blacksmith, approaching at that moment, laid a quieting hand upon the flank of the bay, and then picked up a forehoof to take off the old shoe.

"It's the other foot that needs a shoe," pointed out Colter.

The blacksmith shifted to the other side of the horse, and, after working a moment with his tool, he pried off the shoe and cast it on the floor—a freshly made shoe, at that, but the tip of one side had been broken off.

"There's a sign of the shoddy work that they do now," explained Colter, picking up the shoe. "They don't temper the iron with any care. Look at this one. Chilled it too quick, and took the life out of the metal, the fools!"

But the boy stared in a maze of wonder. For he recognized that shoe. In his pocket, at that moment, was the fragment that had been broken from it. He knew, therefore, who had organized that murderous attack upon the Mexicans in San Real Cañon, who had shot them down, and gone back and forth, murdering the wounded who lay on the trail. It was Colter and his crew. Colter, with whom he had barely finished shaking hands, with such a warmth and swelling of his heart.

Colter, in the meantime, was examining the shoes out of which the smith intended to pick a new one, and, when the selection had been made to his taste, he carried Signal away to the nearest saloon.

At the door he paused with a broad grin. "You know what this saloon is?" he asked.

"Well?"

"It's Mortimer's."

"I can't go in here then. This is the Bone hang-out."

"Of course it is. But you're drinking with me, and, while you're with me, there ain't a Bone in the world that would raise a gun at you. Come on in. It'll give the boys a little shock. They'll kind of half figure that I'm throwin' them down."

They passed inside.

Mortimer's saloon was as fine an emporium of liquor as stood in the town of Monument. Ninety feet of varnished bar ran down one side of the room, with four bartenders working busily behind it, their images rising and bowing rapidly in the big mirrors at the rear of the bar, but what Signal saw, first of all, was a white-bearded old man, with a benevolent aspect, and a gentle eye.

He smiled upon them and waved them forward for a drink.

"This is Daddy Bone," said Colter. "Dad, this is John Alias that you've heard about. This drink is on me. Alias and me are turning bottoms up to a long friendship and a smooth one."

Old Bone nodded again in his amiable manner. "It's a kind of a drink that I dunno that I could swaller," he said. "I jest finished drinkin' with Mentor and Charley to the quick scalpin' of this same young feller. But I'll drink mine afterward."

This singular remark made Signal chuckle. He observed that he had become a bright center of interest all along the bar. There was a shifting away from the end at which he stood with Colter.

"They don't know whether I'm going to pull a gun on you and try to blow your spinal column apart, or what I'm after," said Colter, smiling. "This here bothers them a lot. Here's to you, Johnny Alias . . . a long life and a straight one to you . . . a short life and a bright one for me. Will you drink to that?"

And down went the whiskey.

Old Bone waited until the liquor of the first pair of glasses was exhausted. Then he raised his own brimmer. "Here," he said, "is to the hand that holds the gun that shoots the slug that finishes the fight in Monument." He tossed off the glass and coughed. "And I dunno that I could've drunk nothin' more grand and impartial. Boys, will you have another on me?"

But Colter answered: "I've got something else to do with the kid."

He pointed about the room. There were at least two score of

men of all sizes and ages standing before the bar or sitting in the leather-upholstered chairs, for Mortimer had spent a small fortune to equip his place with the utmost comfort.

"You look around you, John," he said. "Write down their faces in your mind. These fellers are all friends of mine and friends of old Dad Bone, here. You take a long think. Maybe you'll make up your mind that you'll want to pick more than me for your friend out of the lot."

He took the boy back to the street and there found his horse waiting. They mounted.

"You better come along with me," said Colter.

"And where?"

"Out to old Pineta's house. I gotta see Esmeralda. She's cut up a good deal right now."

"And why?"

"Because for two reasons. One is that it's pretty near six weeks since I asked Esmeralda to marry me, and she'll be kind of peeved if I don't pay her that little attention now and then. The other is that she needs cheering up. She's had a couple of cousins killed in that gunfight in the San Real Cañon. You heard about that from Pancho Pineta, I guess."

"Gunfight!" echoed young Signal. "From what I heard of the thing, it wasn't a fight at all. It was a massacre, Colter!"

"Massacre? Massacre?" echoed Colter amiably, as though he hardly placed the word. "I'll tell you what, I don't get your drift there."

"Murder then. That's better, I'd say," said Signal, and looked keenly from the corner of his eye at his companion.

The face of Henry Colter was totally unmoved. "I dunno," he said, "but I never quite been able to call the killing of a greaser or two murder."

Undoubtedly he spoke, to a certain extent, from the heart, and great wonder came upon Signal. He remembered the scene as he had come upon it, and the dead men lying where they had fallen in the hopeless slaughter.

"Ten men!" cried the boy. "Ten human beings! Great heavens! And all for the sake of a few mule loads."

"Few mule loads your head," retorted his companion. "I know one of the boys who worked in that job. They split up sixty-four thousand Mexican silver dollars among the lot of 'em. Was that worthwhile? It was, I'd say. What right had a lot of greasers to that much money? Come along. I'm overdue at the Pineta house already?"

So young John Signal allowed himself to drift on at the side of his companion, the roan swinging out freely, reaching hard at the bit.

Never, he felt, did an officer of the law ride more strangely fitted with a companion who was a wholesale murderer, but against whose arrest his hands were so securely tied by the bonds of mutual service, and by a deeply pledged word of honor.

CHAPTER EIGHTEEN

It was a moment in the life of the boy when he felt that he could add up the list of the forces that were working upon him, although he could not tell the direction in which they would eventually cast him, for although he could enumerate so many, yet he could not tell how each would be applied to him, and how one might reinforce or nullify another.

Yonder was the shooting scrape that had driven him across the mountains, above and beyond the law as he had known it all his life. And here in Monument, he was living in the service of the very law that he had offended.

To Fitz Eagan he was a friend, or wished to be one. But Fitz Eagan was an enemy of the law and, therefore, his own professional enemy.

To all the Bone tribe, and particularly to Charley Bone, and to Mentor of the scarred face, and to Joe Klaus—otherwise Santa Claus—and to Sim Langley, he had devoted his particular hatred. But the chief of all that faction, Henry Colter himself, was his boon companion and sworn friend. Colter, murderer in chief, with the blood of San Real Cañon still fresh upon his hands and upon whatever conscience he might possess.

It bewildered Signal to think of these complications. And there was the sheriff himself, vaguely fumbling ahead, striving to bring law and order to Monument, while he sustained one faction of these villains consciously, and set his face against the rest.

In this wild confusion of impulses and impacts what, therefore, would be the ultimate conclusion? Where was he bound, and how long would he be able to sail with the whirlwind before he struck upon a reef?

He began to surrender all hope of solving the problems. But he told himself that he would follow what compass he could, pointing due north toward his duty. For youth continually struggles toward the absolute; only middle age accepts the world as it finds it and is more or less content to drift with life, asking no perfection, no sky-towering standards.

So the deputy sheriff rode out with Monument's greatest criminal and came to the house of Pineta, cool and retired in a cloud of trees. They found Esmeralda Pineta all in black, which made her face seem pale, and her eyes and her hair more shadowy dark than when Signal, fleeing from Langley's Mexicans, had had his first glimpse of her.

She greeted them cheerfully enough, but turned her attention to Signal at once. She had been waiting eagerly, she said, to see him. Their first meeting had been only an exchange of glances. However, Mr. Langley had had a great deal to say about him. So she laughed with Signal, and softened her eyes at him, and told him as plainly as a musical voice and a beautiful face could that she liked him very well indeed and that there was really no other man with whom she would more willingly spend these minutes of this particular day.

And out of the cold darkness of his doubts and his perplexities and his fears, Signal stepped as it were into a pleasant sunshine, and unfolded, and laughed back at her, and years disappeared from his stern young face.

Colter bore this with a degree of good-humored impatience. At length he said: "He ain't the only hoss in the corral, Esmeralda. You might look around a little."

"Don't bother me, Henry," said the girl. "I'm trying to get

acquainted. Haven't I known you a long enough time?"

"Esmeralda is like poker," said Colter. "Everybody has beginner's luck with her. But after a while she wraps 'em up and puts 'em on a shelf, and the dust begins to filter down on 'em, and the spiders, they come along and spin webs all over 'em, and it takes a dog-gone' good man to get dusted off and brought to light again, once Esmeralda has got tired of him."

"You're rude, Henry," said the girl. "You'd better go out and try to find Langley. He's somewhere about. Keep him from blundering in while *Señor* Alias is here."

She chuckled at the name, but Colter refused to budge.

"If Langley sees that roan hoss, he ain't gonna come near," he said. "You take a dog that's been stung on the nose, and he never takes kindly to bees. Look here, Esmeralda. You gotta take me off the shelf right *pronto*. I brought these out to get your eye, says the fly to the spider." And he took from his inner coat pocket a string of pearls that glimmered from his hand and then fell into his palm and made a pool of rich light.

The girl looked at them critically from the distance. "They're fine old pearls," she said.

"Fine they are, and old," said Colter. "They oughta be old, I guess."

"Family heirloom, Henry, I suppose?"

"It sure is," he answered.

"And what family?" she asked.

"I disremember," answered Colter. "I wasn't properly introduced at the time the lady give them to me. Afterward I seen the name in the paper, but I forgot." He leaned back in his chair, chuckling. "You take a popular gent like me," said Colter, "he can't remember the names and the addresses of all the ladies that gives him presents."

She, chin on fist, regarded him half soberly, and half in a sort of critical amusement. "And I'm to wear these, Henry?"

"The minute that I seen them, I knew they belonged around your throat, Esmeralda. And here you are." He dropped them into her hand, and then turned with a broad grin to the boy. "Come over that in the line of conversation, if you can," he invited. "Trot out all your smart talk, young feller, but I aim to say that I've made the hit of the day with Esmeralda. Am I right?" he concluded, swinging back toward her.

"You almost always do," she said. She held out the pearls toward him. "They're as pretty as can be," she said.

"Of course they are. But it ain't a joke, Esmeralda. Those belong to *you*."

She shook her head, still smiling. "I can't wear pearls that . . . have been given to you by admirers, Henry."

"Do you mean that?"

"Suppose she should see me wearing them? It would hurt her feelings, I imagine."

He made a gesture of the utmost earnestness. "You don't understand, honey. The lady that gave me those was on a train. She just got off for a few minutes and gave them to me, and then she went on again. She wouldn't've been stopping this side of Frisco."

But the girl shook her head still. "You have to understand, Henry. It's the way such things are given that counts, you know. There's so much associated with them . . . so much feeling, Henry. I couldn't wear them, really."

And she forced him to take them back, while young John Signal, entranced by her beauty before, was still more delighted by the mingled good-natured humor and cleverness with which she had finally refused the gift.

Colter groaned as he received them. "I'd counted on this for a fine welcome, a smile or two, and a walk under the trees in the evening," he said with his peculiar frankness, "me holding your hand and wanting to know when we'd take the same turning on the long trail, Esmeralda."

In that oddly effective way that Signal had noticed before, she made her eyes gentle as she looked toward Colter, and that worthy stirred uneasily in his chair and flushed with pleasure.

"Of course, we're always glad to have an old friend like you here, Henry."

"*We*," said Colter. "Oh, stop it. Don't talk to me like a dog-gone' editor, Esmeralda. Save that for my pal, John Alias, will you?"

At this she straightened a little in her chair and looked right at Signal, all softness gone, her glance wonderfully bright, and as direct as the stare of a man.

"You two are partners, then?" she asked.

"We're friends," corrected Signal. He was uneasy.

Colter, however, explained: "He's a deputy sheriff, Esmeralda. He's nothing else. On no side, particular. Refused to hook up with me. Refused to hook up with Fitz Eagan, even. He wants to walk his own dog-gone' straight path to glory, and I suppose it'll take him all of three months to get planted where the other suckers have been buried before him. I only hope that don't make you romantic and interested in him, honey."

The girl listened to this mingling of banter and truth with her head canted a bit to one side, and her eyes half veiled with thought as she watched the boy. "I think I understand," she said at last.

"What do you understand about him, Esmeralda?"

"That he's an honest man."

Colter sank back in his chair. "You can always find a settler for me," he admitted. "But this here honest man hasn't got a background that's strictly Sunday school, y'understand?"

"I understand that from Langley," said the girl, smiling again. "Henry!" she said sharply.

"Aye, ma'am."

"You can give me something that is a thousand times more valuable than pearls."

"Whether it's in a safe or a wallet," he said, "it's yours, Esmeralda."

"It's in neither place. *They* are in Monument, no doubt, drinking with stolen money."

Colter sat rigid, saying not a word, but his face was calm, although he must have guessed what was coming.

"Gregorio and his brother were raised with me, Henry. I loved them. They've been horribly murdered. You have men and cleverness to help you. Find the men who did the thing. That will be a present worth more than pearls."

CHAPTER NINETEEN

Hoof beats paused before the house; steps came up onto the porch.

"That's Fitzgerald," said Esmeralda Pineta. "That's Fitzgerald Eagan."

"If you know him by his walk," suggested Colter, with some sourness, "I should say you know him pretty well all around."

She answered with her usual calm: "A dog can learn that much about a man."

"Sure," said Colter, "if the man's his master."

Here followed a tap at the door and then the entrance of the mighty form of Fitzgerald Eagan. He paused there for an instant, blocking away the light, except for what entered about his head, and it seemed to Signal that just as his shadow now was filling the room, so his personality pervaded the place, also, and made other men seem pointless and weak. Even Henry Colter, famous for cunning, famous for crime, seemed no more important than a boy as the big man stood before him.

Eagan looked deliberately at Colter and at young Signal, smiling and nodding at the boy. Signal was sitting forward on the edge of his chair, very ill at ease. It was generally conceded that Colter was the leader of the Bone faction. Certainly he was their most outstanding figure, and the general talk in Monument was to the effect that all the battle between the two factions would culminate and die when Colter and Fitz Eagan fought it out together. But there was no token of such a battle at hand now.

Colter said: "Hello, Fitz! How's things?"

And the great Fitz Eagan waved his hand almost cordially toward Colter. He said to Esmeralda: "I brought out the kid. He's been wanting to meet you for a long time. Be kind to him, Esmeralda."

He stepped into the room as he spoke, and behind him came a boy of twenty, much shorter than Fitz Eagan, rather of a stocky build, but with the look of a brave man and an athlete. The stamp of the lion was upon him; it was no surprise to hear Fitz Eagan introduce the youngster as his brother Dick. The boy flushed very red, bowing before Esmeralda, and she with a light in her eye like the flicker of the sun on a sword blade, looked young Dick Eagan through and through. Very glad was John Signal that he had this opportunity to see her when, for a fraction of an instant, her guard was down. It made a great deal of his own enthusiasm about her evaporate.

Plainly she was a queen to all these rough fellows. Colter paid homage here, Sim Langley, and even that man of men, Fitz Eagan. The deputy sheriff, keen in observance, watched the girl and Fitz Eagan with all his powers of discernment, and it seemed plain to him that, although Esmeralda took the big man seriously, she regarded him with far less intense interest than he bestowed on her.

"You're getting news from Colter, too?" he asked.

"Henry hasn't a word of news for me," said the girl. "Or perhaps he is holding something back. Perhaps he's heard that you know something about San Real Cañon, Fitz?"

Fitz Eagan looked across the room at Colter, who said with some irritation: "I've hinted at nothing like that, Esmeralda."

"One of the two of you must know," she insisted. "There's nothing that happens in the whole range that one of you doesn't know all about. If I draw a blank with you, Henry, then surely

Fitz can help me out."

She leaned forward a little, her eyes keen and expectant, but Eagan replied: "I don't know a syllable. I know nothing whatever about it. But I came out here to tell you, Esmeralda, that I've had nothing to do with that butchery. My methods ain't shaped that way, and, if you can tell me what trail to follow, I'll ride it. I'm the marshal of Monument, you know." He ended with a faint smile, as though ready to join in any mirth that might be aroused by his legal position. But no one laughed.

"You'd ride for me?" asked the girl.

"I would."

"And, Henry, you'd help me?"

"I? Sure."

"And you, John Alias?"

"It's my business," the boy assured her.

Dick Eagan said nothing. He did not have to. With his eyes he was drinking up the beauty of the girl; plainly he would be the first tool for any of her purposes.

"Then with all this help," she said, "I can't fail. I simply can't fail. And if any of you can find even one man who had anything to do with that . . . murder . . . I'll never forget. I'll be his friend to the death of me. Poor Pancho would take the trail, but he's shot to bits. And because of Gregorio and Manuelo, someone has to die."

She said this with a fiery enthusiasm that shook all her body, and again something in John Signal shrank from her. He thought that she was the most beautiful creature he ever had seen; he felt that she was also the most dangerous, like some wild mustang, hunted by every cowpuncher of the range, but useless when caught, except to put a bullet through its wicked brain. Now she was gathering all her forces to send vengeance down the trail of the murderers of her cousins, and these fighters of Monument were all willing to ride in her behalf.

117

Signal looked again at Henry Colter. That gentleman was as cool as could be, as though he had not the slightest thought that any danger might be gathering upon his path. He now stood up.

"There's no place for us here now, Alias," he said. "When Fitz Eagan walks in, sensible gents walk out. Lemme know your dates with Esmeralda and I'll call in the off season," he added to Eagan.

Signal took the hint and rose in turn, but the girl would have stopped him. They had not had a chance to talk together. Or, if he went now, he would come again? There was no more danger of Sim Langley about the place, she assured him. Besides, Langley was not such a bad fellow—just a little overbearing at times.

"Listen to her purring," observed Colter. "Do you hear that, Fitz? She wants to have Alias on her staff, and I suppose she'll land him. But he's fighting for his head now. He'd even swallow the hook if he could break the line afterward. You're right, kid. It's better to have indigestion than Esmeralda."

At this very pointed banter she laughed, but her glance dwelt wickedly upon Colter as the two left the room. They stood on the porch for a moment, Colter mopping his forehead. He had maintained his poise perfectly, but there was no doubt from his compressed lips and his uneasy eye that he realized that the clouds of trouble that this girl was raising might very soon blow in his direction. However, he merely said to his young companion: "You've seen her now. Better'n a view of the mountains at sunset time, eh? There's only one Esmeralda . . . and there's plenty of mountains, even of volcanoes." He waved his hand before him. "Up here on this here verandah, there ain't a man that would take a pot shot at us. Once down the steps, there'd be a plenty. There by that rose bush is the spot where young Sam Channing dropped and kicked up the dirt until he died.

And where the walk turns a little, that's where Push Aiken flopped when Langley shot him through the brain. Langley had been waiting out yonder where that brush stands. A grand killer is Langley. He's got an Indian streak in him, and he takes no chances. Far as that's concerned, he's apt to be lyin' out there now, with his rifle butt cuddled under his chin, waiting to raise a little dust for us. But so long as we're in or on the house of Esmeralda, we're safe."

"Will you tell me why that is?"

"Why, the trouble began to rise too fast. There was four gents shot up and laid away in the hospital from gunfights here, to say nothing of Channing and Aiken that was killed. After Aiken died, the boys all got together and agreed that so long as Esmeralda was pulling the boys in like moths around a candle flame, we'd better make it a rule that her house was peaceful ground. That rule has held ever since. And a good thing. Some of the worst enemies in the world, that wouldn't've spoke a first word outside of with a gun, have met here at the Pineta place and have made up. She's a great hand at getting the hatchet buried."

As he spoke, he had been scanning every feature of the landscape before him, from the ground to the tips of the trees, as though he suspected that fighting men might be hidden away up there, waiting to kill him the instant his foot descended from the front steps of the verandah. However, he seemed assured, at last, and went down to the garden level. There he and his companion took their horses, and they rode down the driveway to the outer road.

There, Colter shrugged his shoulders with a shuddering force. "I always feel a pile better," he said, "when I've sashayed down that avenue of trees and got into the clear again, where my rifle would have a chance to keep things at a distance. Now, tell me what you think of Esmeralda, kid?"

"She's beautiful," said the boy.

119

"Go on. That's only a starting point."

"I don't know," said Signal. "I've said that she's beautiful. I don't think that I could say anything more about her. I was a little afraid of her."

"Afraid?"

"Yes."

"Why, kid, she's like velvet. Expensive, sure. Expensive kind of a wife, but for three years everybody around Monument has been trying to get her. Maybe . . . maybe you'll be the lucky man?"

John Signal smiled and said nothing. In fact, he was unwilling to let his mind dwell upon the thought of this lovely, strange woman, as a man who loves wine too well dreads the tasting of the first glass.

"But you're right," said the other in a sterner voice. "You're dead right. She's dangerous. Velvet. So is a tiger's paw. And as for the price of her . . . why, I think that she'd throw herself at the head of the gent that managed to kill a couple of the boys that shot up her cousins. I never seen her worked up so much. Who would've thought it?" he moralized in wonder. "Who would ever've guessed that she was so dead keen on them greaser cousins of hers?"

And he looked up at the sky and shook his head, a little mournful at the strangeness of this world.

CHAPTER TWENTY

The heart and the brain of young John Signal still were heavy with his problem when he parted from Colter at the edge of town. He said to the outlaw seriously: "They would have shot me to bits, today, except for you."

"I dunno. Maybe they would," replied Colter. "Take it another way. Maybe that was your chance to get famous. You might've tipped over all three of 'em, and after that you'd've lived in books."

The boy shook his head.

"Anyway," said Colter, "don't worry about gratitude. The most that I've done don't balance what you did for me. I keep a pretty straight set of books about things like this, and I know that things still lean your way. It's tit for tat."

"And so we're square?" asked young Signal.

"Of course we are. So long, and take care of yourself. Mind you, I can oar in and keep back the Bone tribe when I'm around, but not when I'm away. They want your scalp. They're afraid of you, son. And there's nothing more dangerous than a gunman that's scared."

With this he rode off, and Signal found himself, in another few moments, at his boarding house. It was a plain wooden building, shingled on the outside, with one turret rising from a series of bow windows. Those were the selected and most expensive rooms in the house. He had been surprised by the grandeur of one he had glimpsed in passing, but, on the whole, he was well satisfied with his own chamber, in the third story and at the back of the house. It looked upon the laundry lines, the sun-faded, unpainted, high, board fences to the rear of the houses, the garbage cans, the wood and horse sheds, the dogs that wandered and the cats that stalked through this wilderness of wood. Above all, from his window he could watch the door of the shed in which the roan horse was quartered.

As he went up the stairs, he passed at the first hall that same crisply pretty girl who he had seen on the street in the morning. She shrank back from him with a little exclamation, and he hesitated. It was not her prettiness that held him. It was sheerest irritation.

He took off his hat and turned toward her. "Are you afraid of me, ma'am?" said John Signal.

She retreated yet another step. Her eyes glanced toward the head of the stairs with a hunted look, as though she were estimating the probable chances of escape by bolting. Then she gave up, and, turning, she fled into one of those large corner rooms that have been mentioned.

He, angered more than ever, strode on to his own cubbyhole and sat down to take his head in his hand and ponder. He could see no solution for his problem and he had not long to dream over it, for a heavy hand struck his door. He sang out, and immediately there stood before him the alert, strongly built man of middle age who he had seen with the girl that morning.

"My daughter," began the other.

John Signal looked at him with expressive eyes.

"And who are you?" asked Signal.

"My name is Morley Shand. Did you ever hear it?"

"I never did."

Mr. Shand seemed gravely taken aback. "Mister Alias," he said, "since you choose to pass by that name, I wish to tell you that no matter how you may behave among the ruffians of

Monument, with me it will be necessary for you to take a different line. And when it comes to bullying my daughter in this very house where. . . ."

"Is that she waiting outside the door?" asked Signal.

Mr. Shand turned and snatched the door open. He revealed the chambermaid. She was a brown-faced girl from the range, obviously pressed into this work on the spur of the moment. She had not yet had a chance to turn pale.

"What will you have? Why are you here?" asked Mr. Shand in increasing anger.

She leaned her hand against the door jamb. "I heard him speak to Miss Shand," she said.

"*Ah!*" cried Mr. Morley Shand. "If I have a witness of this affair, I think that I can make life fairly hot for you in Monument. No matter what else Westerners may be, they don't allow insults to. . . ."

"Hold on," said the chambermaid. "You start drifting like that with your head down, and you'll hang up on wire before long. I heard everything that was said, and I seen it all. I was cleaning the next flight of steps up. Miss Shand shied when Mister Alias come upstairs to the landing. He only asked her if she was afraid of him."

"And that was enough to make my girl run for her life!" shouted Mr. Shand in increasing fury.

"When a pony ain't bridlewise, you can't blame it for bolting," said the girl.

Mr. Shand, thus balked, turned his anger upon the newcomer. "I've never heard of such infernal rudeness," he declared. "I'll let your mistress know about this, my fine girl."

He burst from the room, and from the door the calm voice of Signal pursued him: "You'd better think that over twice, before you start yapping about her," said Signal.

Mr. Shand whirled about. He was fairly explosive with his

123

fury, but suddenly he turned pale and retreated.

"He thought about guns," said the chambermaid, nodding confidentially at Signal.

"Who are you?" asked the latter.

"I'm Polly. I do this floor and help wash up after meals, and keep the vegetable garden."

"Is that all you do?"

"That's all."

"And what do you get?"

"I get forty."

"A week?"

"What d'you mean? A month, of course."

"Come in and sit down," he said coaxingly.

"Is it right?" said Polly.

"And why not?"

She grinned at him. Freckles spotted the nose and the upper cheeks of Polly. She had hair redder than her freckles. Her nose had never grown up.

"It might get you talked about," said Polly. "Having a girl into your room, I mean." She walked straight in as she spoke. Before the window there was a plain wooden kitchen table. Against this she leaned. "Besides," she said, "I might get fired."

"For what?"

"*Aw* . . . sassing his lordship, you see."

"I don't think he'll talk."

"He will, though. You take a law-and-order gent like him, he can't help talking, no more than a calf can help bawling, or a burro braying."

"If he says a word . . . ," said the boy darkly.

"What could you do?" she asked calmly. "He's too tenderfoot to pack a gun, except in a bag. And he's too old for you to hit him. If you whacked him in the stomach, he'd have indigestion the rest of his life."

"Sit down," he invited, smiling at her.

She perched herself on the edge of the table. "This is breaking all the rules," she said, "confabbing with men guests and sitting on tables."

"You're fine," said the boy, admiring her heartily.

"Get out," she said. "I'm all full of freckles!"

"What are they?" he said gallantly.

"They're a lot. Sulphuric acid and lye won't take 'em out."

"Did you try?"

"Both ways, and it wouldn't work."

"Suppose," he said, "suppose you lose your job here?"

"Well, what of it? It's a pretty big country."

"Look here. Are you alone?"

"Me? I should say not. I'm with the celebrated gunfighter, John Alias. Is that being alone? It is not," she answered herself.

"I'm not celebrated," he told her, "and I'm not a gunfighter. You remember that."

"I'll try to," she said, "but other people won't let me. Not since they've got you into the papers."

"The papers are fools!" he said.

"Sure they are," she agreed, "but they're giving you a lot of free space. I could use some of it, I can tell you."

"For what?"

"Me? For getting on the stage."

"And what would you do on the stage?"

"I gotta swell voice," she said. "Let me sashay out onto the stage of that opera house and I'll tell you what, they'll put me on the payroll."

"Have you tried them?"

"Who, the manager?"

"Yes."

"I tried the manager. He'd been down at Mortimer's saloon drinking gin fizzes. He remembered right away that he'd known me since I was a little girl. He started to hold my hand."

"The coyote!" said the boy with earnest anger.

"I told him that I wasn't a two-year-old and that I didn't need gentling, but that didn't stop him. So I slapped his face and beat it."

"A man like that ought to be run out of town," declared the deputy sheriff.

"*Aw*, leave him alone," she said. "He's all right. Only he was a little sappy that day. He was not seeing his best and didn't spot my freckles," she concluded with a smile. Then she added: "But if they run me out of this job, I'll call on him again."

"If you do, I'll take you there," said John Signal.

"Would you do that?"

"Of course I would."

"Well," she said, "*that* would put me in the papers. Our distinguished young deputy sheriff took a day off from man-eating and sashayed up to the opera house with Polly Noonan, the well-known chambermaid. Say, John Alias, could you stand for that?"

"I don't know," he said, thoughtful. "I don't think they'd drag any woman into print through me. I don't think that even these newspapers would dare to do that."

"Wouldn't they? I hope they would."

"Well," he said, "I'd have to take my chance on that."

She regarded him with a thoughtful frown, her chin propped on one palm. It was not a graceful position in which she sat, but there are some so gifted in creation that they cannot be awkward. And the eyes of young John Signal having been opened toward the beauty of woman upon this day, he had regard to the hand, like that of a child, and the roundness of the wrist. Her smile, moreover, was a flash of good cheer, and her eyes were blue beyond belief. Neither could one say that her hair was sheer red, but it was golden where the sun touched, dark copper in the shadow. For the first time in his life, John Signal thoroughly enjoyed a color scheme.

"You're all right," said the girl. "You're a straight shooter and a good fellow. I'd like to have some way of paying you back, if you would take me down there to the opera house."

"You could pay me back," he said.

She looked down at the floor, and then straight back at him. "And how?" said she.

"I need advice," said John Signal.

She shrugged her shoulders. "Advice?" she said. "I'm fuller of it than Monument is full of dust. You're in trouble?"

"Yes."

"I've seen all the kinds of trouble there are. Go on, Johnny Alias. Maybe I can show you the way out."

CHAPTER TWENTY-ONE

He looked at her with such appreciation of her cocksureness and poise and with such a growing sense of her charm that she shook her head at him and gave him a dark look.

"Don't do that," she said.

"Don't do what?"

"Think about yourself, not about me. What sort of trouble are you in? With the Bone outfit, I hear."

"They don't bother me much . . . just now. I'm in trouble with myself."

"That's the worst kind," she agreed. "Take a horse that interferes . . . he's always liable to give himself a bad fall, isn't he?"

"All right," he said. "I'll put this straight. Suppose you did a man a good turn."

"How good?"

"Well, had him under your gun . . . and didn't shoot. And having a reason to shoot, say."

"I follow that. Go on. Who was it?"

"This is all supposing."

"All right."

"And afterward you fix him up a little."

"Well?"

"Then suppose that you get into a corner afterward. A mighty bad corner. Life or death for you. And this same fellow drifts in and helps you out of the pinch."

"I can see that. It squares you both up."

"Then suppose that you got a lot of bad information about that fellow, and it's sort of your duty to go out and arrest him. . . ."

"You being deputy sheriff?"

"That's it."

She took this gravely under consideration. Then she said: "I'll tell you what . . . there's a lot of different kind of people floating around in the world."

He nodded.

"They're like money."

He nodded again.

"Some of 'em are just copper. They got a face printed on 'em, and they're round as a gold piece, and got the same kind of milling, and all. But they're cheap stuff. They don't amount to much, except just to fill in and make change."

He smiled.

"Then there's paper money. Some of it's worth a dollar. Some of it's worth a thousand. According to the print that's put on it, and who put the print. You pass one ten-dollar bill and get change for it. You pass another and get jailed, because the money's crooked. And there's a lot of men that way. According to the way that you read 'em, they may be worth something, but at bottom they're just made up of paper junk . . . touch a match to 'em, and a lot of million-dollar people would go up in a couple of whiffs of smoke."

"That's right."

"Then there's some coin that's silver. It's all right. It means what it says. It's worth something. But you'd have to have a whole train of mules to carry away a fortune in it. And a lot of people are that way, that I've met. They look pretty enough and bright enough, but you'd have to have a thousand of 'em to get anywhere with such friends."

"That's true as a book. I've known that kind, too. That's the common or garden sort of a man. Every place is full of 'em."

"But on the other hand, there's gold," said the girl. "There ain't a lot of it, but there's some. It's real money. You can rub it thin, and it still passes. With a pocketful of it, you can go around the world. You can take a golden coin and batter it out of shape. You can stamp on it and twist it crooked . . . but still it's worth just the same. You can't light it with a match, and you can't show it up with acids and what-not. And some people are that way. And when you've tried 'em, and stamped on 'em, and picked 'em up crooked, even . . . if they've got the real stuff in them, they're worth something. That's the way, it seems to me, with this fellow that you stood by. That must've been pretty fine, and I wish that I'd seen it. But along comes his chance, and he stands behind you, just when you need him. Well, it seems to me, sort of, that if I was a deputy sheriff, or deputy anyone else, I wouldn't harm that man. I'd just let him alone. I'd keep him for a friend. I'd put him in my pocket and hope that maybe, sometime, I could pick up one more friend just like him, because that would make the real music."

He waited for a moment, turning the idea in his mind, and at last he said to her: "I think you're right. This thing was spinning around in my brain. You see, I'd taken an oath to do certain sorts of things."

"I know that. But an oath is words . . . guns can say a lot more . . . you and your friend have done some talking with guns, eh?"

"You've helped me a lot," he assured her. "I'll go down there to the opera house with you, whenever you say the word. Is that a go?"

"It is! Tomorrow morning?"

"Right."

She slipped down from the table. "They'll be calling for me

pretty soon. I've got to get along. I'm glad I met you."

"And me the same."

"So long, Johnny."

"How old are you?"

"Me? I'm nineteen."

"Nineteen!" he cried.

"Is that so bad?"

"Floating around in the world all by yourself."

"Well," she said, "a young horse can stand a terrible lot of bad weather."

"You were raised on the range?"

"The range raised me," she answered. "And by the way, how old are you, John Alias?"

"Oh," he said, "I'm twenty-two."

She paused by the door and made a face of pretended gravity. "Oh," she said, "you're all of that, you are? Why," she added, "you're a real growed-up man, ain't you?" She slipped through the door and into the hall.

"Hey, Polly!" he called, and followed her in much haste.

At the door he saw her scurrying. But she paused at a little distance.

"What did you mean by that?" he asked her.

"By what?" she asked.

"By laughing," he said.

"Ain't that allowed in the game?"

"Wait a minute, Polly, will you?"

"I'll see you tomorrow," she said, and slipped from view around the corner of the hallway.

He hesitated, and then he went back into his room and began to pace up and down. He felt the oddest change in his mind and in his whole being. He had been, before, vastly depressed, confused, bewildered. He had been walking through a room of darkness. Now the door suddenly had been opened and he

131

stood in sunshine and heard the song of birds.

In his walking, he found himself snapping his fingers softly, smiling to himself. The problems were solved. The difficulties were ended, and that complicated Gordian knot had been cut.

All this change had been effected he hardly knew how. It appeared now perfectly patent that he could not betray his friendship with Colter by arresting him for the murder of the Mexicans in San Real Cañon. There was no necessary plan for his action except to drift with the current of events. Perhaps he would have the fortune to stumble upon others of those who had waylaid the Pinetas. At any rate, he would keep his eyes wide open and hope. Furthermore, there was plenty of crime and criminals about Monument, outside of Colter and his crew.

Then he stopped. He opened his eyes, as it were, and saw that he had been walking all this while in a happy trance. Who had done this thing to him and touched him with such magic? Why, who else but the red-headed, freckle-faced, blue-eyed girl called Polly? Polly who? Polly what?

He sat down on the window sill and rolled a cigarette, whistling to himself, and, as he lighted the smoke, he saw an arm, a shoulder, and part of a head appear around the corner of a barn, and, also, the sun gleamed on a long, steel barrel. He flung himself backward to the floor of the room as the rifle *clanged*. The bullet clipped the sill and a splinter of wood struck him in the face.

Springing up, he flattened himself against the wall and peered cautiously out, but he had only a glimpse of a man darting around the corner of the horse shed.

It did not pay to fall into dreams in Monument!

Chapter Twenty-Two

Well healed of all dreaming, then, John Signal went down from his room to the rear yard as a cat goes down after a mouse. Around the house he flashed, found the rear gate of the yard locked, and, still cat-like, over it he went and came to a horse shed, where a weary-faced man, with a prodigious yawn, was saddling a pinto mustang in the stall next to Grundy.

Grundy, at least, was safe.

"Stranger," said Signal, "you heard a rifle fired around the corner, here?"

"Yes, sure," said the other. "Somebody potting a rabbit, I guess."

"You guess?"

"Yep. And must've hit it. I heard him run off afterward as though he aimed to pick up what he'd plugged."

"And who was it?"

"I never seen his face." The tired man turned slowly to Signal and added: "What's the matter? Was it *your* rabbit he was shootin' at?" And, as he said this, an odd light glimmered into his eyes and instantly passed out again.

It made Signal consider him through a silent moment, staring steadily, and the longer he stared the more uneasy the other became. His weariness left him. He grew tense, and seemed poised on tiptoe, either for flight or for attack. Remorselessly Signal stared at him, and the pressure of that young and brilliant eye began to rob the other of his color. His face grew white and hard. His nostrils quivered. He seemed about to make some desperate start when Signal said: "You know who that was?"

"How should I know?" gasped the other.

"Who are you?"

"Me? What difference does that make?"

"I ask you who you are!" shouted John Signal.

The other leaped back as though a bullet had torn through him. "Name of Pete Graham!" he said. "What's the matter?"

"Is that your rifle that's leaning against the wall?"

"Maybe it is."

"Is that your rifle?" roared John Signal.

"Yes, yes," stammered Pete Graham.

Signal picked it up. He had little fear that the other would attempt a sudden attack upon him. Pete Graham was almost demoralized. His glance would not hold still for an instant, but wavered from side to side, and his color was most sickly.

So John Signal opened the rifle and made sure that no bullet had been fired from it. He dropped the gun back against the wall and stared again at Pete Graham, curiously and savagely pleased to mark the disintegration of the man. It was almost like seeing a figure constructed of sand dissolve in water.

"You didn't shoot," said John Signal. "But who did?"

"How should I know? I ain't got eyes everywhere!"

"No. You only have eyes in your head. Who shot at me?" He advanced a half step.

Pete Graham, with a faint groan, drew himself back against the manger and set his teeth. "I'll see you hanged before I tell," he said.

"I guessed that you knew," said Signal.

Pete Graham started to answer, but only achieved a writhing of his lips. He had begun to tremble violently. With all the bitterness of fear, he was tasting death.

Signal dropped a hand upon his gun. "I'll wait till I count three on you," he said. "Then I want that name out of you."

Pete Graham closed his eyes. He hung by his elbows on the manger, looking ready to faint.

"It was Langley," he breathed. "Lord help me. It was Langley."

Signal turned on his heel and went out from the horse shed. He was filled with cold rage at Langley, and a peculiar mixture of cruel satisfaction and pity as he thought of Pete Graham. Perhaps that had been a brave fellow, or brave enough to pass, but now he was dissolved, and he could never be much of a man again. It reminded Signal of a young giant who had gone forth from Bender Creek to conquer the pugilistic world and who had risen with a dizzy suddenness, until he met the champion. The result of that fight was a crushing defeat, and, when the giant came home, he had altered to a weak pulp of a man; he could hardly look a child in the face.

So it seemed to have happened with Pete Graham, all of whose strength had disappeared. And he, John Signal, had been the burning glass that had focused on poor Graham.

So, if pity was in him, that same cruel pride was in him, too. It had been a terrible experiment; it had been a wonderful thing, as well.

He walked around the house to enter it again, and, so doing, he encountered a gasping, hurrying, little man whose eyes seemed popping out of his head.

"Hey, John Alias!"

"Well?" said Signal with disdain, for he recognized the same little fellow who had been apparently spying on the sheriff, outside that official's door,

"Sheriff Ogden sent me up to find you. He says for you to look out. He says that Charley and Jud Bone are both in Mortimer's saloon swearin' that they're gonna get you, and get you

135

good, and get you today. He says, you better lie low for a while."

Signal compressed his lips to keep back the first retort, which was: *Why did the sheriff send such a warning, instead of putting under arrest the men who were threatening the life of a peaceful citizen in good standing . . . so far as Monument was concerned?*

But he merely said: "You know Charley and Jud?"

"Sure I know 'em."

"You hear me?"

"I hear you, Alias."

"Go to Mortimer's saloon."

"It ain't hardly safe."

"Isn't it safe for you?"

The other moistened his lips. He looked with rat-like eyes upon Signal. "Maybe I'd chance it," he said.

From his pocket, Signal drew $5 and dropped them into the ready palm of the other. "You go to Mortimer's saloon. Is there a crowd there, besides Charley and Jud?"

"It's packed to the doors. They got about a hundred men in there, and Charley and Jud are tellin' what they're gonna do. They're all heated up, and ready for a kill."

"You've seen 'em?"

"I've seen 'em."

"Go back to Mortimer's saloon and make a little speech to the whole crowd, or else talk to Charley and Jud so that everybody can hear. Say that I'm sending them word that I hear that they're after me. That they want to run me out of town. Is that it?"

"They wanna run you into your grave, Alias. That's the short of it."

"Tell them that in a half hour, I'm going to leave this house and I'm going to walk straight down to the sheriff's office. I'm going to be armed and ready for trouble, and, if they're men and want trouble, they can stop me on the way. I'll have nobody behind me. I'll be tackling this game alone. If the pair of them have any nerve, if they're men, tell them that I expect to be met."

The messenger leaned against the picket fence very much as Pete Graham had leaned against the manger in the barn. Then he rallied. "I'll go as fast as I can," he said. "I'll go down there and tell the boys in Mortimer's saloon about everything that's been told to me. *Aw,* say, there's never been nothing like this, even in Monument!" He looked at Signal for a single instant, with a grin of horrible joy, and then he turned and fled.

Signal looked after him with a peculiar interest. In all his life he never had seen such a repulsive creature. There was no manliness in him; he was nothing but a negation, except that he loved trouble and lived upon it—the trouble of others! He was the tool who brought fighting men together and watched them destroy one another. Like the most detestable jackal, he lived upon the scraps of danger thrown into his path when the giants clashed. Now, watching him running down the street, his feet shambling, his rounded shoulders working, Signal knew that the most dreadful greed was driving this pariah.

He stared after him in interest. Pete Graham recently had dropped a long distance. Would he ever drop as far as that? And if Graham had dropped, what had forced him down? The impact of more fierce and savage personalities—like his own, like John Signal's?

What passed through the soul of John Signal then, as he reflected keenly on what he was and what he had done? There should have been shame that there was in him such power over his brother man; there should have been remorse and regret, of gigantic proportions. But in truth, since the truth we must have about him, although there were some faint shadowings of these more humble emotions, all was overridden by a great pride that rose in him like a pillar of white fire—pride, utter self-confidence, and a willingness to lay down his life struggling to maintain his czardom over the wills of lesser men.

He went up to his room and there he took up his rifle and began to unload it, preparatory to cleaning and oiling it, so that all would be in perfect readiness for his march into the throat of danger. He could have burst into song; in fact, he was humming softly to himself and regardless of the fact that his door was open, when the voice of Polly spoke from it, saying: "I've always heard that a cat purrs before it pounces. But I never heard the cat before now."

CHAPTER TWENTY-THREE

He looked up at the girl with a keen interest. She had shown before that she could look deeply through the ideas of men. How deeply would she look through him?

"Cat?" he asked.

She nodded. She half closed her eyes and scanned him from head to foot. "Big, sleek, soft, happy pussy," she said, "about to jump on a mouse. Or a pair of mice," she added.

"Hello!" he said. "What's all this about?"

"Oh," she answered, "Crawlin was here."

"Who's Crawlin?"

"The rat that was looking for you."

"What did he say to you?"

"The same he said to you. That the pair of 'em were looking for you. He was so scared about it that he was happy. 'Maybe they'll all be killed,' says he . . . the rat!"

"He is a rat."

"When they took a shot at you, they didn't scratch you?"

"What shot?"

She pointed at the chip taken from the window sill. "It kept on traveling up," she said. "It went through the floor of my room upstairs and nearly took the heel off my shoe. I came down to find out . . . and you'd sashayed out to ask questions, I suppose?"

"Langley shot at me," he said. He had been working at the rifle while he talked. Now he paused and looked at her with luminous eyes. "The murderer," he said softly.

"Aye," she said. "Langley's a murderer. Everybody always has known that. Indian kind of murder. That's his long suit. But there's other cards in the deck than the aces, such as you play. A straight flush beats four of a kind, Johnny."

"Meaning what?"

"Why should you be so hard on the murderers?" she asked him.

"D'you want me to praise 'em?"

"I'd sort of expect you to."

"Would you?" he asked icily. "What sort of a man d'you take me to be, Polly?"

"A dog-gone' dangerous one," she said.

His swift, well-accustomed hands already had finished with the rifle. He began to slip the bullets into the magazine. "That's fine and friendly," he said. "Dangerous to whom?"

"Why, to pretty near anybody. Man or girl, old man or old woman. Dangerous to everybody, down to the babies in the cradle. That's what you are, Johnny."

"You don't say that seriously, Polly."

"Don't I just!"

"How d'you mean . . . dangerous even to babies?"

"A baby has to have a father, don't it, to keep earning money, and what not?"

"And I'd kill the papa, eh?" He laughed angrily. "Why, Polly, you're talking crazy."

"Perhaps I seem to be. I'm not. You're going to run amuck right now."

"What d'you mean?"

"Instead of lying low, like the sheriff wants you to, you're gonna prance down the street and soak the two of 'em full of lead."

"That Crawlin told you everything, did he?"

"Sure. He tells everything, and then some more."

"I'll give him something else to think about, the next time I see him," said Signal.

"Sure," said Polly. "You'll get down even as low as taking a crack at a worm like Crawlin."

"Say," he cried, "are you trying to get me all heated up, Polly? What's the matter with you? What have I done to you?"

"Made me like you," said Polly, "and that's the worst thing that's happened to me in a long time."

"*Humph!*" he said. "Like me! And you come in here and call me . . . why, you call me a murderer. *Like* me?" He repeated it, very bitterly.

"Oh, I mean it all," she said. "But you fellows who live by the gun are so single track you can't carry two loads at once. You've given me a bigger thrill than a roller coaster."

"I wish you'd stop kidding and talk straight to me," he complained.

"I'm talking nothing but," she assured him. "Never anything like it since an actor I seen on the stage, once. He was mighty cool and slick. He had long white hands. He never raised his voice. He had a slow sort of a smile, and all the girls in the play were always falling in love with him. He made my heart jump right up in high C. But the next day . . . I hadn't slept all night . . . I seen the wind blow off his hat when he was going down the street, and it took off his wig, too. He was about fifty-five, the old liar!" She laughed at the memory.

"I'm a faker like him, am I?"

"You're a lot worse. He never would make any widows, except through the divorce courts. But you'll make a plenty before you're done."

"You think that I'm a low gunfighter!" he exclaimed.

"No, I think you're an ace-high gunfighter. I'd put you right up there with the classy ones . . . with Colter and Fitz Eagan, even. And now that you've got me all in a fuss about you, you're gonna. . . ."

"Look here," cried the boy, "I won't listen to you, the way you're carrying on to make a fool of me!"

"*Bah!*" answered Polly. "You make me tired. *I've* practically fallen in love, I think . . . and here you're walking out to get yourself all shot to bits."

"I won't be shot to bits," he said. "I think the shoe will be on the other foot. I'm not going to miss, I can tell you."

"That's pretty." She nodded. "You ain't gonna miss. You bet you ain't!"

"But look here, Polly. The other thing. . . . What I mean to say is . . . you know . . . speaking about you and me. . . . Jiminy, Polly, of course you're just making a fool out of me!"

Polly regarded him with a bland blue eye. "I got an idea," she said, "that you're tryin' to say something kind to me. Is that right?"

Young John Signal turned the brightest of bright reds. "You're pretty hard," he said.

"To say nice things to?" she inquired. "Not a bit. You try me."

He gnawed his lip. The more he looked at her, the more delightful she appeared. "Polly," he said with a sigh, "you're just badgering me."

"If you want help," said Polly, "I'll help you out if I can. Do you want to say that you're fond of me, Johnny?"

He perked back his shoulders. "How could I?" he demanded of her. "You start right in by calling me a cat . . . and then you say that I'm a murderer. And then. . . ."

"You take things pretty hard," she said. "You're mighty nice, Johnny, but I don't think you'll ever be much use."

"You're just a nineteen-year-old girl," he said. "What right have you to talk so grown up? You're only nineteen. You're just a baby, really."

"Am I?" she asked, smiling. "I wish I was. Oh, how I wish I was."

"I don't pretend to be anything very much," he went on, furiously hot with wounded dignity and spoiled vanity. "But you don't think that I'll ever be any use."

"Not once you've really gone wild. You was raised tame, eating out of the hand and getting used to the halter and the bridle right from the beginning. But once you bust loose . . . well, the hardest outlaw hoss is the one that's come out of a corral, not the one that's always run wild."

"I wish that you'd get away from horses and get down to men," he said.

All at once, she threw out her hands toward him, and the softest of music was in her voice. "Oh, Johnny," she said, "you're such a good boy . . . in spots. You could be so grand. You're so terrible good-looking, too. Why won't you be nice?"

He hesitated. There had been so much banter that he dared not take all for granted, but he was irresistibly drawn closer to her. He took her hands. They were ridiculously soft, and they quivered, and her fingers squirmed, but really she made hardly an effort to get away. She tipped back her head a little. "You're laughing at me all the time," he stammered.

"I'm not. I'm not," she whispered. "Johnny, say that you like me a little, because I know that you do. D'you think that I would've dared to talk this way to you if I hadn't guessed?"

He held her with one arm; she laid her hands upon his shoulders, with her face still raised to his, without the slightest trifle of defense. And still he hesitated. His poor young brain was whirling wildly. Music rang in his ears, red joy floated before his eyes. But he was held back by a silken string of criticism, his mind still acting, no matter how imperfectly.

"Polly," he said, "I know that you'd never come in here like this except that you had some bigger reason than just caring for me. You wouldn't tell me so quickly. You'd hold off. You could see me going to pieces about you. What made you walk in and let me hold you like this?"

"Will you kiss me, Johnny, and be talkin' about it afterward?" she said.

"Aye, Polly, if you'll tell me what it is that you want."

"Only a small thing . . . that you'll stay here and not go prancin' off down the street like a fool for them to shoot at you. Only for the promise of that," she said.

He began to straighten a little, so drawing away from her. "Cannot you see, Polly, that I've got all my honor pledged to walk down to the sheriff's office in the middle of the street, so's to give the pair of them a chance to meet me?"

"What is honor worth? What's that kind of honor worth, honey? Look at me, Johnny. Don't go starin' at yourself in the street. Monument can see you other days, but you'll be stayin' home here with me today, will you? *I'll* make you happy. I'll make you forget the rest of them . . . the gunfightin', murderin' rascals! Oh, Johnny, it ain't only that you might be killed . . . it's that you might kill one of them. And that'd be the finish of you. Oh, honey, will you listen to me?"

He stepped back from her, white of face, his forehead beaded. "They've hired you to try me out this way, too," he said. "They'd do anything to shame me."

CHAPTER TWENTY-FOUR

He saw Polly drop into the nearest chair, with one arm fallen over the back of it, and he felt that he had struck her down, and that he was a brute. Was he wrong, and had grief unnerved her, and horror? Was he right, and had fear and shame struck her?

But he said to himself that the time had come—that he was overdue—that Monument waited for him to make good his boast. And so he snatched up the rifle and went out from the room with long, swift strides, like a hunter on a trail.

All the way down the hall he was desperately drawn to whirl about and run back to her and take her hands and beg her to tell him the truth. But when he had passed the first turning of the stairs, it was easier to go ahead, and, when he stumbled out into the heat of the sun, she danced back into the rear of his mind, until he could hold her at arm's length and remember that her nose was ridiculously short, and that she had freckles.

So, with every step up the street, he grew more certain. His enemies would do anything to break his spirit and shame him before Monument's eyes. And what more natural than for them to use this clever girl, this perfect little actress!

He gritted his teeth, now, seeing that she never could have been drawn to him so suddenly. True enough that he had been swept halfway toward love the first minute he was with her. But that was a miracle. She was hard, quick, sharp, bright; she could not have been involved in the same manner.

So said he to himself, and striding up the street, the action of

145

walking, the heat of the day, the burning brightness of the sun—all acted upon him and enabled him to become his own man again. Nothing was important except the rifle that he carried over the crook of his left arm, his right hand grasping the trigger guard and the trigger. Revolvers were quicker, it was true, but surety was the grand thing. And he wanted to be sure.

He shortened his step. He was coming into the center of Monument; he was turning into the main street itself, and now he saw that all the doorways and the windows were jammed with people, and that the street before him was as naked as the palm of his hand. No, yonder a runabout drawn by a trotting horse came in, but someone ran out from the pavement and headed the driver away. It was as though the street were being kept open by tacit consent for the passage of a procession. And suddenly he realized that his own approach was that which was so expected.

Crawlin must have advertised the coming event with a town crier, for everyone understood, and all were present for the show. Constantly new faces were crowding into the doorways and into the windows. Somewhere Charley Bone and his brother would have to be waiting.

He smiled with a cold and savage content. They were not out in plain sight, walking toward him. They were waiting with rapidly beating hearts, wondering how this affair would turn out—no doubt cursing the stage that had been set for them. For in this battle there was no glory for them whether they won or lost, only the shame of possible defeat, the even greater shame of victory, two against one. But he, whether he won or lost, was glorious. He had faced great danger with equanimity.

Only one shadow troubled his brain. When the bullets tore through his body would he be able to keep on fighting to the end, or would he weaken at the last, and would pain bring from his lips some involuntary cry of agony?

He set his teeth hard. No sound should come from him, except words of scorn and insult. Thus he thought, as he walked in the middle of the street, slowly, his eye running to the right, and to the left, under the lines of pillars of the endless arcades on either hand. But still the two armed men did not appear. He had covered two blocks of this long gantlet.

And then he heard occasional voices that called out to him words of encouragement.

"You'll be our next sheriff, John Alias!"

"That boy has the right stuff."

"We're with you, kid!"

They were with him—in their doorways and their windows, but who was with him in the flesh, walking with weapons in their hands, to face the criminals who waited somewhere for him?

Cool contempt for the speakers and their words possessed him. And his scorn grew, and he went on with a heart of iron, and an eye of fire.

Perhaps each of them would appear upon a different side of the street. In that case, he would put in his first shot to the left—luck send it straight home. Afterward, whirling to the right to bring his gun in line, he would drop upon one knee and shoot again.

So he planned it.

He slowed his pace yet more. He must give plenty of time to them to appear. Perhaps they were weakening. Perhaps the strain was telling on them, as it had told upon Pete Graham. Perhaps, even, they would not come out to face him at all.

And then he saw two men bearing rifles step out from a doorway and pass from the shadow beneath the arcade into the sunlight. They were seventy yards away—pointblank range. One was Charley Bone, and the other was Jud, his tall, massive brother. The crimes laid to the name of Jud Bone would have

147

filled considerable space in a newspaper, even if merely mentioned and not given in detail.

And now John Signal thought of two things. One was that the brothers had come out side-by-side because they needed the reinforcement of their mutual presence. The other was that the first moral victory was upon the side that forced the other to begin the shooting.

There they stood, side-by-side, rifles ready—fine-looking men they appeared, Charley like a brilliant picture, and Jud with his long hair flowing, trapper fashion, over his shoulders. But their fineness was apparently not appreciated by the crowd, and voices called out angrily, loudly: "Two to one! Is that Western fighting fashion? Two to one! Where's the sheriff? Stop this butchery! Give the kid a fighting chance!"

Sweet music to the ears of the boy, John Signal. Bitterest poison to the ears of the brothers as they stood before him. He paused, and allowed those voices to grow in volume. He saw Jud jerk his rifle to his shoulder, then lower it again. Shame must have compelled that change of mind.

And John Signal smiled again. He began to understand. It was as though a voice were speaking into his ear exactly the thoughts in the minds of the two. To Charley it was a horrible affair; Charley was naturally the sort of fellow to want to fight fairly, without odds on his side, but he had been dragged in by Jud, no doubt. And there was Jud, crushed by the scorn and the hatred of the crowd, only to be justified—and thoroughly despised—by dropping the enemy. John Signal smiled, and slowly, deliberately he stepped forward, narrowing the space that intervened—with every step bringing death closer to himself, to yonder pair.

"Keep back, kid! You chuck away your chances by getting closer! Keep back!"

He heard the voices clearly, but they meant nothing. He knew his business. So he advanced, half a dozen, a dozen strides, all slowly taken.

And then the rifle butt again leaped to the hollow of big Jud's broad shoulder.

That instant, Signal dived forward for the ground. He heard the *clang* of the rifle as he lurched. It must have looked, as he intended it to look, as though the bullet had dropped him upon his face. But, in fact, he heard it whistle, harmless, just above his head, and that escape made him feel armored with invincibility.

The thick white dust cushioned his fall and sent up a puffing cloud; some of it entered his eyes, which stung sharply. And, all in a moment, he had time to think several things—such moments as these allow the brain to work swiftly. He wondered if the dust in his eyes would spoil his shooting—if the mist in the air would spoil the aim of the enemy—and he marveled at the heat that the sun had poured into the street. He lay as in an oven.

In falling, he had thrown the gun forward, and now he lay with it trained steadily on the shooting pair, peering at them out of his natural entrenchment, as two more bullets *hummed* wickedly above his body, and again there was the satisfaction of escape, the sense of security unfathomable.

He was taking Jud Bone into the sights, taking him firmly, without haste, using all of a half second to be securely trained upon him. The body was sure, but a man shot through the body may be shooting as he falls, and shoot again as he lies prone. He used another half second to change his aim to the head. Then he pulled the trigger.

Jud Bone stood with a column behind him, and at first he did not seem to have been struck. He merely lowered his rifle, as though to observe what damage his fire had wrought upon the enemy who lay yonder in the street. But, after that, he leaned softly forward. He seemed to be bowing in acquiescence, and so fell dead beneath the arcade.

Already the aim of Signal had been taken on the second and more dangerous enemy. He fired. He saw the rifle flung up from the hands of Charley Bone and saw the latter go back a staggering step. Then, instead of falling, leaving his gun behind him, Charley Bone leaped sidewise into the shelter of the columns and was gone from sight.

John Signal rose, the dust streaming away from him, and the wind catching it and hanging it behind him like a blowing mantle as he walked calmly forward. There were more bullets in his rifle, and he carried that weapon at the ready, for Charley Bone was very apt to open fire again, from shelter. And as Signal arose, the whole street came to life with a shouting and humming of voices, and hundreds poured out to gather around the victor, and the vanquished.

CHAPTER TWENTY-FIVE

With all that outward swirl of people, no one got into the path of John Signal as he walked up to the fallen body of Jud Bone. He turned the dead man upon his back and stared down at him with wonder. He had killed once before, but that had been in the heat of a sudden fury, but this was a premeditated battle, and the enemy had gone down. He kneeled and closed the eyes of Jud Bone, but he did it without a sense of pity. No gentle remorse disturbed him; he was keen upon the trail that he had started. So, springing up again, he said quietly to a man nearby: "I suppose the family of this fellow will take care of him?"

"They will," said the other.

"Did anyone see what way Charley Bone went?" went on Signal.

A panting, eager little man worked through the crowd, fighting his way. It was Crawlin, his face pale with eagerness, his eye more bloodshot and ferret-like than ever.

"I seen Charley Bone! He run down the street. He went into Mortimer's saloon. You would dare to go there, would you?"

Signal already was on the way with long strides, and the other trotted beside him, gasping interjections. But Signal, grimly in part, and part joyously, went forward, dimly aware of the faces about him, men stumbling and crowding to get from his path, shrinking a little as he went by, staring at him as though at a strange being dropped from another world. And he knew that his name had been written into the slender list of Monument's

151

immortals. As for what else this day's work meant—why, he was only twenty-two, and that was enough excuse for a little short-sightedness.

Crawlin was still beside him. "You ain't gonna go in?" demanded Crawlin, his voice shaking with joyous anticipation. "They'd . . . they'd shoot you to bits. Mortimer's is the Bone hang-out. It's full of their men!"

Young Signal went on, unhesitant, turned the corner, struck open the swinging doors, and entered Mortimer's saloon. It was almost empty. Everyone had gone out to join the crowd of spectators in the street except half a dozen grim-looking fellows and the bartenders, and all of these turned blank, astonished faces toward the deputy sheriff.

He could tell at once what they were. They were solid adherents, fighting men in the Bone cause. But he feared them not. In his hands was still the weapon, warm with the death of one man, and the routing of another.

"I want Charley Bone. He came in here," he stated.

"He went on through," said the nearest bartender. "He went on through the house, I suppose."

"Which way?"

"Back that way."

He knew that it was a lie; he knew that he could not find Charley Bone. But what he wanted was the glory of having bearded the lion in his den. So he went on into the back rooms, and walked rapidly through them, opening many doors. There was no one to be found, except a pair of resolute gamblers, weary of eye; perhaps they had been playing since the night before, and certainly now they were blank to the outer world.

He came back into the barroom, looked up and down the line of threatening, dark faces, then turned his back upon them and, without undue haste, stepped out onto the street.

It had been simple enough in the execution, but he felt as

though that pilgrimage into Mortimer's place had been far more dangerous than the actual fight against Charley and Jud. But the second victory was dependent upon the first. Other things still would flow naturally out of this day's work. And the sun was not yet down.

So thought John Signal, walking back up the street toward the spot where the dead man had been left lying. And, as he went, he saw Crawlin darting here and there before him, anxious, eager, ever hungry for dangerous news, ever feverishly spreading what he knew, and pausing here and there to discharge a few volleys of facts that he had learned of the invasion of Mortimer's. He disappeared in the crowd, far up the street. And Signal came back to Jud Bone in time to find that unhappy man being raised and carried into the nearest store. They laid Jud Bone upon a counter and brushed the dust from him. Signal himself composed the hands of the dead man upon his breast.

Then a furtive voice beside him said: "I'm from the *Ledger*. We'd like a statement, Sheriff Alias."

"I'll make this statement," said the boy. "Those fellows let the whole town know that they were looking for me. So I came to look for them and warned them of it. I stand for law and order. I've taken an oath. And I'm going to live up to that oath. That's all I have to say."

He looked about him as he spoke and noted that all eyes shifted away from his glance. They did not believe him. They could not believe him. He spoke of law and order, but they wrote him down as a mere gunfighter, who killed for the joy of seeing the other men fall.

He went back onto the street. This pot had begun to boil, and the cookery was not yet finished, he could guess as he saw the congested knots of people here and there. And then a familiar shuffling figure squirmed through one knot and came hastily toward him—Crawlin, his face fairly purple with excitement. He looked like a glutton faced in time of starvation with a table groaning under an Olympian weight of delicacies. He clutched the arm of the boy and hung there a moment, gasping in his wind again.

"The whole bunch!" he finally managed to ejaculate. "They're coming for you. About a dozen of the Bone outfit. They're all coming. They're gonna get your scalp. They've sworn to get it. Old man Bone . . . and Charley Bone is back with them with blood on his face . . . and . . . I never thought that I'd see such a day. There's gonna be trouble in Monument!"

But it was not horror that made his eyes flash. It was hideous, consuming joy.

Then a dry voice nearby said: "If you're standing for law and order, you'd better go and arrest that bunch of murderers, John Alias."

It was an old, withered man who spoke, fixing his keen blue eye upon the boy.

"And do you think that I'll run away from them?" asked Signal. He never had dreamed of standing against such odds as Crawlin reported, but now that he was challenged, his heart leaped into his throat and forced the answer.

"You'll run your own business," said the old man. "But don't be a young fool. The heroes of Monument won't be remembered many days after they drop."

He said this with a sarcastic smile, as though he had read the very heart of Signal, but the boy answered hotly: "If they come for me, they'll find me. Not sneaking in the crowd, but out where I can be seen."

And he went straight out into the center of the street, and stood there, leaning upon his rifle, and watching the sudden streaking of all the rest to cover, while, far down the street, a dust cloud burst upward, and rolled away across the tops of the northern houses.

There was the enemy. By the first glance of that cloud of white rising, he knew that he could not stand against any such onrush as that. Fortune, a little nerve, and a clever maneuver in the battle had won for him against Charley Bone and Jud. But fortune could not favor him twice so overwhelmingly. And yet he could not budge from his place.

Excited voices called to him. They bade him not be a fool. They told him that he had done enough for one day. They even cursed him for his rashness. And then a pair of miners lumbered out toward him. They caught him by the arms and made as if to carry him away, but he twisted from them.

"You fellows mean well," he told them. "But this is my place, and here I'm going to stay."

"We'll stand by you, then," said one, with a liberal enriching of Irish brogue. "I wouldn't be after runnin' away from a man like you, Alias, when the pinch come."

But Signal smiled upon him and shook his head. "You fellows have one pistol between you. This isn't your business. I've started it and I'll finish it, and I don't want help. You go back where you'll be safe."

They hesitated. Then the Irishman was seized by his friend and dragged away, protesting. Out of the dust cloud down the street men were riding, not any dozen as Crawlin had declared, but seven bold horsemen, armed to the teeth, their rifles flashing, balanced across the pommels of their saddles. In the van and the center rode the father of the family, his white beard divided by the wind of the gallop, and blowing back over either shoulder. He came to avenge the death of a son, and he came fast.

John Signal raised his rifle, braced his feet, and waited. Prone upon the ground would again have been a better position, but, seeing that his case was hopeless, it seemed to him, somehow, a better thing that he should meet death standing, rather than be trampled underfoot by charging horses.

He took his place firmly, therefore, and then he saw the charging cavalcade draw down to a trot, to a walk. They would not unsteady their aim by the motion of their horses. They were not thirty yards away—and still no bullet fired—when from the corner of his eye Signal saw a form move out upon the sidewalk.

He looked again. It was the tall, slender form of Major Paul Harkness, as dapper and calm as ever, but carrying now in his hand a double-barreled shotgun, sawed off short. He came out from the arcade and waved his hand cheerfully toward Signal, then he faced the oncoming brigade.

Signal, confused by the shouts that began to ring out on either side of the street, turned in the other direction, and there he beheld the mighty form of Fitzgerald Eagan, with a revolver in either hand. One of those guns he waved toward Signal, and nodded.

Suddenly the heart of the boy leaped higher than ever. It would be no useless stand against numbers. He could not have found by combing the world two better fighting men than these who now flanked him.

CHAPTER TWENTY-SIX

Now as he listened more closely to the uproar about him, he understood that it was the apparition of the added pair that the crowd commented upon. They had been watching to see the death of a very rash and very young deputy sheriff. Now they changed their minds. It was simply a battle of the first magnitude to which they would be witnesses. Among the columns of the arcade lingered Crawlin, halfway between the two forces, so that he could not be suspected of favoring either, in an agony of terror because so much danger was about him, but, while he wrung his hands in that chilly ecstasy, the attraction proved irresistible, and he could not go back from his place of peril.

The forces of the Bone faction, in the meantime, saw their purpose necessarily checked for the moment. At least, it was one thing to beat down one rash youth; it was another to march in under the converging fire of three warriors, all of whom had proved themselves to be desperate fighters. The horsemen halted. They flung themselves from their horses, but still they tarried at about twenty-five paces.

Suddenly old Bone walked forward, a hand raised in signal above his head. He went straight up to the city marshal, Fitz Eagan, and exploded in the following manner.

"Eagan, I take it uncommon low and mean of you to step in here like this. The kid deserves killin' . . . he's been askin' for trouble, and now he's gonna get it."

"What's he done?" asked the sheriff.

"He killed a man . . . he gets killed in turn. Ain't that fair?"

This naïve argument did not disturb big Eagan, who replied: "He killed one of a pair . . . and the pair was out lookin' for him. How does that sound to you?"

"It was my boy Jud that he killed, and you dog-gone' well know it."

"Wasn't Jud looking for him with a gun, and wasn't Charley along with him?"

"What do I care about that? Ain't I Jud's pa?"

"I suppose you are."

"What kind of a skunk would you write me down if I didn't try to scalp the gent that murdered Jud?"

"I don't deny you got a right to be heated up for losing your boy. But Jud wasn't shot from behind."

"It was the darned low trick of fightin' out of a cloud of dust. How d'you get around that?"

"You're mad and you're sore, Dad. You see this thing all crooked."

"I don't see it crooked at all. This kid is our meat, and you know it, and still you come hornin' in. Is this here gonna be the end of the truce between us all that the sheriff has been workin' so hard to keep up?"

"This has nothin' to do with the sheriff," insisted Fitz Eagan. "The kid played a good, square game. He's got too much nerve to run away even when seven of you come for him. He don't shoot from behind walls, either."

"What d'you mean by that?" shouted the other, apparently touched in a sore spot by this reference.

"You know pretty well what I mean. Now, Dad, you'd better let this job drop. The kid's all right, and you ought to know that he is. He's never looked for trouble from you and your gang. You know that, too."

"He never looked for trouble? How did all the trouble start, then?"

"Who stole the kid's horse?"

"Who says that I did?"

"I don't. But don't Langley belong to you? Ain't that Sim Langley over there right now?"

"That's Sim, and I'm glad and proud to have him," said Dad Bone, deftly shifting the point of view. "What I say is . . . are you gonna undo all the good work of the sheriff and chuck Monument back into a dog-gone' civil war the way that it was before he come in and took sides?"

"I'm not here because I'm against you," said Fitz Eagan, with a good deal of conciliation in his voice and manner. "I'm here because I'm the city marshal."

"*Aw*, quit that kind of fool talk," groaned the old man. "Don't speak like that to me, Fitz. You're too young. And I'm too old and know too much about you. That's the fact of the matter."

"It's not the fact. I'm telling you the truth, and you're aching to dodge it. The kid's a sworn officer of the law. So am I."

"And so's Major Harkness, yonder?" sneered Dad Bone.

"Every good citizen ought to stand behind the officers of the law."

"Then they's a lot of yaller hounds that I can see from down here!" exclaimed the old man, glaring around at the crowded windows that overlooked the streets.

"Leave the rest of them out of it," retorted Fitz Eagan. "Am I town marshal, or am I not?"

"I suppose you are," said the other. "What has that got to do with me?"

"You've come here with six more to get John Alias, and you've admitted it in them words. Well, as town marshal, I ain't going to let you commit that murder under my eyes, and I order you to disperse and go home."

Old Bone fairly sputtered with rage for a moment. Then he roared, so that the bellow echoed from wall to wall: "This here is the end of the peace in Monument, young feller! This here is the undoin' of all the sheriff's good work, and this old town is gonna be painted red before many more days! You hear me talk?"

"I hear you talk," said Fitz Eagan earnestly. "Now you hear me. There are six more with you. That's seven, by any man's counting. There's only three on this side. Why don't you lead on in and start something? We're here to be finished. Finish me and the major off, and there'll be no danger of that there civil war that you talk about so much. I make you my offer, Dad. You take it now, or show the world that you and the rest of the Bone tribe are a pack of sneaking cowards, and odds of two to one ain't enough for you."

Dad Bone recoiled a little, burying both his hands in his magnificent, snowy beard. It did not seem a sign of age in the old man, but a sort of token of reverend iniquity and hardy, seasoned vice of all descriptions.

"Three of you out here in plain sight," he shouted, "and thirty more of you lyin' away behind the windows! You call this a fair fight, do you? It's a trap!"

"It's no trap," answered Fitz Eagan. "It's no trap at all. There ain't a man laid away in hiding. There's three of us alone, and, if anybody else joins in on this here scrap, I'll call him a skunk, and go for him myself, afterward. Lemme hear you talk to that?"

"I don't want to talk to it!" shouted Dad Bone. "And I've done my last talkin' to you, young Eagan. You've been livin' pretty high. You've been lording it over Monument. I ain't cared. I wanted nothing but the peace. Fitz Eagan is just a young fool, says I to myself, and let you have your day. But that time is finished, and I'm gonna tear you to rags, Fitz Eagan. You hear me talk?"

"I hear you talk, and I know when I'll be torn," said Fitz Eagan. "I'll be shot full of holes the first time that you and your ratty crew can shoot at me from behind a wall, the same as you've shot down better men than yourselves before me."

Dad Bone waved both his clenched fists above his head in furious indignation, but, no words coming, he turned and half ran, half stumbled back toward the rest of his party. Halfway there, he wheeled about and delivered a few tremendous oaths at the head of the marshal. Then he went on, and the ranks of his men instantly closed around him.

Fitz Eagan called across to John Signal: "Don't you let up, youngster! Stand tight and keep your gun ready. Those rats are liable to turn and start biting, if they see that you're off your guard."

But Signal had not the slightest idea of abandoning his attitude of care and watchfulness. He keenly eyed the milling group of the Bone adherents and waited to see if the scorn of the crowd would urge them on to battle, for frequent bits of comment were hurled at them from the windows and doors.

"Now you got the Eagans where you want 'em!"

"Put three each on Alias and Fitz . . . that leaves one for the major. Ain't three to one good enough for you?"

"You've showed your bluff. Now call it!"

These and much more insulting cries were hurled at the seven who, suddenly, mounted their horses and turned their heads down the street. But, at this, there was a great wave of derisive, mocking laughter and hate.

And Crawlin, overmastered by exquisite disappointment, in that no more blood seemed about to be shed upon this day, fell back against one of the pillars and beat his claw-like hands against his face.

But he rallied himself immediately, for fear lest any sight or sound of trouble should escape him, and stood against his pillar, turning his wicked head in bird-like activity up and down the street.

So the Bone tribe retreated in inglorious derision, with all Monument left laughing at and scorning them. And a host of congratulations were poured in upon Fitz Eagan and young Signal. Now the brutes of the town had been faced and had been shamed. Was it not the proper moment to strike hard in the interests of law and order? Was it not the moment to rally all forces and clean up Monument for good and all?

Fitz Eagan looked around the crowd and—lion that he was—answered them to their faces: "You talk law and order. You know that you ain't ready for law and order, yet. You ain't shot yourselves out, yet, and your favorite judge is old Judge Colt. If you wanted law and order so bad, why did five hundred of you stand around and watch while one kid stood out there and faced seven murderin' demons?"

To this the crowd did not attempt the slightest answer, and the marshal turned away, wading through the throng of people slowly, with Major Harkness on one hand, and young John Signal on the other.

And behind them the cricket-like voice of Crawlin sang out: "Watch 'em! Use your eyes! Three finer fightin' men never stepped together before. Do you think they will all be alive in the mornin'?"

CHAPTER TWENTY-SEVEN

Now Major Harkness proposed a drink, but young Signal merely wrung the hand of each of his newly proved friends.

"I'd better see the sheriff," he said. "I hope to heaven no trouble comes to either of you fellows for standing by me this way. And night or day, I'm ready to ride with you. Is that understood?"

"That's understood."

"Heaven forgive me if I ever forget," said the boy with fervor.

Even the cold eye of the major brightened and warmed a little as he stared at Signal. The major was dying of consumption, slowly and surely, and that, men said, was why he advanced into the teeth of danger with such calm unconcern.

He clapped John Signal lightly on the shoulder. "Don't burn yourself up with too much gratitude," he said. "Fact is, Fitz was playing his own game as much as yours. He wants to put down the Bone tribe as much as you do."

"Of course," said Fitz Eagan frankly. "You go and talk to the sheriff, if you can find him. He's due back in town in a short time."

So John Signal went straight to the sheriff's office, and found it empty. Peter Ogden had not yet returned from an expedition into the country. Signal, therefore, sat at the window and watched the sunset colors beginning, and wondered if ever before a man had lived through such a thronged day as this.

Across the street stood Grundy, the roan, tethered beside the watering troughs in front of the Metropolis Hotel. It tickled the very cockles of Signal's young heart to see the people stop around that horse and point it out and nod to themselves as they discussed its merits, and turn away still in deep talk. Not of Grundy were their words, he knew, but of Grundy's owner.

And then, darkening in his mind with the day, he remembered the words of Polly. What had she said of guns and gunfighters? And what had she declared about him before he started for the fray?

She's only a girl, he thought to himself, and then he heard footfalls in the hall. The door opened, and the sheriff in person appeared before him against the blackness of the hall behind. For the room was a sea of twilight; in the deeps of it pulsed the cinder at the end of the sheriff's eternal cigar.

He paused in the doorway, and then strode into the room, the flimsy floor quaking beneath his weight. "You been having quite a party, I hear," said Peter Ogden.

To this, Signal returned no answer, for he could see that the way would not be easy before him.

"You been rousin' up the town, I hear," went on the sheriff in a voice more bland than before. "But I see how it is. You figure, back in your own home town, you found things more lively than we got 'em out here. Things are pretty sleepy for you, and you had to stir up a little fun. Was that it?"

Young John Signal said not a word, but he shrank a little in his chair. He had no very profound respect for the sheriff, but superior years have a certain weight of authority and before it Signal bowed.

The sheriff leaned on the back of a chair and puffed at his cigar. "Monument has a new hero," he went on at last, "and Monument has a new grave. Always gotta be that way, I suppose. One man can't go up without another goin' down." He added heavily: "Me, for instance. Young John Alias, he goes up.

And Jud Bone dies. Dies young!" He paused. There was such an obvious injustice in this remark that anger wiped from Signal's mind half of his contrition and depression.

"And Monument has to go down, too," said the sheriff in continuation. "Monument that was beginnin' to float on an even keel, it's struck the rough waters, again."

"I don't know," murmured Signal. "I don't see what I've done to put Monument on the rocks."

"You don't know . . . you don't see! No, you wouldn't. You ain't got the eyes to see that far or that deep into things. You're young."

"I did nothing," said the deputy sheriff, "except what seemed to me to be my plain duty."

"You done nothing except what seemed to you your plain duty," echoed the ironic sheriff. He laughed, a great, harsh laugh. "Your duty," he said again.

"Look here!" protested the boy. "You know what happened? Sitting in my window at the boarding house, they took a shot at me. The Bone people did."

"You saw the man take the shot, did you?"

"No."

"Then how do you know?"

"I found a man in the stable and made him tell."

"You found a man in the stable . . . you made him tell," sneered the sheriff. "He knew, didn't he? He was able to look through the wall of the barn and see?"

"He knew," said the boy quietly, sure of himself.

"Who was he?"

"His name is Pete Graham."

"What?" The sheriff was quiet for a moment. Then he asked: "Who did he say did it?"

"Langley."

The sheriff exclaimed—and then growled: "The fool! The

yellow fool!"

Signal continued: "When I got back into the house after running outside, I got word that Jud and Charley were in town saying that they were going to get me. I simply sent down word that I was coming to give them a chance. And they took their chance. And there you are. Wasn't that my duty?"

"Oh, hang your duty!" cried the sheriff. "You wanted to make a grandstand play. You wanted to get onto the center of the stage where all the boys and girls could see you and get to know you. Tell me the truth. Wasn't that it?"

And John Signal answered meekly: "Yes, there's some truth in that, no doubt. I'm ashamed of it."

This confession seemed to take a good deal of the wind out of the sails of the sheriff. But he gathered strength again as he continued: "Then you smash everything that I've done. You throw in with the Eagans!"

"I didn't. They stood by me to keep me from being mobbed. You weren't there to help!"

"No," said the sheriff, "and thank goodness I wasn't. You know what I've been doing in this here town, don't you?"

"I know that you've been the sheriff for a while, of course."

"When I come here, what do I find? The Eagans and the Bones running everything. Every other stage that run out of town was stuck up. The silver couldn't be shipped out, the half of it. Everything was going to pot. Business was stopping. Two of the biggest mines was shut down, the owners waiting. There were three men killed . . . in self-defense . . . the first day that I arrived here. Monument ate three men a day. Everybody packed guns. The honest men included. Well, what did I do? Kill and hang all the Bones and the Eagans? No, I couldn't do that. But I balanced 'em one ag'in' the other. I made 'em run the other crooks out of town. I got Fitz Eagan, the grandest fighting man in this world, made the city marshal. I cleaned up the gambling dumps. There ain't a crooked roulette wheel in this town. I made the saloons chuck the rotten bartenders that would feed booze to a man till he was crazy drunk. I had Monument started on the way to being a decent town. But . . . I didn't keep it fast enough and entertainin' enough to suit Mister John Alias. I couldn't do that. And when he come along, he seen his duty plain, and he done it . . . with a gun in each hand. Well, kid, d'you think that I couldn't use guns, too? D'you think that I'm afraid of guns? I got my record. Look it up! But there never was a decent job done with gunpowder and lead, and there never will be . . . they're good for nothing but murder, and murder is what you've raised up in these here streets again!"

John Signal was thunderstruck. He never had taken this attitude toward the sheriff; he never had heard people speak of him with any vast respect. It seemed generally admitted that, under his regime, Monument was a better and a quieter town than it had been ever before, but that was all. But now Signal could look a bit beneath the surface and see that everything that had been said by the older man probably was the truth. He was shamed and he was startled. He could see, now, that there might have been a halfway stand taken. The sheriff was right. The girl had been right, too, and the higher courage worked without guns.

So he sat dumbfounded, while the sheriff exclaimed: "I want no more of you! You've smashed all my work. You've put the Eagans and the Bones at each other's throats. You've killed one. You've thrown the law in on the side of the other party. I wish I'd never seen you. I'll pay you a month's salary, and you can get out, and the farther that you get, the better for you . . . and for me!"

John Signal stood up in the thickening gloom of the office. "Look here," he said quietly, "I've done wrong, perhaps. But I meant to do right." He lighted the lamp. He wanted to see the sheriff's face, and he was rather relieved to find nothing but honest indignation on it.

"There's a place," said the sheriff, darkly, "that's full of gents that wanted to do right."

"It's not fair to fire me," said Signal, "and you know it. And how can you tell that your way is the best? You make the law a joke. People laugh at it. All they respect in this town are Henry Colter and Fitz Eagan. And you ought to drive them both out . . . and you know it."

"You want to run the office for me, eh?"

"You swore me into this job. I'll stay."

"You'll stay? I fire you now . . . on the spot!"

"Do you? Then I'll walk down to the street and call every man in town together, and I'll tell them that I've been fired. And I'll tell them why. For killing Jud Bone, instead of lying low, like a scared coyote. I'll tell them that. Where will you stand then?"

The sheriff turned purple with fury. He could only glare for a moment, utterly baffled. Then he muttered: "You want to stay? You want to be kept busy, eh? I'll keep you busy. Tomorrow you start out and collect the taxes outside of Monument. I'll tell you where." And he laughed, brutally, with triumph in his eye.

Chapter Twenty-Eight

The minds of some men cannot be at ease unless their hands are occupied. And the sheriff, having delivered this ultimatum, smiled with grim triumph at his deputy; he took out of his pocket a little golden trinket and began to spin it into the air— not a coin, but something the size of a double eagle.

"You'll go to Hanford and collect the taxes there," he said. "I've got the list here of all the payments due." He went to his desk and from a drawer he took out an envelope. "You'll find everything that you want to know about Hanford taxes in here," he said. And he smiled again at the youngster and spun the golden trinket a second time in sheer excess of spirits. However, he missed catching it in its descent. It slipped from his hand and rolled across the table, tumbling to a stop in front of John Signal.

The latter stared at it hopelessly, as a man will stare when his mind is troubled with problems to which he finds no solution. It was, he saw, no coin at all, but a group of two figures in gold—a man walking with a staff and carrying a small child upon his shoulder, the whole group embraced with a circling band. In another instant, he recognized the figure—that of St. Christopher carrying the Christ Child—and suddenly his heart stopped.

From the dead brother of Pancho Pineta in San Real Cañon just such a trinket had been taken—the patron saint to which the smugglers had prayed in their journeyings. It was most unlikely that a second figure such as this should exist in one community, and the thought that came home with stunning weight upon the mind of the boy was that Sheriff Peter Ogden himself might have been a figure in the robbery and the terrible murder of the smugglers.

He closed his eyes. Monument, he felt, was growing a little too complicated for his understanding. He picked up the ornament and pretended to admire it.

"This is a good bit of work," he said. "I never saw anything better."

"You don't know the Mexicans," said the sheriff. He added with a careless gesture: "Take it along. Maybe it'll give you luck at Hanford. I'm going home. You lock up the office after you."

He left the place, and the boy, as bidden, locked the office as he departed. He did not go straight back to the boarding house, however, but went first to the hospital by the side of the river, where he found young Pancho Pineta lying pale and still, but well beyond danger and promising a quick recovery, as the nurse assured him. Yes, he could speak with the Mexican for two or three minutes.

"Pineta," he said, standing by the bed, "do you know me?"

The youngster looked quietly up at him. "No, I don't know you."

"My name is John Alias. I'm the deputy sheriff. . . ."

The other smiled in instant appreciation. "I've been hearing nothing else all day, *señor*, except about what you have done. Jud Bone was a dog. A cruel dog. I am glad to see your face, *señor*, to remember a man."

"Thank you. I've come to speak about San Real."

"So does the sheriff. Everyone is willing to talk about San Real, but nothing is done, nothing is done until I can ride and shoot again." His face flushed with angry determination.

"I've come to ask you a particular thing. You remember the

figure of Saint Christopher that your brother wore in his hat?"

"How could I forget it? My poor brother used to say a prayer to it, night and morning."

"Was there anything about it that could make you identify it? There might be other figures just like it."

"There are, of course. But that one was marked. Once a bullet grazed the hat of my brother. Saint Christopher saved him, of course, but there was a furrow left across the breast of the saint."

Signal took out the small image. Plainly across the form of the saint was the notch cut by the bullet. "Is this the one?"

"*¡Madre de Dios!*" breathed the wounded man, and lay still, with eyes of fire.

"Listen to me," said Signal. "If you want that trail run down and the murderers caught, forget what I've showed you. Rub it out of your mind. Don't let yourself whisper even in your sleep, because if it's known that I've identified it, there will be an end to that trail. You understand?"

The Mexican held out his hand and gripped that of Signal with surprising strength. "I understand," he said. "My soul rides with you. Good fortune, *Señor* Alias."

Signal left the hospital and stood in the cool of the evening by the river. In Mortimer's dance hall, behind his saloon, the orchestra was running over a new piece for the evening, and the music sounded sweet in the ear of the boy. From the gardens along the river front there was a fragrance of many flowers. The honeysuckle was blooming, and its breath came strongly upon the quiet air. For nothing stirred except sound and scent. All men were home at dinner; no horses clattered over the bridges; the wagons for once were still, with their far-heard creakings. Neither did the tall trees stir a leaf, and the golden faces of the lights along the shore fell with never a wrinkle upon the broad black water.

In the tumult of Monument, there was this pause, not for thought and reflection, but for bacon and eggs. And then it seemed to John Signal that a new sense of life poured suddenly in upon him. It was as though he had turned a corner, not long before, hardly knowing what he did, but now he found himself in a new street, and far from home. A beautiful street, let us say, of splendid houses, but none of them was his.

And then he knew that he had in fact turned out of the old way of his life and come to a new; he was no longer a boy. Somewhere between Polly and the slaying of Jud Bone he had left that lesser self behind him, and it was not a new world in which he stood—it was simply a new self that stood there breathing the odors of the flowers, watching the golden-barred river.

It sobered John Signal. He had galloped into Monument with little care. But suddenly he was crushed under a load of apprehension and of trouble, for it seemed that whatever hand he tried to play, all men were against him—even the sheriff, now, must be hunted down.

He, being of such stuff as should compose men, did not even contemplate giving up the battle, but he was daunted, and hurt, and mystified. It is harder to charge the enemy at a walk than at a gallop.

He walked back to the boarding house, the roan, Grundy, following at his heels, like a dog. Grundy, too, had changed since their arrival in Monument. He was no longer so apt to use his teeth or his heels. The demon in Grundy, by the demon in the town, seemed, apparently, to have been shamed into flight.

He encountered not a soul in the streets on the return journey, put up the horse in the shed, and went into the house for supper. It was already in progress—a dozen men sat around the table, and two waitresses served them as rapidly as possible with thin-cut steaks, and fried potatoes, and cornbread, and great cups of black coffee. When he came in, all heads jerked up or around and stared at him. When he said—"Good evening."—there was a deep rumble of response. When he sat down, all men looked fixedly at their plates and went on feverishly with their business of eating.

Polly brought him his plate, Polly with a face of the utmost indifference, as though bored at waiting upon him.

He ate mechanically, slowly, his thoughts on other things—on the great tangle that made up this day's adventures—perhaps not yet ended. The others broke up quickly. Their last cup of coffee and piece of apple pie consumed, they scraped back their chairs and went out without saying a word. Their voices then sounded in the distance of the hallway. He was left alone with two rows of scattered, emptied plates and coffee-stained cups before him. Polly was clearing them away, taking out great armfuls.

At last he said to her: "Polly."

She paused at the kitchen door, glanced over her shoulder, and then disappeared without an answer.

Polly, too, had disowned him.

And this, somehow, cut much deeper than all the danger in which he was living and all the hostilities that were grouped around him. She came back and paused, close to him.

"Well," said Polly.

"These fellows," he said—he would not speak to her about her own attitude—"these fellows . . . they all stopped talking when I came in. They wouldn't talk to me. Why?"

Polly canted her head a little to one side, as though thought unbalanced it there. "Suppose a dozen house dogs are eating in the backyard, and a big wolf comes along and stands in among them?"

"I don't follow that."

"No, you wouldn't. But just supposin'. Well, the first dog that started barking might have his head snapped off. Ain't that a fact?"

"I suppose so. Am I a wolf, Polly? Do I snap at people?"

"You're John Alias. You're the man from Nowhere. You're the gunfighter . . . the new one. What d'you think? Do people get chummy with dynamite?"

"I'm dangerous, am I?"

"Ask yourself. Be honest," said the girl.

"I'll be honest, then. All I see is that I've fought when I had to fight."

"You went out hunting trouble. You got it. But, oh," said Polly, "I'm not gonna be your conscience. You can handle that for yourself. I . . . I gotta clear the table." And she fell to work noisily, and went out with another staggering burden.

When she came back, he asked her impersonally: "D'you ever hear of a place called Hanford?"

"Of course, I've heard of it."

"What is it?"

"Hanford," she said, "is the headquarters of the crooks . . . Monument is just their playground."

Chapter Twenty-Nine

That remark began to give point to the remarks of the sheriff in sending him out upon this mission.

"Do they pay taxes?" he asked.

"Taxes? Why should they? Who'd make them . . . except the United States Army."

"No one man could do it?"

"Except Colter. He could, of course."

He stood up, burdened with this fresh information. "Polly," he said softly, "I want to explain about today. I had to go. I couldn't've called myself a man, if I hadn't. It didn't mean that I thought any the less of you."

"What did you think of me in the first place?" she asked.

"I liked you . . . a lot. I still do. I mean to take you down to the opera house for that singing, Polly. I mean to take you down there tomorrow morning."

She merely answered sharply: "You'd better take yourself out of Monument. That's the best thing you can do."

She started to turn away, but he touched her shoulder.

"You're tired of the thought of me, Polly, I suppose."

"*Aw*," said Polly, frowning, "can't a poor girl spend five minutes a day flirting without having to go to jail for it afterward?"

He drew himself up, taking the blow in quiet. "Well," he said, "I didn't understand. That's all. I'm sorry that I've been a fool."

She turned and laughed carelessly in his face. "Say, look

here," she said. "D'you suppose that me or any other girl would go nutty about you two minutes after seein' you for the first time? What sort of a guy are you, anyway?"

"A fool," he said, standing, motionless and pale, before her. "I'm a fool. It took you to show me how much of one I am. Good night, Polly."

"So long," said Polly. "Sweet dreams."

And she went off toward the kitchen, and he saw her shoulders still quivering with inward laughter as she went. He, going up to his room, fell at full length upon his bed and lay there, hot with shame. He felt that he had revealed his soul to a stranger, and the stranger had laughed. But even this agony could not keep him awake, for John Signal was only twenty-two, and he was a very tired young man, and all the events of that day—from San Real Cañon and the broken horseshoes to the blacksmith's shop and the gathering enemies, and the trip to Esmeralda Pineta's house, and the arrival of big Fitz Eagan, and the cowardly shot that Langley had fired, and Pete Graham, and Polly, and the fall of Jud Bone, and the manner in which he had fronted the hosts of Bone, and the fury of the sheriff, and the cold cruelty of Polly in the end—drove through his mind like a herd of wild horses, all with trampling hoofs, and a sort of reverberation filled his mind like a hollow cave— and suddenly he slept.

When he wakened, he was not refreshed. It was the cool of the morning, but he got up with a heavy head, as though he had been drinking. His hands hung weightily at his sides; his eyes were dim. And all night long, although he could not recall a single dream, he knew that he had been fumbling with trouble and had found no solution to it.

He went down to breakfast before anyone else in the house, and there he found Polly laying out the long table. She looked at him with a smile and a nod, as though all were perfectly well between them, and he, staring at her with hollow eyes, wondered at her, and at all womankind.

Yes, he could have an early breakfast. The cook had the coffee ready. It would take only a minute to fry bacon and eggs.

"And where does Hanford lie?"

"Straight west, in the hills. Ten trails in, and one trail out, they say. You know what that means. Are you going there?"

"I may."

She nodded at him cheerfully. "That's the way with a lot of fellows," said Polly. "They make a break at staying on the side of the law. But when they get into a pinch, they see that they belong on the other side of the fence. Of course, you can make a lot more easy money working with Colter than you ever could working for the county."

That was her understanding of him, then.

"I'm to go out and join 'em, eh?" he said.

"Well, why else would you be going?" she asked.

He put that question aside with another. "Which is Colter's hang-out in Hanford?"

"He changes from one place to another. You never can tell, they say. But the big white barn . . . it's barn on one side and house on the other . . . is where you'd most likely find him."

He finished his breakfast.

"Are you paying your bill before you leave?"

"I'm coming back," he said.

She frowned, unable to understand. "You're coming back!"

"Yes."

He went to the door, then her voice stopped him. "Johnny Alias, why are you goin' to Hanford?"

"I'm collecting the county taxes," he said, and passed out through the door.

Footfalls pattered after him; the door was snatched open behind him.

"Johnny!"

"So long," he said, and went resolutely out from the house to where he had left Grundy, the roan, tethered at the hitching rack. He had half hoped that she would follow, but she did not. He was gathering the reins before mounting when a panting, shambling figure came up the street.

It was Crawlin, worn out with effort. "Ride hard and ride fast, and don't you come back, kid," he urged.

"And why not come back?"

"Ain't you heard? Ain't you heard?" The lips of Crawlin parted in a grin that showed his broken, yellow teeth, and his little rat eyes blazed with joy. He studied the face of the deputy.

"I've heard nothing. About what?"

"They got the news from Bender Creek. They got all the news. They know all about you!"

"They know all about me, eh?"

"About the gent that you killed there. Hampton was his name, wasn't it?"

"Hampton was his name," said the other quietly.

"They know it all. I guess that they'll have a warrant out for your arrest pretty *pronto.*"

"And who'll serve it?"

"The sheriff, of course. Would you resist it, kid? Would you resist the servin' of it, Signal?"

"They know my name, eh?"

"Aw, they know all about you."

"I don't know," said John Signal. "I might resist arrest, I might not . . . if I make up my mind in time." He added: "I'll let you know, Crawlin, so that you can be there to see the fight." He swung into the saddle.

Crawlin clung to a stirrup leather. He was wheezing and gasping with excitement. "All right. You let me know. I tell you what, Signal, I've always been your friend. I never seen any man that give the town so many good shows in such a short time. I'm your friend. You remember that, will you?"

"I'll never forget," said the boy. And he rode on out from Monument and took the western road.

There were ten long miles, up and down, between Monument and Hanford village, but the roan covered them in less than an hour, and the sun was hardly above the horizon when he went over the brow of the last hill and looked down into the hollow.

There could not have been a more peaceful place, in seeming, in the whole world. It was a pleasant pasture land, coming down smoothly from the hills all around and cut in two by a small stream that cut with arrowy straightness across it. Willows and poplars edged the stream. Bigger and more permanent trees grew in groups, here and there, almost screening the houses from view. And of those houses he made out a small cluster of half a dozen that were evidently Hanford proper, while half a dozen more sat here and there, deeply embowered in covert.

He took the first road to the left, and at the second bending he found himself looking up a gentle slope toward what seemed to be a great white barn, surrounded with lofty trees. From one side of the barn a chimney arose, and from the chimney poured thick puffs of white smoke. That, according to the description of Polly, must be the residence of the great Colter.

He went straight up to the place. There was no real thought in his mind, except to go forward mechanically with the duty that had been placed in his hands. He would go in among the men and read out the list of names of the delinquent tax payers. Henry Colter himself was one. Mentor was another. He would know those two faces, at least. And if he could collect from a single man in Hanford, he would have done far more than actually was expected from him.

He thought back bitterly to the sheriff—he who stood so strongly for law and order—and had in his own pocket some of the spoils of San Real Cañon.

But how to turn back, he knew not. Retreat was closed in the rear by the word that Crawlin had brought him. To go forward into the unknown he had no heart. It seemed better to enter that barn, that sprawling white barn where the outlaws nested like pigeons together, and there to come briefly to an end, in the name of the law.

In fact, the brain of young John Signal, confused and weary, could not find any solution except sheer action. So he bore straight up to the side of the barn from which the chimney arose, dismounted, and without announcing his arrival with a knock, he pulled open the door, and stepped inside of the barn.

He had left his rifle in the saddle holster. He had with him only the long Colt that weighted down his right leg, and in his left hand he carried the envelope that was filled with information about delinquents in taxes.

So he stepped into the interior of the barn, and there paused, slowly pushing the door shut behind him. For he saw that he had dropped headlong, as it were, into a nest of hornets. The very first picture that rose before his eyes was the long, white, divided beard of Dad Bone.

CHAPTER THIRTY

They were all there, all the heads of the Bone power, which so long had ruled the land. Besides the father of the family, Signal saw Joe Klaus, and the scarred face of Mentor, and Charley Bone, with a bandage around his head, where the rifle had struck when it was shot out of his hands by Signal's bullet the day before. There was Langley, too, with his long, hard face, and others of whom he knew nothing. Altogether, there were nine men seated in the long, low room that served as bunkhouse, dining room, living room, kitchen. On the table by the stove the soiled tinware of the breakfast was piled in confusion, and around another table the crowd sat as in conference. They turned their heads toward the deputy as he entered and closed the door behind him.

Old Bone said in a matter-of-fact voice: "You name the devil . . . up he jumps. Here's our gent now come askin' for trouble. Have you got any to spare for him, boys?"

This remark brought no verbal answer, but Langley stood up from his chair with a drawn Colt in his hand, ready. And Joe Klaus picked a sawed-off shotgun from the floor.

"What you want?" barked old man Bone.

"I'm out here to collect the county taxes," said the deputy sheriff, "or else to serve notice on a good many of you. You, Bone, and you, Mentor, and you, Klaus. I have all your names down here and the sums you owe."

This remark caused them to open their eyes at him.

"It's a trap," said Langley hastily. "He's probably got Ogden and twenty rifles hiding around outside the place in a circle."

"Ogden wouldn't be such a fool," said Joe Klaus. "He's got better sense. But I'll go and look." He stepped through a side door that opened from the barn, and went out, rifle in hand.

Charley Bone approached the enemy of his family with the most cheerful of smiles. He said genially: "Twice yesterday I thought that I'd be in at the death of you, Alias. But it don't pan out that way. I was figuring things a day too early, it seems. And nobody can force the cards. Is that right?"

Signal smiled in turn. "Of course, that's right," he said. "But perhaps I'll squeeze through today, too."

"I like an optimist," said Charley. "But tell me, old-timer, how come you to walk out here and step inside, same as a pig walking into a cask of salt pork?"

"The sheriff ordered me . . . I've got to march the way he says," replied the boy.

And Charley Bone nodded with a frown. "You heard that?" he asked of the others. "Ogden sent him out here to collect the taxes."

"Sure," said Langley. "Ogden has a head on his shoulders. If he don't expect to find the taxes, he expects to find the receipt, anyway, on this kid. Signed with guns, too. I aim to write my name in full."

This grim banter had hardly ended when Joe Klaus returned, with a grin of pleasure. "There ain't a man near," he said. "The fool has come out here on his own. He'll go back by a shorter way, I'm thinking."

"Where's Colter?" asked Charley Bone.

"Leave Henry out of it," said Dad Bone. "He's better out. They's something between him and this young rat. There ain't a better way of finishing off this job, I'd say, than finishing it off now."

"You mean fair murder, out and out?" asked Signal, watching the face of the old man. And he saw that face wrinkle with utter hatred and savage meaning.

"I mean the stampin' on the head of a snake that's been in my house," said Dad Bone. "I only wish that Jud could be here to see the finish of you. But maybe his ghost'll know, and grin. Charley . . . Doc . . . Joe . . . are you ready?"

They did not answer. There was no need to answer. They faced the deputy sheriff like a small semicircle of wolves. And Signal, glancing into those hard, bright eyes, knew that he stood one gesture from death. He stood back against the manger, bracing himself for the shock, his hand tingling with readiness to jump to his gun, but up to the last moment he kept his voice calm and fairly steady. Colter was near, it seemed, and, if that were the case, then Colter must be waited for.

"This looks," he said, "like a hand that you fellows can play through to a win."

"We can, and we will," said old Bone. "Talk up fair and square, kid. If you had us cornered, wouldn't you blast the life out of us?"

"I would," said Signal, "but not in one lump. I'd spread the thing out. What's the good of blowing ten fighting men to death in one blast? There's more fun in tackling them one by one."

"You'd take us one by one? You lie!" said Doc Mentor, his ugly face writhing.

"A good many of you have had a shot at me," said Signal. "There's Langley, for instance, who took a crack at me from around the corner of the shed, when I was sitting in my room. There's Mentor, who tried to murder me while my horse was bucking. There's Charley, who opened up face to face, I must say. Now then, I don't grudge you those chances. And if I had you cornered, I'd bring you out one by one and polish you off with my own gun."

"You young jackass," said old Bone. "These here is the best lot of fightin' men in the whole West."

It was plain that these men were all greatly irritated by the calm assumption of superiority on the part of Signal, but since he could not win time by appealing to them in any other way, he determined to entertain them by sheer baiting.

"Fighting men! Fighting men!" sneered John Signal. "What sort of fighting men fight seven to one? Fighting men! One real man like Fitz Eagan would make the pack of you run like curs."

The gun of Doc Mentor jumped up to fire—and then sank again.

"You," went on Signal, nodding at Mentor. "You're a fighting man, are you? Why, let the others stand aside. You and I will have it out together, peaceable and pleasant. And after I've dropped you, then the rest of them can finish me off. If there's any fight or any man in you, step out and answer me to that?"

In spite of themselves, all heads turned toward Doc Mentor for a flash, and his color faded.

"I fight when fighting pays," he growled. "And what's the use of fighting for a sure thing?"

"The pleasure of seeing a man you hate curl up in front of your gun," said Signal. "But I don't need to use a gun. I can look you in the eye and see you curl up like a pack of cheap town dogs."

"Are you going to stan' here and listen to him?" yelled Dad Bone, waxing more savage than before. "Why waste time? There he is, and here we are. If nobody else will start, I will." And he jerked his gun to the ready as the side door opened, and Colter stepped in among them.

"Hold on," said Charley Bone, grasping the gun hand of his father. "Hold on. Here's Colter. He has to have his say."

Henry Colter, squinting so as to accustom himself to the rather dim light inside the barn, flashed one glance over this tableau and then stepped in front of his companions, facing them, and backing toward the boy, so that he covered Signal with his own body.

"This play has gone far enough," said Colter. "You know where I stand with him. You've tried to snag him behind my back before. Now if you want him, take me with him." He was in a high passion, and he proceeded furiously: "Why, I've been your bread and butter for years, and yet you're willing to chuck me like this. What's the kid done to you that you should be after him like so many demons? He made you back up in front of the whole town of Monument. You want to slaughter him now because you're afraid of him. Is that it?"

Old Bone said in a conciliatory fashion: "Henry, you're sayin' more things than you realize. But we know you, old son. And we'd put up with worse than that from you. You know why we gotta get this kid. He's the murderer of my Jud. Ain't that as plain as the nose on your face?"

"It was fair fighting," said Colter. "You know it was fair. You," he continued, turning angrily on Signal, "what brought you out here? Tired of living?"

"Taxes!" croaked Doc Mentor. "He come out here to collect the taxes from us."

"Taxes?" shouted Colter. "Is that right?"

"Ogden sent me."

"Ogden? That's hard to believe."

"D'you think I came for fun?"

"No," answered Colter, scowling.

"But what did Ogden want?"

"The taxes, of course."

"Either he wanted the taxes collected or you finished. How much are those taxes?"

"Seven hundred and eighteen dollars, and the names that have to pay 'em are. . . ."

"Never mind the names. You hear, boys? Seven hundred and eighteen dollars Ogden's in need of. Are we gonna quit on him when he sends in a holler for help, like this? Ain't Ogden worth more'n ten times that much to us?"

There was a muttering of agreement to this.

"Would he've sent out this fightin' kid just to collect money?"

"Who else would have the nerve to ride inside of ten miles of Hanford?" Then Colter added briskly: "We'll have that money out, boys. We're all flush enough just now, I guess. Wait a minute. Here's three hundred for my share."

"All right," said Charley Bone. "I never liked the idea of snagging him by a crooked game. Let him have his fair chance to fight it out, one of these days. I'll pony up a hundred and fifty."

Joe Klaus followed suit. Only old Bone himself refused to contribute. He argued no more for the head of Signal, but stood in the background and waited, his face terrible in its hatred and in its pain.

But $718 were counted into the hand of the deputy, who was immediately dragged outside the barn by Colter and taken down the hillside toward Grundy.

"Kid," said Colter, "you ain't a little touched in the head, today?"

"Things were closing in on me," explained Signal, "and I couldn't think of any better way out. That's all."

Chapter Thirty-One

They stood at the side of Grundy, and a wind shook and fluttered the leaves of the trees above them.

"Don't use up your luck, Alias," said the outlaw.

"I was blue and I was down," answered John Signal, ashamed. "I acted like a fool. But I didn't know how to dodge, when the sheriff sent me out here. I want to ask you one thing. Is Ogden an honest man?"

Colter stared at him. "How long you been here?"

"In Monument?"

"Yes."

"Just two or three days."

"And you don't know about the sheriff?"

"No. I can't make him out."

"Well, son," said Colter, "I wish you all kinds of luck, but that's one thing you'd better find out for yourself."

Signal mounted the saddle. He said in farewell: "I've used up my luck, maybe," he said, "but I'm afraid that I've used up a big chunk of your friendship, too, Colter."

It seemed to him, as he said this, that the face of the other hardened a little, although he replied lightly enough: "Don't be a fool . . . I can always run those fellows to suit myself. You haven't used up my friendship. It's worth more than seven hundred and eighteen dollars. But . . . you really don't figure out the sheriff?"

"No. Is he as bad as all that?"

"Bad? You go and make your mind up about him."

With that, he waved his hand, and the boy rode off down the valley. He went with his courage returning, his heart stronger, his spirit higher. What lay before him in Monument he could not guess, but he knew that a swirl of difficulties of all kinds was certain. All things were against him, it had seemed when he rode out from the town. Perhaps all things were against him still, but a great confidence in his fate, his fortune now possessed him.

He made the journey back to Monument faster than he had come out from it, and jogged Grundy down the main street toward the sheriff's office, conscious, as always, of the faces turned toward him, and that murmur of voices that had become to him the most enchanting of all music.

He was tethering the horse to the rack outside the office building, when the ubiquitous Crawlin appeared before him, always in haste, always with color coming and going, always with cruel, hungry eyes.

"What you gonna do, Signal? What you gonna do?"

"I don't know. Why?"

"You ain't gonna go upstairs, are you?"

"To the sheriff's office?"

"You ain't gonna go there?"

"And why not?"

"They got a man there from Bender Creek. He knows all about you. I told you that before!"

There loomed in the mind of the boy a picture of the big gray sheriff of Bender County, stern, silent, impressive as a craggy mountain.

"What sort of a looking man?"

"Youngish . . . smart-looking. . . ."

"I don't care about that." He was only glad that it was not the sheriff in person. No matter what deputy might have been sent upon this mission.

"You *are* gonna go up?"

"Yes."

"Well, Lord help you. You're gonna walk straight into a jail, because I figger that the Bender man is still there."

But past this croaking raven of ill omen, John Signal walked up the stairs until he came to the office, and marched in, prepared, if necessary, to face drawn weapons. But there was only Sheriff Peter Ogden, bent over his desk, shuffling papers and chewing his cigar. He looked askance at his deputy.

"You made a quick trip," he said sourly.

"I made a quick trip."

"You saw Hanford?"

"Yes."

"But you didn't see no money, I suppose?"

"I found the tax money, if that's what you mean." He placed the sum on the desk in front of the other, and the sheriff tilted back in his swivel chair, amazed and speechless.

"You got that out of your own pocket!" he charged bluntly.

Signal flushed. "You'd better think that over again," he said.

Sheriff Ogden, strangely without pleasure, counted the money. "It's straight," he said. "The whole wad is here."

"Seems to worry you," commented the boy.

"I'm worried," admitted the sheriff. "You got it out of 'em. How?"

"Colter, of course."

"Ah, Colter. You got him in your pocket. I'd forgotten that Colter . . . the devil!"

John Signal was growing more and more angry as he considered the words and the attitude of the sheriff. Then he said: "You don't like Colter . . . you don't like the money . . . then why did you send me out there to collect the taxes? I want to know the truth about it."

The sheriff turned abruptly in his swivel chair, his head a trifle down, his eyes glaring upward. He looked a picture of dangerous strength. "Are you going to force something from me, young man?" he asked.

"I am. I'm going to make you admit that you sent me out there for the sake of letting the Bone tribe murder me. That was all that you had in your mind."

The sheriff did not budge, nor change his expression.

"And," went on the boy, "you came within an inch of having your wish. You wanted to get rid of me, and you failed. Well, you can't drive me out of the county. I see through you, Ogden. You're a crook and a black one. But I won't budge. You swore me in as a deputy. You can't swear me out again. If you fire me, I'll raise this town to a yell. You may be tired of me . . . but they want me. If you doubt that, go out and ask them."

At this, the sheriff slowly raised his head, slowly stood up from his chair, and then with equal lack of haste raised a balled fist toward the ceiling. He spoke not a word, but there seemed an infinite suppressed rage in his face. "I can't drive you out, eh?" he said at last.

"You cannot!"

Alert and watchful—for now he was ready to suspect anything—young John Signal waited, and saw the burly sheriff stride to the window and stand there looking out. But his hands were behind his back, and those hands were clasped and unclasped rapidly, and with great muscular force. The most convulsed face could not have shown more clearly the emotion that was inside him, the baffled straining of his spirit.

It seemed to John Signal that the meaning of Henry Colter was now plain enough. Sheriff Peter Ogden was a scoundrel and, to all the crooked fraternity, well known as such. The fact was apparently so patent that Colter could not believe that anyone had failed to see it clearly.

Peter Ogden whirled suddenly about. "Young man," he said, "my duty to the law is to put you under arrest immediately . . . and for murder. Do you know that, John Alias . . . Signal?"

But Crawlin had prepared him for the blow, and the boy merely smiled. "And why don't you do it, Ogden?"

"Because," said the sheriff, "you're only a kid. I sort of like you. I want to give you another chance. And I shall give you another chance. Alias, you're free to get out of this here town. But you gotta get quick. I'll give you an hour from this minute. If I catch you inside of Monument after that, heaven help you. You understand?"

"I understand as though I'd read the words out of a book," said Signal. "You stand for law and order, don't you?"

"With all my might."

"You lie," said the boy quietly. "You're a crook, and you stand for crookedness, and you play the Eagans and the Bones off against each other so as to line your own pockets!"

The flexible, heavy brows of the sheriff were drawn far down over his eyes.

He waited, however, and did not reply, while John Signal continued: "You want me out of town. Not that you give a hoot about me. You'd soonest of all see me strung up . . . or knifed in the back. Any way so as to get rid of me . . . because I'm interfering with your ideas too much. I'm spoiling your crooked game. Is that right?" Still the sheriff did not speak, and the boy continued: "Besides, I can prove what I say."

The sheriff muttered something beneath his breath.

"I can prove it," said Signal with cruel exultation. "And here's the proof." He held forth in the palm of his hand the golden medal of St. Christopher.

"And what does that prove?" asked the sheriff a little huskily.

"It proves that you were with the gang that did the murder-

ing in San Real Cañon! You were there. This came off the hat of
Pineta."

He shook the little golden circle in the air, and the startled
sheriff stared, agape. There was no doubt that his color had
altered. He was dumbfounded.

"Peter Ogden," cried Signal, filled with horror and disgust,
"I'm going down now to let the rest of the town know what I
know! No matter what they do to me, they'll clean you out of
office. And after that, I'm willing to let the law stretch my neck
with a rope." He backed toward the door. "Good bye, Sheriff,"
he mocked.

The sheriff stared like a man from the deepest sleep. "Hold
on! Alias . . . Signal, I mean. Hold on, for heaven's sake. Don't
go!"

CHAPTER THIRTY-TWO

So John Signal hesitated. It was not respect for Ogden that detained him, but an inborn respect for the office that the man held. For through all the wildness of the Far West, the sheriff is a figure that moves with a singular directness and integrity upon the paths of duty. Bad sheriffs there have been, but they can be counted upon the fingers of one hand, and so the office, even in the wildest days, took on a sort of halo of dignity.

Because of that sense of the office of the man, John Signal now paused and waited. He expected to see Ogden, thus endangered, beg pitifully. But the sheriff maintained a certain dignity throughout.

Perhaps it was a political matter that sustained him.

"My boy," he said, "you haven't lived a very long time in this here world. There's a good many things about the law and the ways of the law that you don't know. I want to tell you, in the first place, that I wasn't in San Real Cañon the day of the murder of the Mexicans."

"You'd swear that, I suppose?"

"I'd swear that, if it would make you believe me."

"It wouldn't," answered John Signal, more brutally than before. "Because I know in my heart that you're guilty."

"You know that?"

"What have you done from the first? You've tried to block me every time I moved to enforce the law I was sworn to enforce. You've worried me from the first. You hated me because I shot down a scoundrel like Jud Bone. You wanted to drive me out after that. When you couldn't budge me, then you tried to send me out to my death in Hanford. And when I came back alive from that, you tried the law on me. The law! Why, damn you, and all the law that you can get behind you. It doesn't have any meaning for me. I despise you and the rest of your kind. And that's straight. You can smoke that, if you've got a match that'll light it."

So, fiercely, he uttered his denunciation of the sheriff, and the latter listened with singular patience, his big head canted a little to one side, thoughtfully.

Finally he said: "I'll tell you this . . . that medal was given to me by another man."

"*Bah!*" sneered the boy.

"I give you my word."

"*Your* word!"

The sheriff snorted impatiently, but then, controlling himself, he said: "It's the truth."

"Gimme the name of the man."

"I can't do that, John."

"You can't do that? Then you can give the name to the crowd that's going to have a chance to see this Saint Christopher and hear the name of the man from whose hat it was taken. You can explain better to the crowd, maybe. You can make one of your speeches to them, maybe . . . unless they rush you before you get well oiled up and started."

At this, the sheriff was so spurred that he actually dropped a hand upon the butt of his Colt. But the gun was not drawn. "Are you going to drag that name out of me?" he demanded bitterly.

"I am. Or let the crowd drag it. I don't care much which."

"I'll tell you the name, then, if you're willing to swear that you'll keep your hands off the man."

194

"A low, sneaking dodge!" exclaimed the boy. "I keep my hands off him . . . that means that I keep him from proving that he didn't give it to you."

"Ah, damn you!" gasped the sheriff in a sudden barking voice, as though he had been tortured past his ability to withstand pain.

"Damn me as much as you like. But who was the man, if there was such?"

"I'll tell you, then. His name is Sim Langley."

"Your friend Sim Langley. I can believe that! He gave it to you for a memento, eh?"

"No matter why he gave it to me. I've told you his name, and now I've got to beg you not to bother him for a few days. Do you hear me, John Signal? I beg you to leave him alone."

"Because of the law, I suppose? Because of some dog-gone' great scheme that you got up your sleeve, maybe?"

The sheriff threw both arms toward the ceiling and stamped.

John Signal drew back into the doorway. "I'm going to find Langley as fast as I can," he said, "and, when I find him, I'll have the truth out of him."

"*You* will have the truth out of him!" exclaimed the sheriff. "You young simpleton, don't you understand that Langley is more iron than he is flesh? What could you do with him?"

"I could cross him off your visiting list, if nothing more," said Signal. "And that's what I'll probably have to do."

"Signal!" shouted the sheriff. "I tell you that the plans that I've been making for months would. . . ."

"Oh, hang your plans, and you with them," said the boy, and turned out through the door. He went rapidly down the stairs. At the first landing, the voice of the sheriff roared after him: "Hey! Hello! John Alias! John A-li-as!"

The deputy answered the wailing call: "Stop the noise . . . I'm not coming back to you till I have news!" Then he went down to the street. He leaned against a pillar, with the sun burning upon the backs of his hands, which were beaded with moisture. There had been more tension than he supposed in his interview with the sheriff.

So, making a cigarette, he thought the thing over and decided that there was much to this Peter Ogden. A bad man he most undoubtedly was, as all the rest of the people in the know—in that county—probably understood perfectly. But there was strength in him, too. Considered as a sheriff, perhaps he was only a political trimmer. Considered as a criminal, no doubt he was very little short of a mastermind.

But this day he had made a slip. It had been only when he was driven into a corner that he had named Langley to take the blame for the stealing of the St. Christopher. He had mentioned as formidable a fellow as he could think of, but that would not stop John Signal. And, by the grace of fortune, he would this day force the celebrated Langley into a corner, and then extract from him that truth that, as Signal felt, was all that was needed for the unmasking of the sheriff.

He could not but wonder at himself and at the intensity of emotion that he felt. Was it more pique, because he was himself outlawed by the crime in Bender Creek? Or was it, unknown to him, the working of a passion for order and law? Or was it, most likely of all, the mere uprising of cruelty and lion-like will to rule and to crush others? Signal, honestly enough, struggling with these ideas, was inclined toward the last and basest of all. His self-respect was not advanced. But his determination was not blunted.

Crawlin, the sneaking shadow of a man, appeared at his side, rubbing his pale palms together, and then expanding them in the fierce heat of the sun. He looked up to the youth with an ingratiating smile. "And here you are, back again, all safe and sound, and no harm done," he said. "Well, well, you're a man in a thousand . . . no, you're a man in a million, Mister Alias. Signal," he whispered confidentially, and winked with meaning at the boy.

The latter looked down at his companion with an odd mixture of contempt and disgust and interest. "You must have telephones hitched to your ears," he said. "How is it that you know everything that happens in town?"

Crawlin cackled with great pleasure. "Now, you never could tell that," he said. "Oh, but there's ways . . . all kinds of ways, if you're wise. There ain't a wall, hardly, that a small enough thing can't crawl through, and there ain't a wall that a tall enough thing can't look over. You take it that way . . . you see how a gent can look over things, and around the corners of things, and so see the truth about everything?"

"I see." Signal smiled. "I follow you, pretty well. You could almost wriggle through a keyhole, I think, if you wanted to see what was happening inside a room."

"I suppose I could," said Crawlin, with a nod of satisfaction. "Take when I was a kid growin' up, before I got my talents all worked up and developed, as you might say. I always knew everything. I could tell in the morning if the old man and the old woman was to have a fight before night. I could tell by one squint at the old man's face, whether he was gonna lick me or not." He laughed again, and again rubbed his pale, cold hands and extended them to the sun. "It ain't nothin' to my credit," he added. "It's just the way I'm made, I guess."

John Signal, peering at this monstrosity of distortion of the soul, merely nodded. The man was beneath advice, just as he was beneath correction. Even amid the booming guns and the hatreds of Monument, this contemptible little serpent was able to writhe through the streets and into the lives of other and stronger men, unharmed.

Then Signal said: "I want to see Sim Langley. Can you tell

me where he is?"

The little man cocked his head to the side with a jerk, and looked at Signal with his bird-like eyes.

"You want to find Langley," he said. "What's he to you?"

"What's he to me? Why, maybe he is a friend."

"Maybe he is . . . and maybe he ain't," said Crawlin. "Bu—
. . . ." He hesitated, agape for more news.

"I've got a message for him from the sheriff," said the boy.

"From the sheriff!" exclaimed the other.

"Yes."

"He gave the message to you, to give to Langley?"

"Yes."

"Well," said Crawlin, "Langley is a pretty hard man to talk to. He's a dangerous gent."

"Here's a dollar," said Signal. "Go find him for me."

Crawlin took the coin with a cringing grin, and instantly disappeared.

CHAPTER THIRTY-THREE

A long half hour passed, and Signal began to think that Langley had not, perhaps, come back to Monument from Hanford, when Crawlin appeared again, snaking his way through the crowd. As always when he carried important news, his face was pale and his eyes glistened like the red-stained eyes of a ferret. He clutched the lapel of Signal's coat, as though partly to sustain himself and partly to make sure of his auditor.

"I've seen a thing," said Crawlin, "that there was never anything like in Monument."

"Who's dead now?" asked the boy, weary of this ceaseless passive savagery on the part of the little man.

"Lemme finish! It was in front of Oliver's hardware store. Fitz Eagan and Champ Mooney, the gambler, was both standing there. Up comes Joe Klaus and walks straight to Fitz Eagan. He pulls out his handkerchief and throws an end of it to Fitz. To Fitz Eagan, mind you."

"I suppose Fitz shot him to bits?"

"Here comes the wonder. Eagan didn't catch hold of the end of the handkerchief that was snapped out to him. He just let it go by. He says to Joe Klaus . . . 'Joe, you're a fool to think that I'll fight with you for fun. I'll wait till I have a warrant for you, and then I'll go get you.' Klaus says to him . . . 'I'm hanged if I thought that Fitz Eagan ever would take water!' And he walked on, just like that. And I was by, and saw it all."

Signal was stunned. "But after all," he said, "that was his

right. He's the city marshal. He would be a fool to fight for no good reason at all."

"He took water," said Crawlin, drawing in his breath with a drinking sound. "I was by, and I seen it."

"Let Fitz Eagan be," said Signal sternly. "I know that he's a man and never would take water from twenty like Joe Klaus."

"Nobody knows that," declared the little man. "I've seen the bravest in the world, and they all have their weak times, the same as Fitz Eagan, even, has had his bad time today. There ain't going to be nothing else talked about in town for a few days, I reckon." He laughed soundlessly, filled with a malicious joy, as though he fed himself upon the contemplation of evil in his fellows.

"And what about Langley? You didn't find him?"

"Didn't I? I found Langley in the back room of Steeven's saloon, playing poker with Sam Tucker and a couple of miners, just down to town for the day. Langley and Tucker is cleaning them up."

"Where's Steeven's saloon?"

"Not four blocks away."

"Did you give Langley my message that I wanted to see him for the sheriff?"

"I didn't. He wouldn't leave as fat a game as that, even for the sake of the sheriff."

"Take me over to Steeven's place, then."

Little Crawlin assented with a nod and scurried ahead to show the deputy sheriff to the spot, and, as they came near the door, he tipped his evil face sidewise and stared up at John Signal. "You're all by yourself," he declared. "The rest of 'em will enjoy a fight, now and ag'in, if they're drunk. But you cotton to it when you're sober. And that's different. Gimme a chance to get around to the window, will you, so's I can look in and see you tackle him?"

"Take your time," said Signal, and began to saunter slowly back through Steeven's array of little card rooms, where the games ran day and night. There were few people in them, at this hour of the day. The all-nighters were hardly up, and the players by day rarely got seriously to work before the afternoon.

But when he came into the last room of all, there he saw at the corner table the layout of four, just as Crawlin had stated—and Langley in the farthest corner, facing the room.

He came out of his chair with a bound when he saw the deputy sheriff, but time was sadly against poor Langley. He was looking into the ominous face of a Colt before he had half risen; he was helpless before he could make a draw.

The other three at the table departed from their places at high speed. One slid down to the floor as though he suddenly had been turned to a wet rag. The other pair dived for the corners of the room—dived as though the hard flooring were water to receive them. So they rolled out of the probable path of bullets.

They left Langley alone—white, stammering, but unyielding.

"It's a damned low trick, Alias," he said. "Give me a half chance and I'll fight you to a finish. You come in here and take the jump on me."

John Signal said with calm: "Put your hands over your head. Walk out from behind that table. Turn your face to the wall."

Langley's eyes flashed wildly from side to side. "Boys," he said, his voice shaking, "are you gonna let me be murdered like this?"

There was no answer. One of the recent gamblers was squeezing through a window too small for him. Another was scrambling through the doorway.

So Signal went up to his victim and relieved him of no fewer than three Colts, and a long and heavy-bladed knife. There was even a slung shot attached at the wrist of Langley by a flexible holder, so that it could be jerked down to the fingertips of the wearer and used to slap a man into unconsciousness with a single gesture.

This array of weapons being transferred, the deputy sheriff walked his man out of the saloon, his hands still in the air above his head. It would have been safer, and easier, to take him in irons by side streets to the jail, but Signal had a very definite thought in mind, and he persisted in driving Langley straight through the center of Monument's traffic, his hands still above his head, and sagging down with weariness. Behind him came the captor, a Colt in either hand, while the crowd gathered thickly before, and split away in a constantly receding furrow to make way for their advance.

There was a shower of questions, but Signal moved through them, unheeding. They reached the jail. It was newly built, of red brick, with heavily barred windows, and a door of special strength, so that it might defy a great battering. Into the jail he conducted Langley, who was now raging and raving against such treatment.

Signal took him into the sheriff's own sanctum, a little room that was lighted by a single window, set high in the wall and crossed with iron bars. It was a dim room. Even in midday, there was use for a lamp, which Signal now lighted. He looked up from that operation and found Langley biting his lips with nervousness, and Signal smiled again with a cruel pleasure in his heart. As he had done with Graham, so would he now do with this man, he thought.

"It's more'n you can get away with," said Langley. "It's a damn' sight more."

"Sit down," said Signal gently.

"There's a law of *habeas corpus*, or some such thing. I appeal to that!" cried Langley.

"Sit down!" commanded the deputy.

Langley shouted in a louder voice than ever: "I have friends who'll see that I get the law! Friends who could crack open this jail like a rotten nut!" He was crimson with anger, and his confidence would have grown great very shortly had it not been for the calm and satisfied manner in which John Signal watched him.

The latter repeated now: "You'd better sit down. You'll be staying a while, I think."

"The sheriff don't know about this!" exclaimed Langley. "He wouldn't stand for it. You hear me? He wouldn't stand for it. He's my friend!"

And the boy smiled coldly, saying: "I have no doubt that the sheriff's your friend." He himself could not have said what he meant this to infer, but the mysterious manner of the speech told shrewdly upon the prisoner.

"I don't know what you're at," he said in protest. "You sashay in and shove a gun under my nose. I dunno what you mean by that, Alias!"

"I ought to kill you," said the deputy. "I ought to have killed you when I first saw you in Steeven's place. But I'm not going to kill you. I want to hear you talk."

"You want to hear me talk?" said Langley. "There ain't a thing for me to tell, but, if there was, wild horses wouldn't make me double-cross any partner of mine. That's the kind of a man that I am, Alias."

"I'm not wild horses," said the boy, "but you'll talk for me."

"I'll see you hanged first!"

"There's ways and ways of making people talk, Langley."

The other suddenly blanched.

"What ways d'you mean?"

"I mean the ways of the Indians, Langley. You've been with the tribes. You know about Apache ways."

"It's a lie," gasped Langley. "It's a lie that I ever lived with them or was a squawman, or that I ever rode in their raids. It's all a lie, Alias!"

This involuntary self-accusation was stored away in the memory of the deputy.

"You rode with 'em," said Signal. "I'm telling you that I know the facts about you. All that I want is to get you to write down a full confession and sign it. That's all I want."

"Why," said the other, laughing in a forced fashion, "you must think I'm crazy if you figure that I'd make out a warrant for my own hanging." He added suddenly: "I suppose you want me to turn state's evidence?"

"No," said the boy, "I got enough to hang you, now. I just want the pleasure of having the whole story out of you."

A flush suddenly drenched the face of Langley. "You know nothing," he said.

"Don't I?" answered John Signal, and he took from his pocket the medal of St. Christopher.

CHAPTER THIRTY-FOUR

Upon this, the prisoner stared, fascinated. But Signal, having given him a glimpse of it, absent-mindedly returned the trinket to his vest pocket.

"It was you, Langley, who tried to shoot me when I was sitting in the window of my boarding house."

"That's a lie and a loud lie," said Langley.

Signal smiled again. He was gathering in this man with a secure ease, he felt. "I have the word of an eyewitness," he said.

"It ain't possible. Who?"

"Graham."

"The sneak," groaned Langley. "The . . . the liar!"

"Liar?"

"Yes, yes! Great guns, man, would I be sneaking around and trying to murder you? I don't like you. I never pretended that I liked you. But murder? That ain't my style."

"You don't lie well," criticized Signal. "But take your time. Afterward you'll remember the truth."

"I've finished talking," said the other, "and I'm dashed if I'll ever say another word."

Signal took from his pocket a stout length of cord and knotted the ends together as he said: "You're a broad-minded man, Langley. And you'll change your mind about answering. I could almost swear that you'll change your mind." He held up the cord.

Langley watched him with a scowl.

"When you rode south into Mexico with the Apaches," said Signal, "did you ever raid a town and catch a few of the men and women and ask 'em where they kept their money? And did you ever urge 'em to talk by twisting a cord like this around their heads and then turning it tighter and tighter?"

Langley's mouth sagged open, and over his white lips he passed the tip of his tongue. The words that he had sworn he would not speak came out with a groan. "You're a white man, Alias. You wouldn't do a thing like that to a gent that ain't got a chance to help himself."

"You lie," said Signal with sudden anger. "You could have pulled your gun and died fighting in Steeven's place. You knew that I'd said that I'd get you the first time I met you on the street."

Langley swallowed. His color was a peculiar pale yellow-green. "I dunno what you want to get out of me," he said.

"I want the whole story," said Signal.

"About what?"

"About you!"

"I could tell you the story of my life," said Langley, with a flash of cunning in his face.

"With everything in?"

"Yes. Everything. I wouldn't try to fool you, Alias. You're too smart for me." He looked keenly at the boy, as he spoke, trying desperately to read around the corner, as it were.

"You'll put in San Real Cañon in full?" asked Signal.

"What should I know about that?" he asked, and blinked hard.

Again Signal took out the medal of St. Christopher. He held it up to the prisoner. "You've seen this before?"

"There might be twenty like that in the world," said Langley miserably.

"There's this one," replied Signal. "There's no more in this part of the world. You gave it to the sheriff."

"And he turned me over to you. Is that it?" shouted Langley in a new fury.

"No matter what he did. Here I am. I'm asking to have the facts out of you. Will you put 'em down in black and white?"

"Not a word."

"You're going to stick it out?"

"I'm going to stick it out."

"Well," said Signal, standing up, the cord ready in his hand, "I don't want to go this far, but I see that I'll have to."

"You'd try torture!" gasped Langley. "It ain't possible! Alias, you're a white man. You ain't a. . . ."

"Will you talk?"

"The mark of it'll be on me!" exclaimed Langley. "If you twist that thing around my head, it'll leave the mark on me, and Monument'll lynch you."

"Monument will do no more lynching," said Signal. "Monument is going to quiet down and be a model town. I give you your last chance, Langley. Will you write the little story for me?"

"They'd kill me!" said the prisoner hoarsely. "What good would it do me to win my life from 'em? They'd bust in here and tear me to bits."

"I give you my word that nobody is going to be able to tear in here. *I'm* going to stay."

"To guard me?"

"To guard you."

"A lot I could trust to you."

"Look here," said Signal quietly, "I'll show you what I mean. Out of what you write down, I can bust Monument wide open. You'll be like a nutcracker. You'll make the inside of the nut easy to eat. Protect you? I'd keep you safer than a watch in cotton batting. I'd keep you safer than I'd keep myself."

Langley flung himself back in his chair. His hands worked at his throat, opening the shirt so that he could breathe more easily, and his eyes were closed. For a long moment he suffered silently. Then he said in a croaking voice: "How would I ever get out of the country alive?"

"*I'd* take you out."

"Into the next county. What's that to me? They'd reach clean to Canada after me."

"I'll see you to Canada, then. I'll see you safely out."

Langley opened his eyes and slowly pushed himself up in the chair. "It started with a roan hoss," he said, "and look where I am now. I've been square. But I've gone bad. I'll have to change my name. After this, everybody that's ever heard of me will blame me for a yellow skunk."

"It's better to be blamed than to be dead," said the boy. "Besides, there's places as far off as Australia."

"There are," said the other with a flash of hope in his face. "And I'll have to head out that way. Alias, what d'you want me to do first?"

"Start writing. There's a desk. There's ink. There's paper."

"All right. Where shall I begin?"

"You'd better begin with San Real Cañon."

"Well?"

"You killed one of the Pinetas. Write that."

"How in the name of wonder d'you know that I killed him?" The amazement of the prisoner almost overcame his extreme fear and trouble of mind.

"You shot him through the head," guessed the deputy sheriff, "while he was lying on the ground."

Langley rose slowly to his feet and as slowly sat down again. "You were hidin' somewhere near!" he cried. "Or," he added, guessing wildly, "you were one of us."

Signal smiled.

208

And Langley, seeing that he had implied everything in this remark, groaned deeply.

"You killed Pineta. Write that down and sign it," said the deputy sheriff. "That'll make a beginning for us."

The other nodded. He set his teeth, took up the pen, and scratched rapidly, fiercely at the paper. When he had ended, he thrust the paper to Signal, and then rested his forehead on his hand. Shame had not prevented him from joining the murderers in the cañon, or from taking a flying shot at Signal, but shame overcame him now, as he thought of betraying his associates. Shame and fear, no doubt, in equal portions. His whole body was trembling.

And the deputy read on the paper in uneven letters that stumbled and shook across the page:

In the fight in San Real Cañon, I took my bead on the older Pineta and dropped him. Afterward, because he wasn't quite finished, I put a bullet through his head while he was lying in the trail.

(Signed)
Simeon Langley

"That's all for the minute," said the deputy.

"I get protection?" demanded the other suddenly. "You swear that?"

"Yes."

"Will you shake on it?"

"I'd rather touch a snake than touch your hand," said Signal.

"Well, let that go. But I got your oath?"

"Yes."

"What happens to me now?"

"You go to a cell. That's the safest place in Monument for you just now."

"Aye," agreed the other with a shiver. "That's the best place for me now, and the safest." He went without a murmur from the little office to the cell room. There was not the usual crowd inside the cells. Only three or four picked up for disturbing the peace the night before were lying on their cots—one asleep, another with eyes closed, cursing feebly, steadily in Spanish.

Langley was locked into a corner cell.

"Nobody can come at your back now," explained the deputy.

Langley nodded at him and even managed a smile. "I dunno how you can steer me through the trouble that's goin' to start poppin' now," he said. "But I gotta trust to you, old-timer."

"Trust to me," answered Signal, "and line up your story ready for writing in full."

So he left him and went to the sheriff, and found Ogden still in his office, furiously chewing a cigar and lost in thought.

"You got Langley," he said. "But how'll you hold him? Where's the warrant?"

"Here's a confession of murder," said the deputy. "Will that do?" And he held the paper before the eyes of the sheriff.

CHAPTER THIRTY-FIVE

The sheriff appeared as one appalled with wonder rather than one shocked with horror. He stared at the paper and then at the youth. "How in the world," he said, "did you manage to make him put his head inside the noose in this fashion?"

"He turns state's evidence," said the boy.

"And who authorized you to offer him that chance of saving his skin?"

"I knew," said young Signal, "that you'd agree with me that it was the easiest way to get one of them to confess, and through him rope the rest of 'em."

"And who may the rest of 'em be?"

"I'm going to pump him later for all the details."

"Did you warn him not to start talking on his own?"

"About what?"

"About the thing he's arrested for."

"No. I didn't think of that."

The sheriff did not seem greatly annoyed. Neither did he seem greatly shocked. Indeed, his attitude was not that of a man who is violently guilty or violently innocent. For one thing, the deputy had proved that the sheriff was not the slayer of Pineta, although as a matter of fact he might have been present in San Real Cañon. His attitude was rather noncommittal.

"You didn't think of that," repeated the sheriff gently.

"And why is it important?"

The sheriff put away his ruined, battered cigar and took out a fresh one, which he lighted. And all during the process of select-ing the new cigar, and cutting off the end of it, and lighting and rolling it, he gave his work not so much as a glance, but kept his gaze constantly fixed upon the face of the boy.

"You wouldn't see that," he said. "But suppose I try to show you. I dunno that you'd agree, but I could show you my side of the idea."

It occurred to Signal that there was a deep, hidden irony in the air and in the words of the sheriff. He flushed a little. and then he said: "Maybe you think that I'm a fathead. I don't think I am. If I've been playing out of a high hand, it's because, as far as I can see, you've been wanting to give me the run out of this county, and I still think that nothing would please you better than to see a chunk of lead go through my head."

"Nothing would please me much more," admitted the strange sheriff, "than to see you out of this here county. But nothing would please me much less than to see you dead. Now, if you'll let me point out something to you, I'd like to say it's probably all over Monument already that you've jailed this gent, and the reasons why you jailed him, and the confession that he's made."

"How could it?" asked the deputy. "Langley would be a fool to get himself into such trouble."

"What trouble?"

"Why, the minute the gang knows that he's apt to confess, won't they try to kill him, to stop his mouth?"

"You've thought of that?" asked the sheriff genially.

"You're trying to make a fool of me," said the deputy.

"No," said the sheriff in the same gentle manner. "I couldn't try my hand at that. Nature has done too good a job for you, without no retouching from me."

This plain insult was made easier to swallow, in a way, by the smile with which the sheriff spoke. It might have been called a sad smile, or an indulgent one, had there not been a bright light of rather foxy inquiry in the eyes of the speaker. It was enough, however, to rouse the boy, who was always listening for the call to war.

He said angrily: "I won't take such talk from you, sir. I don't have to, and I won't."

The sheriff sighed. "This here love of duty that you've got," he said, "will make you murder me before you're out of the town. I can see that. Ah, and how many murders will there be before the finish of this here?" He did not allow the boy to answer or comment, but continued hastily: "This is gonna be the final crash, of course."

"The final crash of what?"

"Monument, I'm afraid."

"I don't know," replied Signal, "how you're going to link up the finish of Monument with the jailing of one self-confessed crook like Langley."

"You don't know," said the sheriff, "and I don't suppose that you could learn."

"Look here!" cried the tormented youth. "If you're gonna keep on talking down to me, I'll leave your office and do things my own way."

"Will you?"

"I will."

"Go on," said the sheriff. "Every river has gotta run down to the sea. Go ahead and do your work the way that you see that it should be done."

"I'd like to know. . . ."

"Something from me?"

"I'd like to know what you mean when you say that Monument is about to go bust because I've put one crook called Langley in the jail?"

"I'll try to explain," said the ironical sheriff. "Suppose you look at it this way. Men were killed in San Real Cañon."

"Yes."

"Langley was one of the murderers."

"Yes."

"He wasn't the only murderer."

"No. Of course not."

"He belonged to a gang, then?"

"Naturally. Everybody has always known that."

"He belonged to a gang that was so slick and so strong that they could eat up that whole mule train with its load of Mexican silver and Mexican goods and never show no signs of indigestion."

"What do you mean by that?"

"Why, the most ordinary sort of an ordinary robbery, when the goods are shared, leads to some fights on the distribution, as you ought to know. And after the split has been made, someone is always sure to get drunk, and talk about what easy money it is that he's spending, and where that easy money came from."

"I suppose that's likely. Matter of fact, I never would want a crooked life, Sheriff."

"It'd sort of scare you, maybe?" asked the sheriff, with a curious question and amusement in his eyes.

"It'd scare me to death, sir."

"Well, you'll never be scared to death in that way. I was pointing out that the whole Mexican mule train was eaten up and no sign of it ever showed. Well, that shows that the organization is pretty big, wouldn't you say? And the dog-gone' gang has numbers and brains to run it, and experience, and nerve, eh?"

"I suppose it shows all of that."

"Now, look here, one of that gang is caught, and he begins to get ready to confess."

"That's right. I've said that. The gang is apt to try to get him set free . . . or to kill him."

"Or kill you," said the sheriff.

"Why me? Out of spite, you mean?"

"If they could have you out of the way, they're pretty sure that they could handle me."

"They are?"

"Yep. They're sure of that."

"And so?"

"They'll be trying a couple of things quick . . . to bump you off. To kill Langley by raiding the jail."

"I can see that there's sense in what you say there."

"And so the battle's sure to come on . . . I mean, the battle that I've been trying to stave off all these months."

"What battle do you mean?"

"You've heard about the Eagans and the Bones, lad?"

"I'm not deaf."

"You ain't? I sometimes wonder. Now, it ain't hard to find out that Langley is a member of the Bone gang."

"With Colter at the head of it?"

"Yes."

"Colter is a friend of mine."

"Colter ain't the friend of anybody who is going to get a confession out of Langley."

"He might try to kill Langley. He'd never put a hand on me."

"You're sure?"

"I'm sure."

"You're crazy," said the sheriff, heat breaking through his talk again.

"Maybe I am. I trust Colter."

"Now, I'll tell you what you'll be inside of one day."

"And what is that?"

"Dead and smashed between two parties."

"Which two? Bone and Eagan?"

"Yes."

"How do the Eagans come in?"

"They hate the Bones, don't they?"

"Yes."

"And Fitz is the city marshal besides?"

"That's right."

"Very well, then. Fitz is sure to come and offer us his help for the defense of the jail. And there you are. The battle is on. That means that every out-and-out crook in the town will throw in his hand with the Bones. And that means that there will be trouble boiling on all the street corners in no time. Am I wrong?"

"I don't know."

The sheriff laid his hand suddenly on the shoulder of his deputy. His voice was rich with kindness. "Here in Monument you can do nothing but get yourself killed. Take this advice from me . . . out of my heart. Leave Monument. Get out, and get quick, and stay out."

"And leave the work to you?"

"Naturally."

The boy laughed. "I've got to go," he said, "but not out of Monument."

"Very well," said the sheriff. "I ain't a prophet, but I'll predict that you'll be dead before tomorrow morning."

CHAPTER THIRTY-SIX

When he left the sheriff again, his sense of the importance of his achievement was reinforced, but he had two new impressions—one that the sheriff might very possibly be an honest or partially honest man, after all, and the other that Monument might soon be devastated by the most terrible strife because of the imprisonment of the robber and killer. But, first of all, it required that the city marshal should actually volunteer his aid on the side of the law for the defense of the jail. For this he could wait. But without some such assistance as the Eagans could give, he despaired of ever keeping the prisoner against an uprising in the town.

One thing at least was certain—that he must remain in the jail from this moment forward, until the fate of the prisoner was assured one way or the other.

So he turned straight toward the boarding house, prepared to take up his pack and go with all his possessions to the jail, and camp there.

He met the inevitable Crawlin again in the street, as he came out. That little spirit of evil grinned and smirked at him in the most detestable manner imaginable.

"Things are buzzin'! Things are buzzin'!" he declared to the deputy sheriff.

"In what way?"

"You wouldn't be knowing that, would you?" he asked with unctuous cheerfulness, giving his hands a brisk rub. "You wouldn't know what's happening. You wouldn't suspect it, even. Not you." He laughed again. He could not keep still, but had to twist himself this way and that in the excess of his joy. He looked like a dope fiend, after too great an excess of a drug. And the deputy sheriff, with that idea in his mind, looked upon the other with a more tolerant and pitying eye, prepared to excuse the base spirit in this man by some such pathetic and contemptible reason. But the closer he looked, the less the fellow seemed afflicted by any such trouble. It was sheer evil of mind that influenced him, and unable to stop any longer to find out what Crawlin might mean, filled with uncontrollable disgust, such as the lion would feel for the jackal, Signal mounted the roan gelding and rode off. At least he could use his imagination. What Crawlin meant was that certain elements in Monument were in a ferment because of the arrest of Langley.

He had not gone two blocks before, passing the door of Mortimer's saloon, he had sufficient proof, for out of the door half a dozen men poured at that instant, recognized him, and halted. They had showed their dislike of him before this. But now they glared at him with a grim frankness. Someone called out something sharply, and a gun actually flashed.

The deputy sheriff made ready to drop over the side of his horse, gun in hand, and open fire, Indian fashion, from under the throat of the gelding. But here Henry Colter appeared, like a guardian spirit, and pushed through the crowd, barking at the men, thrusting them and their weapons aside. He jumped into the saddle of a very fine black mare that stood before the saloon and rode to the side of the deputy. Signal was now moving down the street, keeping a most watchful eye behind him.

Colter, coming up to him, showed a stern and excited face. He said: "Youngster, what sort of trouble are you stirring up in Monument?"

"Do you mean about Langley?" asked the boy.

"I mean that, of course."

"I have my job and my duty," said Signal.

"Oh, cut that sort of talk!" answered the other angrily. "The fact is that your scalp is sitting damned loose, just now. You're good for a pretty short life, young feller."

"You're worried, are you?" asked Signal, pointblank.

"Worried about you. Yes."

"And not about yourself?"

"What do you mean? What is there for me to worry about?"

"Suppose Langley confesses everything?"

"He'd never mention me," said Henry Colter with an expression of peculiar grimness. "The cur wouldn't dare to mention me, even if he knew something against me."

"He'd mention anybody," replied Signal. "Besides, I don't have to have his story in order to get you into the affair. I know that you were there at the cañon when the murders were done."

Colter narrowed his eyes. "Kid," he said, "we've been friends. I've tried to steer you straight in Monument. I've tried to help you out. But this is pretty large talk for me to take from any man."

"I'm not trying to badger you," Signal assured him. "I knew the other morning, when I saw the old shoe that was taken off your horse."

"What?"

"I had the broken piece from the old shoe in my pocket at that minute. I knew all about it, Colter."

"Well?" snapped Colter.

"I let the thing drop. Do you think that after what's happened between us, lately, I ever could raise a hand against you?"

Colter suddenly smiled with relief, and with a shade of surprise, also. "I believe you, kid," he said. "But I want to beg you to turn Langley loose. He's a dead man, anyway. But if he dies right now, *pronto,* then maybe I can save your hide as well."

"I'll have to take my chances with my hide," said the boy. "As for Langley, they can kill him when they can get him."

"You'll chuck yourself away for that rat? The fellow that tried to murder you?"

"I've an idea that Langley may be the tool that will clean up Monument."

At this, Colter laughed with an ugly abandon. "All right," he said. "I like you, kid. But I pity you, if you try to work out this dodge in Monument. Nobody wants it . . . Monument wants to stay itself."

He waved his hand and abruptly left Signal, leaving that young man extremely disturbed. He never before had seen Colter so thoroughly worked up in excitement, and yet he had seen that notable outlaw in many circumstances before this. The mere words of warning that the sheriff and Crawlin had given to him were doubly confirmed by Colter.

He swung down the next street, taking a short cut for the lodging house, when he heard the rapid *spatting* of hoofs behind him, and turned to see a dashing, flashing form whirl around the next corner, the brim of the sombrero furled with the wind—a slender rider, swaying with the speed of the gallop. And so Esmeralda Pineta loomed suddenly behind him, distancing the escort of two *vaqueros* who spurred behind her.

She had no sooner seen the deputy sheriff than she threw up her hand and flung her mustang upon its quarters. So she slid it to a halt beside Signal, and a great cloud of dust went belching down the street, like smoke from the mouth of a gigantic cannon.

She swayed out to Signal and took his hands. Her face shone with deepest delight. "The moment I heard," said Esmeralda, "I came at once. Oh, but I knew the first moment that I saw you. I knew that you would make the curs run. I knew that you'd hunt them down. They never would dare to face you. And now . . .

now you've got one of them. Oh, keep him safe. Keep him safe. Never let him get away. Never let the crowd break in at him. They'll want to kill him. They'll want to do away with him, of course. They know that what he says will hang twenty of their best rascals. But I trust in you, *Señor* Sheriff, oh, brave, brave Juan Alias!"

She was in an ecstasy. She began to laugh with the extremity of her joy, and Signal thought that he never had seen a thing so beautiful, or so sinister. She was all in black—black habit, black boots, black sombrero. The very riding whip was ebony-handled and black of lash. But at her breast, where the white blouse showed, she had fastened a red rose. And this she now took and kissed, leaned forward, and pinned it on the coat of young Signal.

Now, with the nearness of her beauty, and the radiance of her eyes so close, and the breath of sweetness that went up from her as from the body of a flower, John Signal was more than a little dazed and bewildered. And he felt as though a great procession and flashing bursts of music had poured past him, and as though, somehow, he had been a part of that procession, and had been cheered by great throngs.

So he was stunned by the beauty and by the nearness of Esmeralda, when a glance over her shoulder cleared his mind.

For into the mouth of the next street, he saw Henry Colter ride, drawing rein as he saw the close group of the boy and Esmeralda. Only for an instant did Henry Colter remain there, and then he jerked his horse about and was off. But, in that instant, even in the distance Signal had seen the outlaw's face contracted with all the pain of jealousy. And that sight pricked the bubble of romance and left him clear-headed and himself, as Esmeralda reined her horse suddenly back, laughing at him, and nodding.

"I wish that it were one great ruby!" she cried. "And set in diamonds, too. But those two poor dead boys will have a proper vengeance now, Juan Alias!"

"I'm going to do my best," he said.

There was a perceptible shadow on her face. She had not succeeded half as well as she had hoped in bewitching the youngster. But she went on to more practical measures. She said: "You'll do your best, but you need men to work for you. Here are two men, Juan Alias. You see? Eduardo and Ricardo are both brave men. They can shoot straight. Oh, I've seen them do it. And I want you to take them along to the jail. I'll pay them double wages for it."

He looked keenly at the pair. They were, in fact, seasoned cowpunchers in appearance, hardy enough to tackle any sort of dangerous work, but when they were directly hailed, they looked blankly at one another.

"No, *señor*," they finally said in one voice. "We ride night herd on cattle, not on men."

"Listen!" cried the girl. "I'll give you three times your regular pay. I . . . I'll pay you a week's wages for every day that you guard the jail."

One of them shook his head. The other spread out his hands, with a shrug of the shoulders.

"And how shall one ever spend even a week's wages in heaven?" he asked.

CHAPTER THIRTY-SEVEN

It took some of the blood out of the cheeks of the deputy sheriff, this apparently common opinion of the town of Monument about the security of the jail that held his prisoner. But although John Signal was daunted, he set his teeth, and that Esmeralda saw, and cried to him: "You'll never lose heart because a pair of cowards flinch like this! And . . . I'll find you other men . . . somewhere," she said rather desperately.

Plainly she had counted greatly upon this pair, and her lip curled with her scorn and her anger as she stared at them.

"I'll find you other men, no matter what I have to pay for them," she repeated.

"That's no use," Signal told her. "That's no use at all. The reason is that some fellows who are really on the other side might be willing to take your money and work at the jail . . . but they'd be there only to shoot me in the back when the pinch comes."

"And the sheriff? The sheriff?" she cried. "Won't shame make him do something?"

"I don't know."

"Don't leave the jail!" she pleaded. "Go back to it now . . . and stay there, stay there. Oh, *Señor* Alias, if you bring up to justice only three of the scoundrels who did the murders in San Real Cañon, what would I not do for you?" And she made a gesture, a small gesture, with both hands, as though literally she placed her soul in his keeping.

223

He waved good bye to her and thanked her, and went on hastily toward the lodging house, rather upset because he had met her in this fashion. And, arriving in front of the house, he threw the reins and ran up the stairs.

The door swung suddenly open before him—and his Colt almost jumped from the holster in response before he saw that it was that same gentleman of the testy manner and the haughty air—he whose daughter had fled from Signal in the hallway of the house.

The gentleman hesitated now for an instant, and then lurched forward with a crimson face but a determined smile. He caught the hand of Signal and wrung it. He said earnestly: "The other day I was a simpleton. I didn't understand you or what you represented, young man. My . . . *er* . . . my daughter is also waiting to apologize to you at the first opportunity. I thought . . . *er* . . . in short, I was a fool. But now that I recognize the magnificent work you are trying to perform for law and order in Monument, I tell you I feel honored to have even laid eyes on you, Mister Alias . . . since you choose to wear that name. I have been at a business meeting. I've heard twenty men just speaking. I tell you, young man, that because of you, we begin to see our way through the storm, and law and order not so very far off."

This speech was delivered with a good deal of mingled embarrassment and dignity and with real admiration, so that John Signal blushed in turn.

He said to the other: "If you and other honest men in Monument want to help, it's at the jail that you could be used."

"To keep the man with whom you've baited the trap? By all means. We'll see what we can do." But most of his ardor had vanished, and hastily he went away from the boy.

Signal, glancing after him, understood. The honest men of Monument were at the present time quite willing to applaud the efforts toward law and order. But they were not yet willing to risk their necks for that fine project.

He turned again toward the door and saw Polly there, her arms folded, leaning her shoulder against the jamb of the door.

"Nice feller, ain't he?" Polly said. "If words was bucks, he could pay his way. You'll see him at the jail, all right . . . when you arrest him and snake him there at the end of a lariat. No quicker, old son."

He looked at her with a sudden, strange relief. "Polly," he said, "I'm tired as can be. Can you get me a cup of coffee?"

"You'd better have some lunch," she advised him.

"I don't want any. I want to stay awake and think. I'm fagged."

"Go into the dining room. I'll fix you up."

By the time he had washed his hands, she had a steaming cup of coffee before him. "That's the way with brain work," she said. "It tires out some people. Thinking about going on the stage has worried me a pile more than just the singing ever would do."

"I haven't forgotten," he told her. "I'm going to take you down to the opera house tomorrow."

She smiled faintly at him.

"I mean it."

"You look kinda vague, though."

"I feel a little vague, too," he explained, surprised at himself. "But it does seem a long way off . . . tomorrow, I mean."

"It is," said the girl. "It's a long way off, all right. Lord knows if you'll ever see the crack of the day beginnin'."

"You know all about everything," he said.

"I know about you and your job pretty good," she said.

"And how, please?"

"Nobody can keep anything from Crawlin. He spreads everything around."

"He ought to be in jail."

"He has been. It don't make no difference. He can start in the jail a whisper that'll bust through the walls and circulate all around the town." She added: "You'd better go up and lie down for half an hour."

"I've got to go to the jail."

"You gotta sleep first. A half hour now in the middle of the day, and you'll be fit as a fiddle for the rest of the time."

"Sleep?" He smiled.

"Go on," she said. "I'll go up and pack your duds for you."

"Who told you I was moving?"

She winked. "*Aw*, I could guess that."

It was true that he was very sleepy. Much had rushed through his brain and over his head since he rose that morning. He went up the stairs with a stumbling step. When he entered his room, the heat of it rolled into his brain like a wave of liquid, but he fell on the bed and stretched himself out. A cool towel was laid over his forehead. From the opened window a breath of air touched him kindly.

He looked at Polly. She was moving quietly and dexterously about the room, getting his belongings together. And suddenly peace dropped upon the wearied, confused brain of the boy.

"This is great," he murmured, and dropped instantly into heavy, dreamless sleep.

Almost instantly, a hand dropped upon his shoulder. He opened startled eyes and found her smiling down at him. "You've had your half hour," she said, and he, propping himself up on the bed, saw his pack made up and laid upon the chair. His head was clear, his brain was quietly ordered again, and the tangled mystery of all the actions and the motives that lay behind the sheriff and the Eagans and the Bones and the Pinetas and the Crawlins of Monument now appeared less confused, and less important. He stood up, stretched himself, and heaved the pack over his shoulder. She opened the doors for him all the way down to the street, and there he paused again, towering above her.

She nodded and smiled at him. "Good luck to you," said Polly.

"In the whole town," he said, "you're the only person that seems to want me to go to the jail and fight this thing out."

She smiled a twisted smile. "The only one?"

"Yes."

"Who put that red rose on your coat, Johnny?"

He clutched it, surprised. He had quite forgotten about it.

"Why d'you blush?" she asked him.

"Why, it don't mean anything."

"There's a considerable hedge of roses just that kind beside the Pineta house," she said.

"Is there?" he muttered. And he plucked the rose from its fastening and slowly crushed it in his hand.

"D'you mean to do that?" she asked him, frowning.

He answered her indirectly. "If ever I get through to tomorrow," he said, "I'm going to come back here and see you, Polly."

"You'd better," she said. "We got the best coffee in town in this house."

He hesitated. There were other and more serious things that he wanted to say.

"Well, so long," said Polly.

"So long," he murmured.

And she closed the door behind him, and shut him out into the bright desert of the open day.

At that he turned again and laid his hand on the knob of the door, but the catch had caught. He could not turn it. "Polly!" he called softly.

There was no answer. But suddenly he knew that Polly was inside that door, leaning heavily, limply against it, and hearing his voice, but held back from answering it.

He turned again and went down the steps and into the blast and burden of the sun that burned through his coat and scorched his shoulders. The pack he fastened behind the saddle upon the roan.

A pair of cowpunchers, jogging down the street, brought their horses down to a walk and began to mutter to one another with side glances as they went past.

He was known to them. He was known to everyone, apparently. But that was not worth his notice at this moment. Other and more important things filled his mind. So he climbed into the saddle, slowly and stiffly, like an old man, and rode down the street.

But at the next corner he turned and glanced back at the house, and he had a glimpse of Polly at an upper window, her face looking oddly white and old, as he thought. Then he went on toward the jail.

CHAPTER THIRTY-EIGHT

The jail, rather oddly, was the last building of public utility of which Monument had thought, and, when they came to build it, all the center of the town was closely occupied with frame and brick and adobe buildings, and Monument could not afford to waste money in the purchase of these, together with the land on which they stood. Prices, it must be understood, were soaring, and there was not too big a fund set aside for the jail. So they had to go to the outer edge of the town, where it stretched away toward the northern hills.

Here they bought a plot between a rambling old adobe house and an abandoned barn that even the careless, reckless population of Monument did not care to use as a habitation, for its back was broken and sagged sharply down, and at all the four corners its knees were gradually giving way and breaking in. This space between the two structures was completely filled by the jail, which was constructed of red bricks. A fly could not have walked between the wall of the jail and the wall of the house, and there was only a small alley between it and the side of the barn. Toward the town there were a couple of empty lots, filled with tall brush; toward the hills the trees began, here and there cut down and thinned away by the seekers after fuel, but still a dense enough screen rolled away like smoke to the north.

And young John Signal, riding toward the jail on this fatal day, noted all these things with a new interest. Never before had he been so aware of the vulnerability of the jail. The stoutness of its walls and the thickness of its bars of iron always had given him an impression of strength, but it is an old maxim in a fighting country that a man must keep his back to the wall and his eye upon the door—and this was impossible for the jail. The house leaned perilously against it. The barn was in jumping distance of the roof. And the trees to the rear and the brush in front rolled dangerously close. Five hundred rifles could have been packed away in such a covert.

At the first view, rounding the corner, John Signal had reined in his horse a little, and now he noticed a small figure slouched against a telephone pole on the right-hand side of the street.

Crawlin, of course. Suddenly he wondered what news that scavenger of trouble could have gathered within the last hour, so he rode close to the little man, and, although he hardly glanced down from the saddle, he heard a gasping voice say: "You wanna die, kid? Keep right on down this here street if you do."

John Signal rode on—straight down that street toward the front of the jail, but he rode now with his eyes alert, probing at the windows of the house, at the yawning black entrance of the door of the mow, high on the side of the barn, and, most of all, at the tangle of the brush to his right.

And he saw two things all in one instant—the movement of a human shadow behind a bush, and the glint of steel deep behind a second-story window of the house. Signal twitched the reins of the roan. Not for nothing had he called it a cutting horse. Now it spun around like a top and darted back the way it had come while two hornet sounds flew with sinister humming past the ears of the boy, followed instantly by the reports of two rifles, which sounded like two hammer strokes.

He swerved the roan to the side and swerved him back again; well and valiantly that practiced worker dodged, as though wending through a dense crowd of cattle at high speed. And this time half a dozen hornets were on wings about the head of John Signal. With a twitch, his sombrero was lifted from his head and sailed off into the air, and a loud Indian yell of triumph rang behind him.

But he was unhurt as he jerked Grundy around the next corner out of the path of the fire. He leaned from the saddle upon either side to examine the roan; Grundy showed a long rip across his right shoulder, and the blood was streaking down from it. But his spirit was not hurt, and his long ears were pointed forward. It made the heart of Signal boil with anger; it was more to him than the sight of a dead man lying in his way—a dead friend. And now, gritting his teeth, he wondered what he could attempt next. There was the way by the trees at the rear of the jail, of course, and, although the Bone tribe must have planted some look-outs here, perhaps he could break through them.

He cursed the delay he had made in going from the sheriff's office to the jail again. For the tactics of the enemy were perfectly apparent. They would strive to keep him away from the jail during the day. In the night they would rush the building, and, without Signal in it, it could not make any strong defense.

He rounded the group of sheds just before him and saw an old Mexican woman squatted at the door of one, patting out tortillas on a flat-topped stone.

She grinned at him, toothless and cheerful. "Death is the friend of no man, *señor* . . . that is true, is it not?"

"That is true, mother" he said. "How does your house open to the rear?"

"On the barn for the horses and the mules, *señor.*"

"And beyond that?"

"The back of the barn is against an old house, *señor.*"

"And the old house?"

"It rests against the jail, *Señor* Alias."

He marveled a little at this. Even this ancient bit of wrinkled humanity knew him. Yet he could not take pleasure in this for the moment. The better he was known, the more surely could rifles be aimed at him by skillful hands.

He dismounted on the spot. He stripped off the pack and the saddle, carried them into the house, and laid them in a heap in a corner.

"Mother," he said, "here are my belongings. Tell your man that I have left them here. If I am alive tomorrow, I shall come for them. If I die, they are all yours and your man's."

Her old eyes flashed at him, like lights through a mist. "Saint Christopher carry you back to us, my child."

And he knew that she meant it with all her heart. He took his rifle under his arm. Two heavy Colts burdened his thighs, and so, bareheaded, he made his way back through the house and into the narrow open yard behind. Then through the barn, where a moldy-looking mule stood with flopped ears and pendant lower lip.

At the rear door of the barn he crouched for a moment. It hung a little ajar, and through the crack he could look out at the side of the house that leaned against the jail, as the old woman so aptly put it. Earnestly he peered up at all the windows within view, and suddenly one on a level with his eyes was thrust up. The head and shoulders of a man appeared—a bandaged head, and Charley Bone climbed out and reached back his hand. He drew up an unknown man to join him.

"He'll never try again today," said the second comer, pulling his tipped hat straighter over his eyes.

"He'll try anything. That's how he wins . . . by doing the wrong thing," said Charley Bone. "Cut down there behind that tree. Be careful that they don't get a bead on you from the jail. Kid, if we can snag Alias, yonder among the trees, we'll never be forgotten."

And they worked off from the house to the north.

Signal, listening with a beating heart, smiled fiercely to himself. It was vast temptation to step out of the barn and hold them up as they hurried off, but it was more important to get himself into the jail than to get this precious pair into an early grave. Besides, his heart was softened a little toward them by the praise that he had received—the sweetest of all tributes, coming from enemy lips. And he felt, more than ever, that he never could be shuffled aside in the memoirs of Monument now as a mere lawless, reckless boy. He was a man, and doing an honest man's work. Let the world balance this against the killing in Bender Creek, and make up its mind. With mercy, he thought.

He had not, really, a thought that he could live through this mortal danger. He had received too many warnings. It was merely hope for the next moment that sustained him and sent him forward, step by step, like a blind man walking against a storm.

He pushed the rear door of the barn a little more ajar, and, creeping out, he cast another glance up at the windows of the abandoned house. To him it was as a cage filled with lions, hungry for his life.

All those windows appeared glimmering, black, empty, and, glancing to the left, he saw that Charley Bone and his companion both had disappeared among the trees.

So he left the barn and leaped across the distance that separated him from the wall of the house of his enemies. Down this he stole, and, turning the corner, he looked toward the jail. If he got there, would he have to stand outside the door, calling for the door to be opened to him? Five seconds of such a pause would bring fifty bullets into his flesh, as he very well knew.

The house blocked away most of the view of the jail, as a

matter of course, but he could see two windows, one on the ground floor and the next on the floor above. And, as he watched, the dim outline of a man appeared at the second.

Frantically Signal waved his hand, but the image disappeared from the window.

No, in another moment it reappeared, closer to the glass, and then went out of sight again. Surely the man had been able to see him, and, no matter which of the prison guards it might be, he could be reasonably sure that they would be glad to see him.

He would wait thirty seconds to allow the man time to run down and open the rear door and thus receive him on his dash. He counted, found that his tongue was racing—and counted the thirty twice over, faster than the ticking of a second hand. Then he rose to bolt for the rear door of the jail—surely it must be opened by this time. And, as he rose, a rifle spurted fire from the trees, and he received a heavy blow across the forehead that staggered him.

Charley Bone and his companion had spotted him, at last, from among the trees.

CHAPTER THIRTY-NINE

The impact of the slug from the rifle had knocked the greater part of the wits of young Signal out of his head, and yet, as he slumped against the wall of the house, he knew certain things with a dreadful distinctness. He knew, for instance, that it was only a glancing wound, although perhaps the bullet had furrowed the bone of the head. He knew that he must flee with all the speed he could manage. And, turning his head, he had a clear view of Charley Bone who, rising from behind a log, excited at the success of his first shot, stood with rifle at his shoulder, about to fire again. But, for the least part of a second, stunned and helpless, the boy could not stir. Only his brain was active to this degree. Then a second shot plunged through the wall just beside his head, and suddenly he was himself again—just as a boxer, stunned and helpless from one blow, suddenly is shocked into his right senses by the impact of a second stroke.

So John Signal came to himself and lurched away. If he really had been in his best senses, he would have shrunk back around the corner of the house, and from this position tried to get in a shot at Charley Bone and his wicked companion. But he did not think of that. He was sufficiently recovered to be able to move, but he was only sensible enough to plunge straight forward toward the rear door of the jail.

The next shot went past him on hornet wings. They had opened upon him with their two repeating Winchesters, and they were fairly pumping the lead at him. And, as he went past the rear of the vacant house, he stumbled on a hummock of soft ground and fell headlong. He heard the wild, exultant yelling as he fell, not of the two among the trees, but of many more as well, and, as he lurched to his feet again, he knew that the entire rear of the house was covered by the tribesmen of Bone, looking out on the fall of this young enemy.

Anger gave him strength and speed. He dodged forward with hardly another shot fired, so greatly did his sudden rise from the ground surprise the others. And so he reached the rear door of the jail and plunged through it to safety, past a chalky-faced jailer who instantly wrenched the thick door shut behind him. It closed with a heavy iron *clanking,* and here was safety for the moment. But for how long?

Of the two guards, if this white fellow was a sample, the pair would not be worth the assistance of a single armed child when the attack was delivered at nightfall. But there was Simeon Langley in the cell, white, also, but resolutely erect, and gripping at the bars of his cell as though he were anxious to get out and share in the defense. That instant the young deputy made up his mind. With the first falling of the night, in case no other succor were at hand, he would free Sim Langley, and so increase his force. But even that would hardly improve matters.

The first glance around him showed how desperately difficult it would be to defend the place. There were many windows, well secured with bars of the best tool-proof steel, but for all that, windows to which anyone could climb from the outside, and through which anyone could fire. There were shutters for these windows, but every one of them was now open and hooked back—for who had use for shutters, here, in summer weather? Into the big cell room looked no fewer than eight windows. During the day they were simply convenient portholes through which the garrison could keep their watch. But during the night they were sure to provide loopholes for the enemy to fire through. Ordinary rascals might not have had the resolution for such feats, but the Bone tribe would without doubt furnish many volunteers for this work.

All this the boy thought in the first glance that he threw around him. And in the meantime, the trembling guard was saying: "*Aw*, but I'm glad to see you, Deputy Sheriff Alias. I never was so glad to see nobody. I thought that I was gonna be left here to die an' rot. I thought that they was gonna leave me here to be murdered."

John Signal said to him sharply: "Murdered you will be, unless you buck up and take a part, and work with your own hands. I never can defend this place by myself."

There was a noise at the front door, and the guard clutched at the wall, half fainting.

"They're sneakin' in through the front way now. Heaven help us. We're done! We're done! Stop 'em, Mister Alias. Stop 'em, sir!"

In fact, there was enough danger in that sound to make the boy quake. Fear, catching like disease of the most deadly nature, breathed coldly in his face. Then he rallied and forced himself forward.

He heard Langley calling softly: "Alias, lemme loose to help you. Lemme loose to fight for myself."

But he had not a key; moreover, he had no time, if the enemy actually were breaking in through the front door. At this moment, he heard a sudden crashing of shots, and a roar of voices from the front of the jail, instantly answered by the rush of heavy feet, and then a great shout inside the front door.

Into that front hallway, the boy himself sprang. For he felt that he was cornered, and, if the enemy were indeed inside the door, his one fighting chance was to drive them out—before they were solidly entrenched. For that purpose he delivered a quick attack, leaping through the doorway with a revolver in either hand.

He saw before him Fitz Eagan, and with him the tall, pale major. Two forms more welcome he could not have seen among all the hosts of the fighting men in Monument. If he had to choose two from the multitude, he would instantly have named these very men. The guard, who had evidently managed to catch the signal of the pair in some manner when they were able to dash for the jail, was now bolting the door behind them, and was laughing hysterically.

"Say," cried young John Signal, "but I'm glad to see you!"

"Not half so glad," said Fitz Eagan, "as we are to see you. I thought you'd be done and down, young game chicken."

"How did you manage? How did you manage?" stammered the deputy sheriff.

"We managed when we heard the roaring of the rifles behind the jail. If that many of the Bone outfit were shooting back there, it stood to reason that not many of them could be watching from the front of the house. So we made the dash. Skinny, here, had been spotting us through the window . . . we passed him the signal, and here we are."

So, carelessly, Fitz Eagan commented on their arrival, but Signal did not need to be told what danger had been endured. He had heard the crash of the guns only a few seconds before.

"This will go down as one of the great battles of the West," Major Paul Harkness declared, sneering. "Fifty fighting men. All outlaws. All desperadoes. All dead shots. And out of the first hundred bullets fired, there's one small wound. That's the wild and woolly West." He laughed, and his laughter turned abruptly into a racking cough. The spasm brought a flush into his face.

Fitz Eagan, in the meantime, was asking after the boy's wound more seriously, and then he attended to it with his own hands, washing it at the sink in the corner of the cell room, and then dressing it. He had brought over ample materials for the dressing of all kinds of wounds. He had with him, moreover, a quantity of bread, meat, and salt, and two very large flasks of whiskey.

The spirits of the deputy sheriff rose high. He danced and swore softly as the stinging medicaments entered his wound, but still he chuckled. "When they open this box," said John Signal, "I've an idea they'll get pepper into their eyes."

"Of course they will," said Fitz Eagan genially, "but when they sneeze, it may be the finish of us."

"What do you think?" asked the boy of Major Harkness.

The latter smiled. It was not really a smile, but his nearest sneering approach to one. "It's the first time in years," said the major, "that I've been asked for a thought. Usually it's for money or a gun. D'you really mean it, Mister Deputy Sheriff?"

"Paul, don't be ridiculous," said Fitz Eagan angrily. "Open up and talk like a sensible man if you can. The kid is serious."

"Why," said the major, taking no notice of this rebuke, "I'll do my best. My idea is that there'll be no more trouble. We're here, and the Bones won't bother us."

"How do you work that out?" asked Fitz Eagan.

"It's simple, ain't it?"

"I don't follow it at all."

"The Bone gang is a pack of Indians. They'll never give away three lives to get three . . . or three to get four. And it's pretty plain that they're apt to pay that high for the inside of this package. Or d'you think that we'll be cheaper meat than that, partner?" He asked it with a drawling viciousness.

But Fitz Eagan turned to the deputy sheriff. "What do you think?" he asked.

"I don't know what to think," said young John Signal. "I'm pretty badly scared, I guess. I'm not thinking very fast or very straight, as a matter of fact. I only know that we're on the inside and a lot of trouble is on the outside. But there's the whole city of Monument that can hear the guns. Surely some of the fighting men will come to help us."

Harkness stepped closer and laid a hand on the shoulder of the deputy. "You're a good kid," he said. "I thought you might have a little case of swelled head after what you've done in Monument, but I can see that you've eaten your raw meat with salt on it. But about these fighting heroes in Monument . . . well, lad, they won't come near us. Why should they?"

"Except the sheriff," said Fitz Eagan. "He's sure to turn up."

"Then why isn't he here now?" asked the major.

"I don't know. It rather beats me, I confess. I looked to find the old fat boy here."

"He's changed his mind. He's one of the heroes that would rather be alive to read books than be dead and put inside the covers of one."

So said the major, and John Signal heartily agreed.

CHAPTER FORTY

Before they attempted any definite conclusion, they went over the jail with the greatest care, passing together from the top to the bottom, and from one end of it to the other. The farther they went, the more complicated the task appeared. To begin with, above the first floor there was a large attic with a barred window at either end, one pressing against the wall of the vacant house that the Bone tribe had seized, and the other looking upon the barn. This attic was littered in part with broken furniture and odds and ends. In part, it was cluttered with several big packing cases.

"A pretty neat place for twenty thugs to hide out," as Fitz Eagan commented.

"But how could they get in?" asked John Signal.

Both the major and Eagan turned curious eyes upon their companion. Then the former said quietly: "The wall of that next house is just thin boards. What's wrong with peeling off those boards and going to work on this brick wall with a crowbar? Six licks would break a hole through it."

"It would," agreed Fitz Eagan, and Signal was silent, for he saw the truth in what had been said.

They went down to the main floor of the building, and there they took note of the eight windows that yawned upon the cell room. Peering out through one of these, Fitz Eagan called the attention of his friends to the houses that were nearest to them upon the town side of the building. Every window was crowded, particularly the upper ones. And sheltering themselves from the sun under big umbrellas, whole families were picnicking in the open air, ready to enjoy the show when the attack upon the jail should commence in earnest.

"There're your honest citizens who ought to be falling in and right-shouldering arms to come to help us," said Major Harkness to Signal. "There they are."

Signal stared, amazed. "I don't make it out," he said. "I don't understand it at all."

"You wouldn't, kid," answered Fitz Eagan. "But the fact is that you don't understand the lie of this land any too well."

"Are there no honest men in Monument with a little nerve?" asked Signal desperately.

"Tons of 'em," said Fitz Eagan. "Tons and tons of 'em. But why should they mix in on this? They shouldn't and they won't. They don't know which side is straight. That's the mistake that Sheriff Ogden has made. He's had to play both sides against the middle. I admit that. But he ought to have let the crowd see where *he* stood."

"How could he let the crowd see and not let both sides see?" asked Major Harkness.

Fitz Eagan appeared to agree. It was a tight hole and a bad fix for the sheriff, he admitted. This defense of Ogden seemed very wonderful to Signal. Finally he exclaimed: "If the sheriff really is honest, why isn't he here now to help us fight?"

"I dunno," answered Fitz Eagan. "But I do know this . . . that you can't judge a man until you've seen him finish the race. This one is barely started. Give Ogden another chance to come through."

They continued their investigation of the main floor. There were three small rooms across the front of the building. One of these was the room of the sheriff himself, where Signal already had sat. Of the remaining two, one was devoted to supplies and guns of all necessary kinds, together with fetters of various sorts; the other served as a cooking and living room for the jail guards. Each of these rooms contained a window. Eleven windows, therefore, looked in upon the main floor of the jail.

"We're like water in a sieve," commented Fitz Eagan. "How can we keep from leaking out, I ask you? What can we do?"

They went down into the cellar. It was practically as large as the floor above it, and that floor was supported by a small forest of timber pillars.

"They could fire this," said Fitz Eagan at once. "And once they fired it, they could burn us out like so many rats. Isn't that right?"

"That's right enough. But how would they get fire into this?" asked Signal curiously.

"By bashing a hole through the cellar wall, the same as they could do through any of the floors above," said Fitz Eagan. "This jail is a fine fort. I'd as soon be in a glass house. They can do everything but look through at us. And we'll have to have a man on every floor, every minute of the time." This seemed obvious.

They posted the two regular jail guards, one in the attic and one in the cellar. Their fear, which they plainly showed even after the arrival of such reinforcements, should be enough to keep their senses upon the alert.

The fighting corps, as Eagan, Harkness, and John Signal might be called, was to take charge of the main floor, since, if there was an attempt to rush the jail, or to get possession of the windows from the outside, of course the attack would have to be met at that level.

There remained the moot question of Sim Langley. The moment he saw Fitz Eagan and Harkness, he ceased his clamoring for freedom from his cell. Harkness walked up to the cell and rolled a cigarette while he eyed the prisoner.

"Sim Langley," he said, "you always have known that I look on you as a rat?"

Langley made no answer, but, with an equal coolness, he rolled a smoke of his own, and regarded the other placidly through the bars of the cell.

"A poison rat?" repeated Harkness calmly.

"Harkness," said Langley, "you've got a great name for yourself around Monument by bumping off a few tenderfeet. I never laid no stock by you. And I ain't ready to change my mind now. I figure you for a low four-flusher, and if you want to call my turn, let me out of this cell and gimme a six-shooter. When I've finished with you, your partners can finish with me. But finish you I can, and I will, if I get the smallest half of a chance."

"This is something pretty good," declared Harkness. "Do you hear this, boys? Langley is getting a heart inside him. The yellow doesn't show such a broad streak today. Will you let him walk out and talk to me, Alias?"

"There'll be no fighting here," answered Signal. "Not a little bit of it. Langley, you've chucked your chance to come out and help fight for your own hide."

To this Fitz Eagan replied that the fault was Harkness's, and not the prisoner's. Still, Signal would not permit Langley to leave the cell until he had finished writing out his confession. And that, most unwillingly, he did.

It was not a long story. It simply told how Henry Colter had called together his clan of fighting men and informed them of the scheme that he had on foot. He was to ride down into Mexico in order to get sure details of the start and the progress of the caravan of mules. After that he was to retire into the upper mountains, east of Monument. There he was to wait, peering down into the lowlands and the hills to spy certain far-off fire signals that the smugglers, he was led to believe, usually used in order to communicate with their friends.

All went as he had planned, and, among those wild uplands where Signal first met him, he had been keeping his watch and had spied out the train. In answer to his own call, his men then went up to meet him, and they descended into the lower lands, paralleling the course of the mule train. They did not come upon a perfect spot for ambuscade until the train was in San Real Cañon, where the blow was delivered with sweeping effect. Only one man had escaped, and that man was badly wounded. Colter, Dad Bone, Charley Bone, Joe Klaus, Langley himself, and several more had worked in the raid. They had planned to leave no living men, when they saw the pocket into which the Mexicans had ridden. But luck prevented the carrying out of their plan.

This confession Langley signed.

"I'm signing my life away," he explained gloomily. "They'll never leave me alone, now, until they've snagged me for this. Never." He added with more bitterness: "It never would've happened . . . we'd've got away with everything, if it hadn't been for the kid here." And he paid John Signal with a glance of uttermost hatred. But however much he might hate the boy, his interest was now plain; his own skin was more endangered than that of any other man. It was his life that the others chiefly wanted. As for his confession, that might well be discredited in a court of law, but his personal testimony would be utterly ruining to too many lives. So Simeon Langley was loosed from the cell and furnished with a rifle and revolvers—his own.

The plan for the defense was now thoroughly established. To the two regular guards of the jail, the outlook from the top floor and from the cellar was to be entrusted. Langley, Signal, and Major Harkness were to go the rounds of the various rooms on the main floor continually, and Fitz Eagan, whose fame and whose fighting experience caused him to be entrusted with the command, would move from one part of the building to the other, wherever he saw fit to go.

Dusk was now coming on, and through the windows they looked gloomily forth upon a world of yellow and pale blue, constantly deepening to purple and gold. Every moment brought their danger nearer and still nearer.

Then Fitz Eagan made a little speech to his assembled garrison. He said: "You been brought up around here to believe in speed. Forget that tonight. Never fire until you get a perfect bead. Always make sure. Nothin' encourages the other gent so much as to be missed. Nothin' discourages him so much as to be shot . . . even if you don't nip off no more than a finger. Besides, we don't want the air in the jail to get all smoked up. Keep your eyes open. And the best way to keep them open is to keep moving. Once every round, stop short and listen hard. Then walk again. Take a slant out of every window as you go past it, and don't forget to look down, because they'll have to come up to get us through the windows. Now, boys, we're in a tight hole. The worst I ever was in in my life. There's about one chance in ten of seein' sunup. Let's forget about that. Let's aim to die well."

CHAPTER FORTY-ONE

Now John Signal well could remember similar instructions often received from his poor mother, from the schoolteacher, from the minister—that the greatest thing in life was to die well. But they had meant death met with a composed mind, with good will and forgiveness to our enemies, with prayers upon the lips, and upward intentions in the soul. The meaning of Fitz Eagan, however, was plainly different. He wanted them to die well— each man fighting to the last gasp—each man shooting straight.

"I take it," said Fitz Eagan, "that we're uncommon fighters, all four of us. The only shame is that the other pair of rats has to be classed with us, so's folks can say afterward that the jail was kept with six men. But if we've got any luck, the four of us should be able to down three apiece, and that would make a pretty fair total. If we can do that, there won't be enough left of the Bone gang to steal a hoss tomorrow." And at this thought he laughed.

Major Harkness said suddenly: "What about your brothers? Why didn't they come in on this with you?"

Said big Fitz Eagan sourly: "I don't know what brothers you mean."

"You don't? Well, everybody else does. I say . . . where are they? Why aren't they, here, fighting beside you?"

Fitz Eagan answered again heavily: "I've got no brothers. They're worse'n dead to me."

And this caused even the hardy major to blink a little. It

247

shocked and appalled John Signal, for he understood that for their failure to follow their brother into this nest of danger, he disavowed them forever.

The dusk gathered, deepened. Now they could see the lights of the town, and finally the long yellow rays began to pass through the barred windows, casting the faint, tangled shadows upon the northern wall of the jail.

The time of danger truly had arrived, and the guards began their watchful procession from room to room. Passing the southern windows, John Signal paused at each to make sure that no enemy crouched beneath it, and he also glanced out to see the crowds who still patiently waited at windows and on roofs to see the commencement of the long-expected battle. He was grimly amused by this worthy patience, and by the thought that one percent of those worthy citizens would be enough to swamp the Bones, and set free the defenders of the jail from all danger. But such a step did not occur to them. The newspaper reporters would be waiting feverishly, too. This was their opportunity to make national copy.

Signal was passing the big front door for the third time after utter darkness fell, when he heard a faint knock, rapidly repeated from the outside. He stepped close and called in a guarded voice: "Who's there?"

"It's me!" gasped an unmistakable voice.

No hesitation made Signal pause. He was thrilled by a vast wonder, and then he unlocked, unbolted the door, and dragged it open. A prostrate form lay before it. He reached out, collared the man, and jerked him inside. The door was already closed again when a rifle pumped two bullets from across the street, but the lead splashed like water from the iron bindings of the door. And John Signal leaned over the limp body of Crawlin.

He exclaimed: "Are you hurt, man? Have they winged you?"

Crawlin recovered a little. "I dunno!" he gasped. "I think

they just shot me twice."

"Where?"

"Through the heart," moaned the wretched man.

Signal smiled. "You're scared half to death, Crawlin," he said. "Stand up and shake yourself. You're out of the water now."

Crawlin, supporting himself on one elbow, fumbled at his body. He groaned with relief as it began to dawn upon him that he had not actually been struck by anything more real than terror.

"But how did you manage to take the chance and get across to the jail?"

"I dunno," mumbled Crawlin. "I'd rather die quick and here than to face it again. I'd rather die. It makes me sick with fright to think of what I done."

"Well, and how did you do it?"

"I just walked down the street. They knew it was me. Nobody never pays no attention to me. When I come to the jail, I turned in toward the door. Then I rapped and you answered. I got faint with excitement and fell down . . . then they began to shoot. I heard the bullets go thumping . . . into my own body, I thought. And then I woke up in here." He clutched his face with his hands to shut out the terror of the picture.

"Look here," said John Signal, between contempt and wonder. "You've done a brave thing, Crawlin. You've done a darn' brave thing that's going to be remembered. Why, the newspaper will be full of what you've done tomorrow."

This suggestion acted as a tremendous tonic upon the coward. He got up from the floor and began to laugh a little shakily. "You think they'll notice me, do you? Nobody's ever noticed me. I never had a fair chance to get on. I never been in a newspaper in my life. You think that they'll notice me?"

"Of course I think so. I know so. You've been a hero."

Crawlin clutched the arm of the deputy. "Sure?" he asked.

"Will people say that about me?"

Signal swallowed a smile. "Why, look at the thing for yourself, will you?" he said. "What do you make of it? Don't you suppose that there's hundreds of people in Monument that would like to see us out of this scrape? But of the whole lot, there was only one man that dared to come and break through and help us."

"Yes, yes," gasped Crawlin. "I'm gonna fight for you, too. Gimme a gun, Signal, and you show me how to shoot, will you? I'm gonna stay and show everybody that I'm a man."

"I'll give you a gun. Don't you worry about that. But still I don't understand why you came."

"Ain't you answered that yourself? I come to help you fight. Besides, the sheriff gave me a message for you."

"The sheriff?"

"Yes."

"For me?"

"For you or for Fitz Eagan. But you're more important in Monument right now than even Fitz Eagan." He slipped off a shoe, and, beneath the false sole, he found and drew out a thin fold of paper. This the boy opened and lighted a match to read. It said:

Fitz Eagan, or Alias: They've shut me off from you, they think. Perhaps they have. I've tried to get through, and they have every inch of ground well covered with their rifles. First of all, I want to give you warning that if you try to make a rush in any direction from the jail, you're probably done for. They've arranged light bombs that they'll throw at the first sign of a break, and, if you try to rush out, the light of the bombs will show you up almost as clearly as the daylight.

I think they have more than forty men scattered around the jail. I've tried to drum up a posse in Monument, but the boys can't see the worth of risking their necks to kill a Bone and save an Eagan. You see that I'm talking straight.

They think that I'm mixed up on one side or the other, as well. I realize that I've been playing my cards like a fool.

At any rate, I want you to know that I haven't stopped trying. If I can't do anything else, I'll try my single hand to get into the jail, and, if I can't get in, I'll die trying.

This isn't mere guff.

Get Langley's written confession and try to hide it where not even fire could find it. But give poor Langley a fighting chance for his life.

I have in mind a desperate last chance—which is to try to get at the jail by getting into the house next door. From the cellar of that, I might be able to break through to you.

At any rate, I want you to know that I'm working hard to get to you.

The Bone tribe has some grand scheme under way. They've brought several barrels of oil into the house, and perhaps they'll try to drench the outer wall of the jail with it. But I don't think the fire from the oil could spread through the brick wall to the woodwork inside. At any rate, keep on the watch for that.

Yours to the last,

Ogden

With this letter, the boy hastened to Fitz Eagan, who read it over with much care. He declared that the light bombs worried him more than anything else, for, as he said, their one real chance of safety had been to depend upon a break from the jail. Neither had he thought of the possibility of an attack with oil. And, as he pointed out to Signal, oil could be flung in quantities through the windows, and then fire thrown after it. In this way the jail would instantly be rendered untenable, and, when the garrison attempted to flee, the burning jail, vomiting flames from the windows, would provide the light by which the fugitives would be shot down.

John Signal agreed, for the thing was only too palpable. They also decided that Harkness and Langley should not see the letter, and Fitz Eagan tore it to shreds.

"But," said Signal aggressively, "after they've thrown in the oil, what will become of the men who have thrown it? Will they be standing doing nothing?"

"They'll show the wits of demons," answered Eagan calmly. "I know the tribe, and I know what they can do. We can only stand tight and watch."

They returned to their posts to watch, but as John Signal went his rounds, little Crawlin shrank along beside him, a pitiable figure, wincing and shrinking from every sound and from every stir of the shadows.

But, not ten minutes later, he clutched the arm of Signal with a feverish grip. "Listen," he said.

As Signal paused, he heard at first a light tapping against the wall that adjoined the vacant house, and that tapping rapidly increased to a violent pounding. They were trying to burst through the brick wall.

CHAPTER FORTY-TWO

No sooner did that pounding develop than the whole garrison of the jail gathered to watch in fear and foreboding.

"What's up?" gasped Crawlin. "What can they do? Here . . . here's seven guns to shoot 'em down faster'n they could enter. Are they crazy? Would they try to rush us through a hole in the wall?"

"You're stupid," answered Fitz Eagan. "They ain't going to rush us. But. . . ."

At that moment there was a noisy fall of bricks into the cell room, and Signal, with leveled and ready rifle, sent a bullet through the hole. Plainly they could hear the exclamation of fear or pain beyond the wall, the noise of the voice almost drowned in the echoes that rang through the jail.

"Will that hold 'em?"

So asked Crawlin, but instantly they distinguished the voice of Colter, crying loudly: "Give me the crowbar! The yellow skunks!"

And the attack upon the wall began again.

With converging fire, six bullets crashed into the widening hole in one volley, but still Colter labored on, mysteriously shielded from the effects of the fire. And the hole was now a gap a foot in diameter.

At this point, the smashing of the crowbar stopped. The garrison of the jail ceased fire. Crawlin was coughing heavily, his throat stung by the gunpowder. But still he clung to Signal, as a

253

man in fear of shipwreck clings to a life preserver.

"They haven't the nerve to keep on," guessed Fitz Eagan, "and Colter probably has been badly wounded. Nothing but wounds would keep that fellow back now. Look here, Alias. Colter is your friend. You might try to talk to him and get us terms. This job looks worse than ever to me."

"He'll get no terms from Colter," broke in little Crawlin. "He hates Alias now worse than he hates even you, Fitz."

"Why, in the name of common sense?"

"Because of Esmeralda Pineta. She smiled a little too much on Alias to please Colter. He wants to carve his name on Alias, now. He'd carve it with his own hand if he could."

"What's that?"

"Look!"

Glimmering in the dim light that flickered through the windows of the jail, they saw a stream of liquid pouring through the hole in the brick wall and washing in a broad ripple across the floor. The next instant the rank odor of oil was penetrating their sensitive nostrils.

"It's the oil, the oil," groaned Fitz Eagan. "The fiend himself taught Colter that trick."

They rushed back to the rear of the room. Crawlin, half collapsing in panic, had to be supported by John Signal. Skinny, the guard, started up the steps to the attic, but Fitz Eagan caught him and pulled him back. "You're crazy," he said. "Don't you know that fire climbs faster than a squirrel?"

Signal, desperate and swearing beneath his breath, sent five rifle bullets through the gap in the wall from which the oil was pouring. It ceased. But instantly it began again, as though another barrel were being emptied. And now the wash of the oil had carried clear across the floor of the jail, and, as they hurried down the steps into the cellar, the liquid filtered after them.

"But d'you hear?" screamed Crawlin, fighting against Signal

as the latter dragged him on. "We'll be roasted in here . . . the oil'll drop through . . . the burnin' oil! The floor'll collapse. We'll be fried like pigeons. Oh, stop . . . oh, stop!"

This cry of despair was hardly ended before a half-stifled, heavy explosion shook the building, and a rain of mortar and bricks showered down into the cellar. The oil had been ignited, and now a pungent odor of burning reached the men.

The roar of the flames went up, now, and, far off, they heard the distant outcries of the watchers, and nearer at hand there were savage shouts of triumph that sounded in the ear of John Signal like the voices of wolves, howling.

That danger that Crawlin had prophesied was almost instantly on the way to fulfillment. The explosion of the first ignition of the oil had knocked many small holes in the floor, and through these holes the flaming oil streamed down, widening in fiercely burning pools upon the floor. Skinny, trying to beat out one of those fires, was caught by the blaze, and rolled, screaming, on the floor until Fitz Eagan wrapped him up in his coat and thus stifled the flames.

But everywhere the danger was streaming down upon them; the floor was puddled with blue, squirming fires, and the air heavy and smooth with the oil smoke.

"Look!" cried Crawlin. "They're comin' at us with fire through this wall, too!"

A considerable section of wall was seen to crumble inward at that instant, but in the dusty mouth that opened there appeared an unsteady figure, whitened with dust of mortar, and a hoarse voice called to them: "This way, boys, and quick, for heaven's sake!"

The voice of Sheriff Ogden.

They lurched toward him wildly. From the safety of that chamber beyond they looked back to an increasing inferno, for the whole cellar of the jail now was bursting with flames as fresh currents of the oil dropped through the crumbling floor.

Crawlin, nearly insensible with terror, was dragged on by John Signal, while Fitz Eagan laid his hand on the shoulder of the sheriff.

That one touch was all the thanks that Ogden received at that moment, although he had appeared, indeed, like an angel of grace. He led the way back through the moldy cellar of the house, merely saying: "I was here a whole hour. I didn't dare to tackle the wall until they began to make enough noise upstairs to cover the sound. I thought I'd never get through. The mason who put up that foundation wall made it as strong as iron."

They gathered at the foot of a narrow stairs, the sheriff and Eagan in the lead, Signal and Langley just behind, and the major in the rear.

"They're up there, somewhere," said the sheriff. "Go soft, boys. Hear 'em dancing their jig and whooping it up? To think that I've let them reptiles live safe here in Monument." And he pushed up at the side of Eagan.

At the head of the stairs they found a door through which they suddenly charged, and before them was a sudden flaring of guns. Signal saw the sheriff plunge forward on his face, while Fitz Eagan leaped powerfully to the side. That left the way clear for John Signal, and he saw before him first of all Charley Bone, a gun flaming in his right hand, his face convulsed with wild laughter. Beside him stood Henry Colter with two six-shooters booming. He looked like a tiger. His dark hair was on end, his face grimly set. Straight at that face the boy fired, and saw his man go down.

He swung on Charley Bone and fired again, and Bone dropped his gun, clutched his breast, staggered, and went down on his face under Signal's third bullet.

Clear of the doorway, now, Signal could see the whole scene. Old Dad Bone, his white hair flying, his beard divided, was heaving a sawed-off shotgun to his shoulder. That maneuver must be stopped. Joe Klaus was running into the hall from an adjoining room, which appeared to be filled with oil smoke. He came like a giant out of a cloud, with the white mist clinging to his shoulders.

There were other fighting men right and left. The cream of the whole Bone faction was gathered here.

To meet them, Langley came shouting through the doorway, ready to die, and Major Harkness, fighting with a rifle for surety, even at this close range, followed.

In the first half second, as Charley Bone pitched forward, Signal saw these things, and then a heavy impact struck his left shoulder and jammed him against the wall. He sank to his knees, and, looking across the room now rapidly darkening with smoke, he could see Henry Colter, already on his knees and driving another bullet after the first. That second shot skimmed past the cheek of Signal, and he fired in return as a burning pain leaped through his right side. The revolver began to wobble in his fingers. He tried to take it with his left hand, but his left arm hung helpless, useless, and still Colter, like a maniac, was firing through the mist.

Then a giant charged through the smoke fog—Fitz Eagan who had found his man. And the boy saw Henry Colter swaying to his feet to fight out the battle.

After this, John Signal saw little more. It was not merely the smoke that clouded his vision, but a dimness of his eyes, and the last thing that lived in his senses was the lion's roar of Fitz Eagan, grappling with his foe. Then bursts and red jets, as it were, of consciousness, returned to Signal. And he was aware of little flashes of the things that passed around him. He saw a narrow, fear-strained face close to his, and vaguely he recognized Crawlin and heard the whimpering of the little man: "Signal . . . Signal . . . are you dead? Are you dead?"

Afterward, frightful agony seized upon him. He looked up; he saw through a fiery mist of agony that Crawlin, laboriously was dragging him off. Again consciousness snapped back to him. Through wildest chaos he heard the voice of Major Harkness vowing that he would get one more before he died.

But that was the end for John Signal.

He heard and he saw no more until a sense of cool dampness crept up his spine, and then bitterly stabbing pains through his right side, and through his left shoulder. There was a sting in his cheek, also.

He wakened.

Strong bandages gripped his body. He could look out from one eye only, for the other was shrouded by a tightly fitted strip of cloth. But through that one eye he saw the leonine face of Fitz Eagan, and nearer, leaning above him, the freckled bridge of Polly's nose, and Polly herself, looking a singular greenish-white.

CHAPTER FORTY-THREE

They made a peaceful party on the verandah of Fitz Eagan's house by the river. John Signal had been carried out for the first time to enjoy the evening coolness. His face was thin and covered with a long scraggling, pale beard, but his eyes were bright again. Fitz Eagan and the sheriff had carried out his cot, each blaming the other for carelessness and stumbling, while Polly moved beside him, giving crisp orders.

Major Harkness, his left arm in a sling, stood nearby smoking a cigarette that Crawlin, perched at the top of the verandah steps, had rolled for him. "The papers are still playing it up," said the major. "They've lighted on Crawlin now. They've made Crawlin the real hero."

"And so he was," said the sheriff. "Without Crawlin, how would we have won through? You boys would have tried to break loose, and then you would have been fairly peppered. Who but Crawlin would have dared to even try to get through into the jail?"

Crawlin stood up and cleared his throat. "Aw," he said, "a man has to take a chance, don't he?"

They did not smile. They looked gravely at Crawlin, and then at one another.

"A lot of rot," said the sour major. "This talk about the Wild West makes me sick."

"Well," admitted the sheriff comfortably, "Monument is getting tolerable quiet now."

"They got a branch of the prevention of cruelty to animals in town now. D'you know that?" commented Fitz Eagan.

"I always knew that Ogden would spoil our fun if he got half a chance," said the major. "And he's gone and done it. But it never was really wild."

"No, nice and quiet you'd call it," said the sheriff.

"Look here at the little old fracas in the jail," said the major. "You'd think, to hear the talk, that everything was dripping with red. Well, no. Charley Bone and Colter dead on one side, and Langley on the other, if you can say that Langley was on the other side." He laughed. "Is that a pitched battle . . . as they called it?" asked the major in conclusion.

"It was pitched enough," said Polly. "They nearly did enough harm." She glanced at the wounded boy, and he smiled frankly up at her. "Are you better, honey?"

"I'm fit as a fiddle," said John Signal.

"But Monument is only a monument now of the good old days," said the major, pursuing his tone of bitterness. "It's not a shade of what it used to be. You did it, Sheriff. You and Signal, of course. Confound him."

He scowled at the boy, and John Signal smiled at the ceiling.

"I didn't want to use him," said the sheriff. "I'll let you ask him if I did."

"You tried to run me out of town," said Signal. "I never quite understood it."

"You're tolerably young, Johnny," said the sheriff. "You gotta admit that you're tolerably young, I guess."

"I'll admit that. But when you sent me out to collect those taxes . . . that looked as though you wanted to get rid of me."

"D'you think I ever dreamed that you'd do it? I never thought that any man in the world was young enough and fool enough to risk his life like that. I was only giving you a good man's chance of resigning."

"And what made you so hot to have me resign?"

"Because I saw from the way you'd started that you'd soon have everything in a mess around here. Of course, I saw that, and that you'd be at the throats of the Bone outfit before long. I didn't want that . . . I wanted more time. I was crowding them . . . and the Eagans . . . into a corner."

He paused to chuckle, and Fitz Eagan freely joined in.

"Besides," said the sheriff, "I knew all about you before you'd been in Monument a day."

"You did?"

"Yes."

"About the shooting in Bender Creek?"

"Yes, I knew that . . . but not the truth about it. I knew that you'd been forced into that fight. I didn't know that your man hadn't died, though. But I knew that you were a straight kid. When you came, I was glad to have you for a new deputy. In about one day, I thought you were going to burn up Monument."

"He didn't, though," commented Fitz Eagan. "He only burned up a house, a barn, and the jail!"

They laughed, all of them, with much good nature.

"Where're the flowers?" asked the major suddenly.

"What flowers?" asked Polly.

"Didn't Esmeralda send any today?"

"They're doing perfectly well inside the house," said Polly sharply.

"Look here, Polly, hasn't she got a right to send flowers, even to Johnny?"

"Stuff!" said Polly.

"Poor Johnny," said Fitz Eagan, "he's got a claim filed on him, and he'll never be a free man again."

But John Signal merely smiled at the ceiling.

"Hey," said Crawlin, "ain't that one of those reporters comin' down the street?"

"It is, sure enough."

"I'll do the talking," said Fitz Eagan.

The reporter, young, straw-hatted, paused at the gate and raised his hat. "May I come in?"

"You may not, son."

"I see the major is much better."

"Who told you so?" asked Harkness sharply.

"I would like a few words with Mister Crawlin, if possible."

"Not possible," said Harkness, as Crawlin eagerly started up. Crawlin sat down, greatly disappointed.

"About Mister Signal," continued the reporter, "we would like to know if it is true that the *Señorita* Pineta and Mister Signal have become betrothed."

"About that," said Fitz Eagan, "I dunno what to say, but I could introduce you here to the next Missus Signal." And he waved to Polly.

"But it isn't true!" cried Polly. She cried out so faintly, however, that the reporter did not hear.

"And now you'd better run along, me son," said Fitz Eagan.

That lion's voice did not need to repeat itself. The reporter went off with a halting step as he scribbled notes frantically. He had his dearly prized scoop at last.

"Why did you say that?" stammered Polly to Fitz Eagan. "There . . . there isn't a word of truth in it."

"Ain't there?" Fitz Eagan grinned. "You mean because Johnny is too much down to talk to the papers for himself? But I'll do his thinking for him, Polly. Or, if you've got any sense, look at the fool expression that Johnny is wearin' now."

There was no doubt about it. John Signal was pink with pleasure, and Polly turned and ran suddenly into the house.

Said John Signal: "D'you mind, one of you, going in and telling Polly that Fitz spoke for me?"

"I'll do it!" cried Crawlin, and was gone through the door before a more dignified messenger could be selected. There was only a brief silence on the porch, and then Crawlin came sauntering out again with an absent-minded expression.

"What happened?" asked Fitz Eagan.

"About what?" asked Crawlin.

"Why, what did she say?"

"Aw, she's all right," said Crawlin carelessly.

"What d'you mean?"

"I was just wondering."

"About what?"

"Why . . . you know this newspaper talk about me?"

"We know it, well enough."

"About me and my fearless work in the jail?"

"Yeah. We read all of that."

"I wanted to say, bein' frank and open, that, while the fightin' was goin' on, I was scared. Not much, y'understand, but a little bit."

ACKNOWLEDGMENTS

"Silver Trail" by Max Brand first appeared as a six-part serial in Street & Smith's *Western Story Magazine* (10/27/28–12/1/28). Copyright © 1928 by Street & Smith Publications, Inc. Copyright © renewed 1956 by Dorothy Faust. Copyright © 2009 by Golden West Literary Agency for restored material. Acknowledgment is made to Condé Nast Publications, Inc., for their co-operation.

ABOUT THE AUTHOR

Max Brand is the best-known pen name of Frederick Faust, creator of Dr. Kildare, Destry, and many other fictional characters popular with readers and viewers worldwide. Faust wrote for a variety of audiences in many genres. His enormous output, totaling approximately thirty million words or the equivalent of five hundred thirty ordinary books, covered nearly every field: crime, fantasy, historical romance, espionage, Westerns, science fiction, adventure, animal stories, love, war, and fashionable society, big business and big medicine. Eighty motion pictures have been based on his work along with many radio and television programs. For good measure he also published four volumes of poetry. Perhaps no other author has reached more people in more different ways. Born in Seattle in 1892, orphaned early, Faust grew up in the rural San Joaquin Valley of California. At Berkeley he became a student rebel and one-man literary movement, contributing prodigiously to all campus publications. Denied a degree because of unconventional conduct, he embarked on a series of adventures culminating in New York City where, after a period of near starvation, he received simultaneous recognition as a serious poet and successful author of fiction. Later, he traveled widely, making his home in New York, then in Florence, and finally in Los Angeles. Once the United States entered the Second World War, Faust abandoned his lucrative writing career and his work as a screenwriter to serve as a war correspondent with the infantry in Italy, despite his fifty-one years and a bad heart. He was killed during a night attack on a hilltop village held by the German army. New books based on magazine serials or unpublished manuscripts or restored versions continue to appear so that, alive or dead, he has averaged a new book every four months for seventy-five years. Beyond this, some work by him is newly reprinted every week of every year in one or another format somewhere in the world. A great deal more about this author and his work can be found in *The Max Brand Companion* (Greenwood Press, 1997) edited by Jon Tuska and Vicki Piekarski. His next Five Star Western will be *The Quest*. His Website is www.MaxBrandOnline.com.